Timely Revelations

By Tempie W. Wade

Timely Revelations
By Tempie W. Wade

Printed in the United States of America

First Edition Print - ISBN: 978-0-9600257-6-3

Digital Edition - ISBN: 978-0-9600257-7-0

For more information, please visit
www.TempieWade.com

Timely Revelations

By Tempie W. Wade

Book Four

The Timely Revolution Book Series

"Life belongs to the living, and he who lives must be prepared for changes." – Johann Wolfgang von Goethe

"I have noticed even people who claim everything is predestined, and that we can do nothing to change it, look before they cross the road." – Stephen Hawking

ACKNOWLEDGMENTS

To all those who have supported me and
encouraged me to continue writing…

THANK YOU!

1 CHAPTER ONE

Beechcroft Estate
Williamsburg, Virginia
Spring 1780

After supper later that night, Maggie, Duncan, Gabe, and Quinn sat in the four chairs that created a circle by the fireplace. John had left earlier that morning, and they were tossing around ideas on how to save him from the hangman's noose.

"It has to appear that he is actually dead from being hanged by the neck?" asked Gabe. "How do we do that?"

"The same way magicians and illusionists do it in my time," said Maggie. "A trick of the eye; a distraction to cause the crowd to look elsewhere while you make the magic happen. I suppose we need to break it down into steps."

"So, what's the first one? asked Duncan.

"The noose!" replied Quinn. "It has to go around his neck, but somehow not catch, while making everyone in the crowd think that it has."

Maggie nodded. "The rope has to be rigged somehow so the knot doesn't tighten, but I have no idea how to make that happen." She tapped her fingers on the arm of her chair. "And, no matter what we do, every person present has to be completely convinced that what they see is real."

"We would need access to the rope beforehand, and the executioner is always the last one to check it," said Quinn.

"Isn't that person usually hooded to hide his identity?" questioned Maggie.

"Yes, that is standard protocol when carrying out the sentence," said Gabe. "It would be a great deal of help if there was some way that one of us could manage to take the hangman's place, but that still won't solve the problem of the noose itself."

"Aye, John has to appear dead," said Duncan, "or they will carry out his punishment in another way, one that we will not be able to anticipate or have enough time to make arrangements for."

Quinn snapped his fingers, recalling something that he had read. "There is a concoction I can brew up that will give the appearance of death. I remember seeing a recipe in one of the books downstairs, but it would have to be administered just before the hanging. The timing would have to be perfect for it to work."

"I am afraid that might be the easiest part," said Maggie, rubbing her temples. "From what I remember, they will immediately inter John's body in a coffin brought for the occasion and bury him on the spot. We have to figure out how to get him out of that wooden box and put something else in his place, all while making sure that no one notices."

"This is not going to be an easy job by any stretch of the imagination, Maggie. As much as I hate to say it, I am not sure this is something we will be able to accomplish," cautioned Gabe sincerely.

Duncan rose from his chair, knelt in front of Maggie, and took both her hands in his. "Gabe is right, my love," he said softly and as gently as he could. "There is a good chance we will not be able to come up with a viable way for this to work. Ye need to prepare yourself for that likelihood."

Maggie simply stared back at him with an expression of desperation upon her face. "Surely, we can figure out a way," she whispered. "We have to at least give it a try. I will never forgive myself if we do not do everything humanly possible to save him, especially given all that we know in advance."

Duncan leaned forward and kissed her forehead. "Of course, we will do all that we can, and I was not suggesting otherwise. I just want ye to be realistic about the outcome."

He embraced her tightly and glanced over at Gabe and Quinn with a solemn, rather grim, look on his face.

The next afternoon, Maggie put the babies down for their nap. Her frustration from not being able to figure out a suitable way to save John had been growing by leaps and bounds, and she decided that it was a good time to try and clear her head. She went into their bedroom, changed into her trousers and top, and looked at herself in the long mirror.

She fiddled with the ties, slid her hand over her stomach, and made a strange face. "They still fit..." she said aloud, "kind of ...sort of?"

"What are ye up to in here?" asked Duncan, leaning against the doorjamb with his arms folded, a broad, amused smile across his face.

"Trying to get back into my pre-pregnancy clothes for one thing." She poked at her stomach with her index finger. "I'm still a little...lumpy and bumpy, in some places more than others."

Maggie grimaced, wrinkling her nose at herself in the mirror. She sighed and turned to face him.

"My love, ye are still as beautiful and desirable as the day I met ye," Duncan crossed the floor, took her in his arms and kissed her.

"Flatterer!" she teased. "I have some nervous energy that needs working out and I have not practiced in a very long time." She tugged on his shirt. "Up for some swordplay with your wife?"

Duncan grinned. "Oh, aye I am."

Maggie moved from his embrace to where she kept her blade, unsheathed it and held it out; it had not been in her hands since before the babies were born and she had missed it. She felt the little surge of energy that she always did when she handled it. Now recognizing it as Fae power, she twirled it back and forth, getting reacquainted with the feel and weight of it.

"It's been a while," said Duncan, coming to her side. "I will go easy on ye this time."

Maggie smirked. "Don't do me any favors." She waved her sword in the air.

Duncan retrieved his own weapon and they moved outside to the side lawn where it was grassy and well maintained.

They spent the next hour practicing, meeting each other, lunge for lunge and step for step, only stopping for a little 'love-play' in between. Duncan finally stopped to strip off his shirt when he became soaked with sweat from all the activity.

"Shall I take my top off as well?" teased Maggie, playfully.

Duncan laughed out loud. "If ye do, we will be having a different sort of 'swordplay' out here, one that ye might not want the whole household to see," he growled, coming over to kiss her ravenously.

Gabe and Quinn, who had noticed them from the drawing room window, came outside to enjoy the show.

"You are looking a little rusty there, Mags," goaded Gabe.

Maggie put one hand on her hip and pointed her sword in his direction. "Perhaps my teacher would like to take my husband's place for a bit." She cut her eyes towards Duncan, holding the back of her hand up to her mouth, mockingly. "Between you and me, I think he is getting a little tired and worn out."

"Worn out?" Duncan exclaimed, amusingly affronted. "I was going easy on ye because ye are the mother of my children."

Maggie blew a kiss at him and winked.

I will show my appreciation later.

"Looking forward to that," he responded aloud.

Gabe shook his head. "Why don't you let me have a go, Duncan?" he offered. "She is not the mother of *my* children!"

"Be my guest," he replied. Duncan tossed his sword to Gabe and went to join Quinn off to the side.

"Wait!" Gabe held up his hand. "It isn't your time of the month, is it?"

Maggie scowled at him. "No, it is not! But I can make an exception for you and we can pretend if you like."

Gabe laughed, "Let's not." He readied himself, then came at her with all he had.

She anticipated each move, and swiftly disarmed him in an unusually short amount of time.

Reaching down, Maggie picked up his weapon from the ground. "Rusty, huh?" She tossed his sword back to him.

"I stand corrected," he bowed. "You have not missed a beat. How long has it been since you picked that thing up anyway?"

"I am not exactly certain." Maggie scratched her head as she pondered. "Since long before the babies came."

The side door from the house flew wide open and Kat ran out, straight for Gabe. He scooped her up with his free arm and she hugged him tightly around the neck and planted a big, smacking kiss on his cheek.

"Hello, princess."

Gabe tossed his sword to Maggie, and wrapped his other arm around his daughter, tickling her to make her laugh.

"I'm sorry, Colonel Asheton," waved Cora as she bent over and rested her hands on her knees, completely out of breath. "She got away from me."

"It's alright, Cora. I've got her." Gabe looked Kat directly in the eye, in a vain endeavor to be serious. "Stop giving your nanny such a hard time," he whispered.

She leaned back and giggled at his failed attempt to scold her, which only amused him more. "You're incorrigible, young lady," he grinned and kissed her repeatedly on the cheeks.

Gabe walked over to join Quinn, and Kat reached for him next.

Quinn took her in his arms, and she hugged him and kissed his cheek, the same as she had done for Gabe.

Maggie smiled at them, her heart warmed by their little family and the wonderful love they shared for each other.

He was running, chasing after Kat through a meadow of wildflowers. Every time he got close to her, she pulled away, laughing and calling out for him. He reached the edge of a cliff, and was searching all around for her, when he finally spotted her, balancing on the very edge. He ran towards her and was almost there, when her foot slipped, and she tumbled over the ledge. He sailed for her, desperately grabbing for her hand while screaming out her name. He caught it for a moment, but she slipped free of him, and was gone. He fell to his knees and cried out in pure agony.

Gabe woke with a start and sat straight up, in a cold, clammy sweat, tears in his eyes, his heart pounding so fast that it made his chest hurt.

Quinn—his arms wrapped around Gabe from their earlier lovemaking—awakened as well, raising up. "What is it? What's wrong?"

Reclining back on the bed, Gabe took in deep breaths, attempting to calm his heart rate. "I just had a nightmare, that's all. Go back to sleep," he said, his breathing still hard.

Quinn propped up on his elbow and rubbed his arm, comfortingly. "Do ye want to talk about it?"

"No!" He shook his head. "I want to forget about it."

Gabe pushed back the covers, swung his feet over the edge of the bed, placed his face into his hands, and tried to pull himself together.

"I am going to check on Kat," he finally said. "I will be right back."

Gabe made his way into the hall and leaned against the wall as soon as he was out of Quinn's sight, still trying to settle his mind. He blew out a few more deep breaths as he looked towards her room.

Pushing her door open quietly, Gabe peeked over into her crib, only to see that she was smiling in her sleep, safe and sound.

Gabe bent at the waist and rested his forehead on the edge of the crib, silently thanking God. The ache from his dream refused to leave him as quickly as he had hoped. He felt Quinn, who had come up behind him, slip his arms around his waist, and plant a light kiss on his back.

"She is perfectly fine. I take it your nightmare was about her."

Gabe nodded and he wiped the sweat from his face with his palm. "I dreamed that I had lost her. I woke up terrified that she was gone."

Quinn turned him around and lightly touched his face as he pushed the dampened hair away from his eyes. "It was only a nightmare and nothing more."

"It was so real." Gabe leaned his forehead against Quinn's shoulder, grateful that he was there.

Winding his arm around Gabe's waist, Quinn guided his husband back to their bedroom. Once they were in bed, Gabe laid with his cheek on Quinn's chest and his arm across his midsection. Quinn pulled him tighter, kissed the top of his head and did his best to comfort him by getting him to talk about menial matters until he drifted off to sleep.

Gabe was still rattled by his nightmare the next morning. He and Maggie were trying to go over the final paperwork for the new house and office in New York, but his mind was elsewhere.

"The house is on the edge of town and close to the shipping dock. It will be perfect."

"Whatever you say," answered Gabe, his mind not present in the conversation.

Maggie lifted her chin, knowing full well that he was not paying attention. "John and I will be able to sneak in fifteen or twenty people for orgies after we remove all the furniture and line the walls with pillows and blankets. I have artists coming to paint nude women, well-endowed men, and pages from the Kama Sutra on the walls and we can probably sacrifice a few virgins while we are at it, if we can find any, that is. I am sure Duncan won't mind at all if I have sex with three or four different men in front of him. He might like to watch, especially if John decides he wants to take me on the floor right there in front of him. Duncan may even want to join in, so we can make it a threesome."

"Hmmm…that sounds wonderful," replied Gabe. "Why don't you take care of that straightaway?" Finally, he blinked and looked up at her. "Wait? What?" he asked, her words sinking in.

"I was checking to see if you were paying attention," said Maggie with her hands on her hips. "And it is apparent that you are not. What's going on with you today?"

Gabe shook his head. "I'm sorry. I had a nightmare about Kat last night, and I cannot seem to shake it."

Maggie poured him a drink as he moved to one of the chairs. She stepped behind him and handed him the glass over his shoulder.

"What sort of nightmare? Tell me about it." She came around to take the chair across from him.

"I dreamt she got away from me and fell over a cliff before I could save her. I had her in my grasp, and she just slipped right through my fingers. It was the most awful thing you could imagine."

Maggie leaned forward and touched his arm. "All parents have those fears, Gabe. I get up at least three times a night to check on the babies, just to make sure they are breathing." She grinned. "And, with Duncan's four times a night, we are basically checking on them every hour."

Gabe reached over and laid his hand on top of hers. "It's crazy what these babies do to us, isn't it," he chuckled softly. "Who would have thought that you and I would end up like this after all of our adventures together?"

"I have a feeling that these children are just the beginning of our adventures," said Maggie, sarcasm dripping from her tongue. "It's normal, Gabe. I wouldn't let one nightmare concern me so much."

"You are right, I know. Quinn said the same thing."

Standing, Maggie kissed him on the top of his head. "Well, you should listen to him. Your husband is a very wise man."

2 CHAPTER TWO

A few days later, Duncan went to the Native American village to check on them, as he often did.

Maggie was writing some correspondence at her desk when a knock at the front door interrupted her. "I will get it, Hettie," she called out, crossing the floor.

She opened the door and was pleasantly surprised to see Duncan's mother standing there.

"Maggie!" The woman said and they rushed into each other's arms and warmly embraced.

"Lady Aurnia! What a marvelous surprise!"

"Maggie, you look wonderful!" Lady Aurnia stepped back for a better look.

"Come in," said Maggie and she took her by the waist. "What are you doing here? We were not expecting you for a visit."

"I know. I am sorry for the short notice, but it could not be helped." Lady Aurnia stopped, looking back at the door and calling for someone else to come in. A little boy, about seven or eight, stepped shyly inside as Lady Aurnia bent down, and took his hand. She turned to Maggie with a guarded expression on her face.

"Maggie, I would like ye to meet someone very special. This is Alastair...my grandson."

"Grandson?" asked Maggie, stunned. Her gaze shifted to the boy, and she took an involuntary step back. She stared at the child before her, confused and unsure of what her mother-in-law meant by 'grandson'. There was no doubt that the little boy carried MacGregor blood in his veins, having the same dark hair and features they all had. He looked exactly like...

Lady Aurnia spoke cautiously. "I have come to bring the boy to his father."

Maggie felt as if she had been punched in the gut. She leaned back against the staircase and reached for something to hold onto for balance, blood rushing to her head and making her feel a little shaky. She looked back and forth between Lady Aurnia and the boy, in utter shock.

His father? Surely, he isn't...

She forced herself to slowly kneel and take a closer look at the boy. "It is...nice to meet you...I am... Maggie," she stuttered and forced a half-smile.

The little boy shyly turned and buried his face into his grandmother's skirt as Maggie looked up at Lady Aurnia, her mind full of a million questions, but with only one that truly mattered.

Hettie came around the corner at that moment, wiping her hands on a towel to see if she was needed.

"Hettie...this is...our new friend.... Alastair...and he looks hungry. Why don't you...take him to the kitchen...and find him something to eat?" Maggie managed to get out.

Hettie noticed how pale Maggie looked and became concerned. "Yes, Maggie," she spoke slowly and held out her hand to the boy. "Are you hungry?" she asked him. He looked back at his grandmother, before he nodded his head.

"It's alright," smiled Lady Aurnia, reassuringly. "Ye can go with her."

He took Hettie's hand, and she led him away as she looked at Maggie warily.

As soon as they were gone, Maggie turned to Lady Aurnia and forced herself to breathe. "That boy...is he?"

At that exact moment, Duncan came through the front door with his arm around Logan, laughing.

"Mother!" he exclaimed gleefully, and he came over to embrace her.

"Oh Duncan, my dear boy! I have missed ye so much!"

Maggie's breathing had become irregular; she started to hyperventilate and leaned against the wall.

As soon as Duncan caught sight of her face, he realized something was terribly wrong. He darted to her and slipped his arms around her waist, catching her just before she collapsed into a heap on the floor.

Duncan recognized the look; the one he had not seen for a while. He gathered her up, carried her to a chair in the drawing room, poured her a drink and forced it down her.

Lady Aurnia and Logan followed with disturbed expressions on their faces.

"Maggie, what is it?" He cupped her face and knelt before her. "Ye look like ye have seen a ghost."

Once Maggie was finally able to speak again, she looked up at Lady Aurnia.

"I think you should explain about that boy!"

"What boy?" asked Duncan.

"The one in the kitchen…the one that looks exactly like YOU," replied Maggie. She turned to Lady Aurnia, "Is that child... Duncan's?"

Duncan looked to his mother, the blood draining from his own face. "Mother? What on Earth is Maggie talking about?"

"Wait!" exclaimed Logan as he held up his hands. "Ye two need to calm yourselves. Ye are making the wrong assumption here."

"But you said that you were bringing him to his father," said Maggie.

Duncan's eyes grew wide and he turned back to Maggie. "Father?"

"Aye," said Lady Aurnia, "we are bringing him to Quinn."

"Quinn?" asked a dumbfounded Duncan. "Quinn has a son?"

Lady Aurnia waited while Duncan went to pull the doors closed.

Maggie moved to the liquor cabinet and blew out a long, slow breath.

"Forgive me, Maggie," she said. "I did not get the chance to clarify things before Duncan came in. I did not mean to cause ye such distress."

Maggie pulled out several glasses for the drinks. "You definitely got my heart pumping." She poured them all whisky and they moved to sit in the chairs by the fireplace.

Lady Aurnia began her story.

"I received an urgent message from his mother on her deathbed two months ago. She lived out at the village that we look after. She told me that eight years ago, she was working as a barmaid in the local tavern when all of ye came in."

"It was the day of Dougal's funeral when we stopped in to have a drink in his memory," added Logan.

Maggie looked to Duncan for clarification.

"Dougal was our father's best friend. They were closer than brothers and when Father died, he stepped in and helped to raise all of us, to teach us all the things our father didn't get the chance to. He and Quinn were especially close because he was so young when it happened. Quinn was beside himself when we lost Dougal."

"And that day, Quinn had more than one drink," said Logan.

Duncan searched his memory. "Aye! He was very upset, and he drank far more than I have ever seen him drink."

"Do ye remember the barmaid that was flirting with him?" asked Logan.

Duncan slowly nodded, memories of that day starting to fill in.

"She told me that they went to one of the rooms upstairs, that she and he...that...well, she became with child that night," whispered Lady Aurnia.

"If that is so, why didn't she come to him sooner?" asked Maggie.

"She said that she wanted to raise the boy herself. She had no one else in the world, and she was happy with it being just the two of them. She loved Alastair very much and when she found out she was dying, she wanted him to be with the only other family he had, so she sent word for me to come." Lady Aurnia took a sip of her drink. "There is no denying that he is Quinn's son. He is the spitting image of him at that age."

Maggie and Duncan exchanged bewildered looks.

"Where are Quinn and Gabe?" asked Lady Aurnia.

Duncan looked in Logan's direction warily.

"He knows about Quinn and Gabe," said Lady Aurnia, as she read his face. "He needed to know."

"They are at their home. I can send someone over for them." Maggie set her glass down and stepped out to call Hettie.

Lady Aurnia smiled. "In the meantime, I would like to meet my newest grandchild. Is it a boy or a girl?"

"Mother, did ye not receive my letter?" asked Duncan.

"Nay. The mail has been very sporadic from the colonies and we may have missed it in passing."

Duncan grinned. "Well, then ye are in for a treat and ye are going to be a *very* happy woman."

Maggie and Duncan motioned for them to follow and led them upstairs to the nursery.

"Three?" laughed Lady Aurnia, picking up Morgan first.

"Well, I guess we know who the favorite son is now, don't we, Brother? Ye outdid all of us in one shot," said Logan as Duncan handed him Kendric and Maggie took Alanna.

"Meet Morgan, Alanna, and our oldest, Kendric," said Maggie.

"Ye named him after your father?" smiled Lady Aurnia. "That pleases me very much and he would be very proud."

"It was Maggie's idea." Duncan kissed his mother's cheek. "Your cup runneth over with grandchildren now. Two boys and three girls, counting little Kat."

Lady Aurnia scoffed. "It took ye long enough!"

"Well, if Finn is right, you will have plenty more to come," mumbled Maggie.

"Who is Finn?" asked Logan while he rocked his nephew in his arms.

"Finn, the King of the Fae," replied Duncan.

"What?" demanded Lady Aurnia who was completely taken aback. "Ye have actually seen him and spoken with him?"

"Aye. I did not write ye in case the letter went astray, especially since nearly all correspondence is being read by the armies on both sides, but there are many things that ye do not know. He paid Maggie a visit on the ship ride home, and he has also visited the babies."

"Why would the King of the Fae come to see these babies?" Aurnia asked, puzzled.

Maggie sighed. "Because, he is my grandfather."

Lady Aurnia cocked her head, even more confused. "I do not understand."

Maggie patted Alanna's bottom lightly as she moved to the rocking chair. "My mother was the goddess Danu before she fell in love with my father and gave up her immortality to spend her life with him."

"Danu? Your mother?"

"And he left Maggie with a few gifts while he was here," added Duncan. "Some of her mother's own abilities."

"Which ones?" asked Logan.

"Fertility for one," laughed Duncan. "She can grant it and she can get things to grow in barren places simply by touching the ground."

Lady Aurnia looked at Maggie with wide eyes. "It seems there is a great deal I need to be filled in on."

"Well, hopefully, ye can stay a while," said Duncan. "We could use your advice on many levels around here."

Cecile knocked on the door.

"Excuse me, Maggie, but they are here."

"Thank you, Cecile. Can you get someone to take the babies and Kat for a while? We have some things to discuss. Please make sure we are not disturbed."

"Of course."

"And Cecile, where is the boy that was in the kitchen?"

Cecile smiled. "Hettie sent him out to play with some of the other children at the school. She has been keeping an eye on him and he is having a good time."

"Thank you, Cecile."

Maggie was the first in the drawing room.

"Oh, there you are," said Gabe. "What's so important?"

"We have guests," said Maggie and Lady Aurnia and Logan followed her in.

"Mother!" exclaimed Quinn, standing to hug her.

"Oh, Quinn!" she said as she squeezed him tightly. "It is so good to see ye."

"Logan!" He and Quinn embraced next.

"Hello, Brother!"

Gabe kissed Lady Aurnia on the cheek and she cupped his face smiling. "Hello, Gabe!"

"It is wonderful to see you, Lady Aurnia," he said.

Logan came over to Gabe and held out his hand.

"Hello Gabe, or should I say 'brother-in-law'?"

Gabe and Quinn froze and cut their eyes to each other.

"It's alright, Quinn," he said. "I know about ye two and I am very glad that ye have found someone that makes ye so happy. I am proud to have Gabe as part of this family."

Gabe shook his hand. "Thank you."

"Yes! Thank ye, Brother! I appreciate that more than ye know," said Quinn and he softly squeezed Logan's shoulder. "What are ye two doing here?"

Duncan closed the doors while Quinn and Gabe watched him nervously.

"This must be serious," whispered Gabe.

"Maybe you two should sit down," said Maggie, and she went to pour them drinks.

After looking at the size of the glasses, she set them back down and reached under the cabinet taking out two full bottles instead. She handed them to Gabe over his shoulder where he and Quinn were already sitting on the sofa.

Gabe looked back at her with a strange look on his face and reluctantly accepted them.

Maggie shrugged, then held her hand up to her mouth as if she were drinking the bottle, indicating that he should probably do the same.

"What on Earth is going on?" asked Quinn.

"We should start keeping count of how many times that question gets asked in this house," mumbled Maggie.

Duncan nodded his head in agreement.

Lady Aurnia sat down on the table between Gabe and Quinn and faced them, while Maggie stood behind the sofa they sat on. Duncan and Logan stood next to each other off to the side.

"I have something to tell the both of ye," she started. "It is going to come as quite a shock."

Quinn and Gabe exchanged nervous looks as Lady Aurnia continued to speak.

"Quinn, do ye remember when Dougal passed away and we all went to the village for the burial?"

"Aye, his wife had been laid to rest in the churchyard there many years before and he wanted to be buried next to her. It was his last request."

"I left to come home and ye boys stopped by the tavern to raise a glass in his memory."

"Ye had a great deal to drink," reminded Logan.

"I did." he agreed. "But, what does that have to do with anything? It was a long time ago."

"What do ye remember about that night?" asked Duncan.

Quinn looked down at the floor. "Not a great deal. We drank…"

Logan looked to Duncan as he took a step closer to Quinn.

"Do ye recall the barmaid who was flirting with ye that day?" asked Logan.

"Aye," Quinn closed his eyes, and said softly, "Her name was Fiona. Why do ye ask about her?"

Maggie laid one hand on Quinn's shoulder and the other on Gabe's.

"Ye went upstairs with her and ye took her to bed," Lady Aurnia whispered.

Quinn looked over at Gabe who was watching him intently, before he turned back to his mother and his jaw tightened.

"Did ye come all the way from Scotland to cause trouble in my marriage? To bring up something that happened…"

"Eight years ago," she finished for him.

She took his hand. "I did not come to cause problems between ye and Gabe; I would never intentionally hurt ye of all people, my dear, sweet, tender-hearted boy. I only came to bring ye… your son."

Maggie felt the breath go out of Quinn and she tightened her grip on his shoulder. His face drained of all color as he stared back at his mother with his mouth agape.

Gabe tensed, and slowly turned to look back at Maggie before turning back to his husband.

"My… what?" Quinn choked out.

"Your son." Lady Aurnia reached over, touching his face compassionately. "Fiona passed away two months ago, and she confessed to me on her deathbed that your union that night created a child. And, he *is* your son. I know it as well as I know that ye are mine."

Quinn leaned forward, pale, with his face in his hands, as he tried to absorb the words his mother had just uttered.

"I have a son?" he whispered. "By Fiona?"

Gabe looked down at the floor and placed his hand on Quinn's back.

"His name is Alastair, he is seven years old, and he is the sweetest child ye will ever know."

Quinn stared straight ahead, stunned, and a few tears dripped down his cheek and the end of his nose. He sniffled, looked back at Gabe with a lost look in his eye, and wiped his face with the back of his hand.

Gabe's face was devoid of all sentiment, blank and unreadable as Quinn silently prayed that his husband would somehow understand why he did what he did. His voice was full of raw emotion as he spoke.

"I was as close to Dougal as I was my own father. When he died, I was so distraught that all I wanted to do was forget about how much pain his absence caused me. I drank far too much that night and I continued to drink until I could barely stand up on my own. I stumbled outside to take a piss and she just appeared out of nowhere. I remember her putting her arm around my waist and helping me up the stairs and onto a bed. I curled on my side and broke down crying like a child. She laid down beside me, telling me it was going to be alright, pulling me closer to her as she tried to comfort me in my grief...and the next thing I knew, we were kissing and then she...and we..." He paused. "I was so out of it, I hardly noticed that she had undressed me, then herself and after that…God help me… I didn't even try to stop her, and I just let it happen. I was numb and having someone there, anyone there, touching me in that way made the pain go away, even if it was only for a little while. When I sobered up and finally realized what I had done, I felt like a horrible person for having used her like that, especially knowing that I would have never taken comfort with a woman had I been in my right mind. I apologized to her over and over, but she said not to; that she had no regrets because she had wanted me, as well. I gathered my things, dressed and left. I never saw her again after that day. The next time I was in the village—a few weeks later—I stopped in and asked about her but the tavernkeeper said she had moved on; he did not know to where. I had no idea that I had left her in that condition. I would never have deserted my child if I had known he existed."

Quinn turned to his mother. "Why wouldn't she tell me? Where has he been all this time?"

His mother shook her head. "I don't know any more than what I told ye, Quinn. All I do know is that your son is here now, and that boy desperately needs his father."

Gabe cleared his throat and brushed away a tear from his own cheek.

Maggie looked to Duncan.

They need some time alone.

Duncan nodded, touched Logan on the back and tipped his head towards the door, then took his mother by the hand and helped her up.

Maggie squeezed Quinn and Gabe shoulders lovingly, before she leaned over and kissed each of them on the top of the head. "We will be right outside if you need us," she said quietly before she followed the others out and closed the doors behind her.

After everyone else had cleared the room, Gabe and Quinn sat in deafening silence for a long while.

Quinn finally leaned forward with his elbows on his knees and looked back at his husband with watery eyes.

"Gabe, I don't know what to say to ye. This is not only a lot for me to take in at one time, but for ye as well. Ye did not sign up for this and if it is too much for ye...." A choked sob escaped him.

Gabe's face softened and he pulled him over onto his chest, stroking his hair as he whispered, "It's alright. You didn't know and there isn't anything you could have done differently."

"I am sorry, Gabe," he whispered.

"Listen to me," Gabe took his face in his hands. "You have nothing to apologize to me for. We have both done things in the past to get us through difficult times and God knows, I have no room to judge anyone. I refuse to call this a mistake, because now, another part of the man I love more than life itself, exists in this world...and that could never be a bad thing. We love each other and we will work through this."

Gabe kissed Quinn and they embraced each other tightly.

"This is not the worst news," said Gabe. "As a matter of fact, you and I should actually be celebrating. We have talked about how much we would love for Kat to have a sibling, and we knew that would not likely ever happen, but now...*NOW*, we have been blessed with a son, one that I expect already sleeps through the night, unlike our daughter," he teased as he tried to lighten the mood.

Quinn pulled back to look Gabe in the eyes and let out a little chuckle through his tears. "God, I hope so!"

Gabe kissed him again. "We are going to be just fine. It will be an adjustment for all of us, but we love each other and there isn't anything we cannot work through together. In the meantime," he said, straightening his husband's collar and now-wrinkled shirt, "you need to pull yourself together and make yourself presentable. You cannot meet your boy looking like this." Gabe smiled and leaned his forehead against Quinn's as Quinn nodded.

"I love ye so much, Gabe."

"I love you too, Quinn."

Maggie leaned against Duncan's chest and he pulled her close as she looked towards the drawing room nervously.

Lady Aurnia moved over to the front of the fireplace, her arms folded and a slight smile on her face, to get a better look at the wedding portrait that hung above it.

"You received one, as well. We were surprised to find it with the others in the chamber after ye left."

"It was a gift from Finn," said Maggie, glancing in that direction. "He also said that he delivered one to my parents in the future to reassure them that I was fine."

"Do ye trust Finn?" asked Lady Aurnia.

Maggie shrugged. "He has not given me any reason to distrust him. He leaves out a great many details on things, yes, but his heart seems to be in the right place, and he *is* my grandfather."

Lady Aurnia shifted her attention to Duncan. "And, ye?"

Duncan looked down at the floor. "I am not as sure."

"What?" asked Maggie, stunned, as she pushed back from him slightly to look him in the eye. "Why would you not trust Finn?"

He exhaled loudly. "Finn paid me a visit the night the colt was born."

Maggie narrowed her eyes at him with a look of disbelief on her face. "Are you kidding me? That was months ago, and you never thought to mention it until now?"

"I did not want to upset ye, my love," he said softly.

"Why would I be upset? What exactly did he say?" she demanded, perturbed that he had been holding out on her.

"He said that the babies were very special and that the new colt, along with the two to follow, would protect our children as Onyx protects ye."

Maggie frowned. "And?" she coaxed. "Obviously, he said a little more than that if you are concerned."

Duncan sighed. "He said ye had another purpose in this world, but he would not elaborate on what it was to me."

"Now, that *is* typical Finn!" She closed her eyes and rubbed the spot between her brows with her index finger. "He isn't big on disclosure."

Duncan took Maggie by the shoulders. "He unsettles me, Maggie. I am concerned that ye are becoming a pawn in some cosmic chess game that he is playing. We need to tread carefully when it comes to all things Fae, especially Finn."

"But he is my grandfather, Duncan. Why would he use me, especially knowing how much he loved my mother?"

"I do not know, but I have a very uneasy feeling about this whole situation, and he seems to be using ye for his own intents and purposes. You and our bairns are my only concern, and I will not let him or anyone else harm my family."

Maggie laid her face on his chest. "I do not think he would. Would he?" she asked, doubts creeping into her mind.

Duncan's refusal to answer that particular question did not sit well with her.

"Do you ever wonder what it would be like to just have one normal day? No Fae, no Culper Spy Ring, no fires to put out, no trying to figure out how to save someone from hanging—just one whole day to do and think about absolutely nothing?" she asked.

Duncan hugged her. "Aye, I do sometimes wonder. Maybe one of these days we will find out."

Quinn and Gabe eventually emerged from the drawing room holding hands and Maggie met them at the doorway.

"Are you two good?" she asked, cautiously optimistic.

Quinn looked to Gabe, smiled, and kissed the back of his hand. "We are."

Maggie hugged them both. "I love you two so much and everything is going to work out just fine."

"We love you too, Mags," said Gabe.

Lady Aurnia stepped forward. "Well, Quinn, are ye ready to go meet your son?"

Quinn blew out a deep breath and gripped Gabe's hand even tighter. "*WE* are ready to meet *our* son."

Alastair was playing tag with some of the other children around the communal kitchen while Hettie sat on a nearby bench keeping watch over them. Maggie sat down next to her as Lady Aurnia led Quinn and Gabe over to him. Maggie looked on as Quinn knelt and spoke to the boy who was hanging onto Lady Aurnia's dress for dear life; Logan and Duncan observed from very close by. Her heart melted when two little arms went around Quinn's neck. Quinn wrapped his arms around him and held on as tight as he could and buried his face in the child's shoulder while Gabe stood behind him, smiling.

"Quinn's boy, huh?" whispered Hettie. "At first sight, I thought for sure that he was Duncan's."

"You and me both," sighed Maggie, leaning towards her. "My heart is still pounding like crazy!"

"I see another brother has shown up. He sure is a handsome fellow." Hettie grinned devilishly in Logan's direction.

"Hettie!" laughed Maggie and nudged her. "Don't tell me you have eyes for my brother-in-law!"

"Aw, you can't help but look at *all* of them, Maggie. They are some mighty fine-looking men. Everybody in town talks about them, you know. Lord have mercy, I'm surprised there ain't women dropping by here every time you turn around."

Maggie covered her mouth with her hand and snickered. "I reignite the murder story every now and then just to keep them away. It seems to work pretty well," she whispered.

Hettie burst into laughter. "It sure does. I reckon you are one smart woman, Maggie." She smiled and maneuvered her neck to get a better look at Logan, a happy look on her face.

3 CHAPTER THREE

They enjoyed a late, leisurely dinner that day. Quinn could not stop staring at Alastair the entire meal, while Gabe remained mostly quiet, lost in his own thoughts, even though he would occasionally look over at Quinn and smile.

Kat was also fascinated by the arrival of her new brother and took right to him.

Lady Aurnia and Logan filled everyone in on the news from home before Maggie and Duncan told them of everything that had happened with them.

After dinner, they all moved into the drawing room to enjoy some time with the children together. Alastair, most of all, seemed to thoroughly enjoy being around Kat and the babies.

Maggie noticed Lady Aurnia's peculiar look as she watched Kat climb up on Duncan's lap.

"Is something wrong?" asked Maggie.

"Oh no, not at all! I am just enjoying being around all of these little ones." Lady Aurnia smiled. "It's just that...Kat...I never noticed it before..."

"Noticed what?"

Lady Aurnia furrowed her brow. "I am sure I must be mistaken. I have to be."

Maggie raised her eyebrows at her. "Oh, just go ahead and say it. You are among family. What have you never noticed about Kat?"

Lady Aurnia looked to Maggie than back at Kat. "How much she looks like...the MacGregors."

Maggie turned her gaze to Kat who sat on Duncan's lap, and noticed it for the first time as well.

"Do ye see it?" whispered Lady Aurnia, "Or, am I imagining it?"

Maggie frowned and looked even harder. "No! I don't think you are. I see it as well, now that you point it out."

Duncan noticed Maggie's stare, and sent her a questioning look. Maggie replied with a silent message.

Did you ever notice how much Kat looks like your family?

Duncan made an odd face and reached down, gently tipping Kat's chin up to see for himself, before he looked back at Maggie strangely.

Lady Aurnia was captivated. "Gabe, what can ye tell me about Kat's family?"

Gabe shrugged. "Not much, I am afraid. Her mother was my sister-in-law, but I do not know anything about her real father's side."

"What about her grandparents? Were there any relatives from Scotland by chance?"

Gabe tapped his fingers on the arm of the chair as he tried to recall. "Not on their father's side, but Penny and Hannah's mother was raised in an orphanage from the time she was a baby, so I cannot say for certain. Why do you ask?"

Maggie had become even more curious. "Gabe, look at her next to Duncan. Do you see the resemblance?"

Gabe turned his head. He slowly stood up and moved to stand beside them, as if seeing Kat for the very first time.

"My God!" He picked up Kat. "How did I not see this before?"

"How did *none* of us see it?" asked Maggie, stunned.

Everyone looked around the room at each other and the room grew quiet.

"Is it possible?" asked Maggie, "Maybe, Kat's grandmother was from another line of MacGregor's?"

"I suppose anything is possible," said Lady Aurnia," but it would be quite a coincidence, don't ye think?"

"I am starting to think there are no such things as coincidences around here," mumbled Maggie.

That night, it was decided that it would be best for everyone to stay under one roof until Alastair became more comfortable with Quinn, Gabe, and his new surroundings. Maggie and Duncan retired to their bedroom after getting the babies to sleep. Maggie leaned back against the bedpost with her arms folded and gave Duncan a dirty look.

He came over to her and placed his hands on her hips. "I know that look a little too well," he said. "What did I do *this* time?"

"I want to discuss why you never told me about your visit from Finn."

Duncan brushed her hair back from her neck and playfully nibbled on it. "Ye discuss," he growled. "I have other plans in mind for the evening and they involve using my mouth for better things than talking."

Maggie pushed him back. "Oh, no you don't! You are not distracting me with your body this time, mister."

Her husband pulled her back to him and traced the top of her dress where it covered her breasts with his finger. "I am sorry I did not tell ye, but it was the night the midwife released ye, and I became completely distracted. It simply slipped my mind and, as I recall, we weren't exactly 'talking' that much that particular night," he winked. "Making other noises, aye, but definitely not speaking."

He moaned slightly and ran his hand down her backside, and his lips moved to the top of her breasts.

Maggie picked up his chin with her finger so that she was looking him directly in the eye. "I need to know any and all matters concerning Finn. You did not forget, I know that, and I know that you are trying to protect me, but when it comes to him, I need every single detail as soon as it comes available."

"Yes, my love," he said, catching her finger playfully with his teeth and grinning.

Maggie shook her head and laughed as she pulled him into a long kiss.

He unexpectedly grabbed her, lifted her off her feet, and plunged them both back onto the bed which caused her to let out a little squeal.

After their lovemaking, Maggie lay curled against Duncan as they talked.

"How is Quinn doing with the news?" she asked as she glided her fingers over his mid-section.

"He is dealing with it. He was as shocked as the rest of us, but I think he will be just fine."

Maggie kissed his deliciously bare chest. "You know, there were a few moments when I thought Alastair was *your* son."

Duncan stroked her arm. "How did ye feel about that?"

"Much the same way I am sure that Gabe is feeling right now. I am greatly concerned about him."

"Ye think he is awake?"

"If I know Gabe, he is downstairs drinking right now," she replied.

Duncan kissed her. "I will keep your spot warm for ye while ye two talk."

"I love you so much," she said and slipped off the bed. She put on her robe, peeked in on the babies, and headed downstairs to the drawing room—where she found Gabe drinking alone in the dark.

She sat down on the sofa next to him. "I had a feeling you would be awake," she said softly.

"Yes, well...it has been a day, hasn't it?" he replied.

"How are you doing, Gabe?"

He rested his hand on her leg. "I am not sure," he said, looking down into his drink. "I am worried about Quinn, of course. Today has been quite a surprise for him; for all of us really."

"Well, I am worried about *you* right now," she said.

"I have no reason to be upset," he assured.

Maggie leaned against him and he put his arm around her. "Then, you are a better soul than I am, as much as I am ashamed to admit it."

Gabe looked down at her, puzzled. "What do you mean by that?" he asked as he sipped his glass.

"Well, for a red-hot minute, I thought Alastair was Duncan's son, and I was on the verge of a full-blown panic attack. I didn't know how to feel. I mean, if he had been Duncan's son, of course, I would have grown to love him as much as I do my own children, simply because of who his father is, but I think it would have taken a while to work my way up to that point. There would be a great many feelings I would have to deal with first and I expect that you and Quinn will have a few things to work through as well."

Gabe looked down at the floor. "That does not trouble me. Quinn and I will be fine. Our relationship is solid, and this new addition will only strengthen our union in the long run. It will just take a little time to adjust. Besides, that is not what I am fretting over."

"Then, what is it?" she asked and pushed herself up.

He blew out a deep breath. "Maggie, do you think that Kat does indeed carry MacGregor blood? I cannot help but think back to the nightmare I had and wonder if it was not some sort of omen."

She took his hand. "Honestly Gabe?" she asked.

He eyed her warily.

"If this were a normal situation and we were a typical family, I would just say that it was mere coincidence, but with all of...Finn's Fae fuckery... going on around here, I cannot help but think that there may be some merit to it."

Gabe cocked his head. "Did something else happen?"

Maggie nodded. "Finn paid a visit to Duncan one evening."

"When?"

"The night the colt was born."

"And you just mention this now?" he exclaimed.

Maggie scrunched up her nose in an annoyed expression. "I just found out myself. Duncan conveniently forgot to inform me. He claims it slipped his mind, but I know damn well he did it intentionally, thinking that he was protecting me."

Gabe turned to be closer to Maggie. "What did he say during this visit with Duncan?"

"He told Duncan that I had a bigger purpose here, but he would say nothing else. Duncan thinks he has something up his sleeve."

"Duncan does have excellent instincts."

"Yes, I know and that is what scares me." Maggie stared straight ahead, completely lost in her own thoughts.

Gabe noticed the pensive look on her face. "Fuckery? Is that a new word in our vocabulary now?" he asked, trying to lighten the mood.

"Can you think of a better one?" she asked sarcastically and rolled her eyes.

"No, it seems pretty fitting actually." Gabe tightened his arm around Maggie. "So, what else is bothering you?" he asked.

"The same thing that has been bothering me for a long time now."

"John!" he said, compassionately. "What if we cannot find a way? Will you be able to live with that, Mags?"

"No, I will not. And, if I have to take extreme measures to save him...." she trailed off.

"How drastic are we talking?" asked Gabe, gravely.

"Whatever it takes," she whispered.

"I wondered where ye went," called Quinn from the doorway. He pointed to Gabe's glass as he walked in. "Please, tell me there is more."

Gabe handed Quinn his own half-full glass after Quinn plopped down on the other side of him.

"I peeked in on Kat and Alastair a few minutes ago," said Quinn, sipping the drink. "They are both sound asleep."

"At least they are both able to get some rest," said Gabe.

"Indeed!" Quinn looked over at his husband with a certain look in his eye.

Maggie felt like she was intruding on a private moment. "I think I am going back to bed," she said. "You two enjoy the rest of your night."

She kissed each of them on the cheek after she stood. Gabe grabbed her hand and gave it a reassuring squeeze before she left. Smiling at Gabe, Maggie went back upstairs to be with Duncan.

"How is Gabe?" asked Duncan as he held open the covers for her.

She dropped her robe, climbed into bed, and snuggled in close to him. "I think he and Quinn will work through this just fine."

"That is good news."

Maggie stretched out on her back, looking up at the ceiling. "He is more concerned about Kat and, truthfully, so am I." She turned to face Duncan. "What are the chances that she carries MacGregor blood?"

Duncan shook his head. "I have no idea."

"It is too much of a coincidence, isn't it?" she whispered.

Duncan slipped his arm around her. "Aye, it probably is."

"More of Finn's Fae fuckery!" she muttered.

He looked confused, then burst into laughter. "Finn's Fae fuckery? What the hell?"

"Yes! It is my new description for all of this," laughed Maggie softly.

"Sounds more like the name of a brothel," said Duncan. "And a fairly interesting one at that."

"I would hate to see his prices!" she scoffed.

Maggie scooched closer to him to look into his eyes. "My mind will not quiet tonight. Can you please help me, my love?" she asked seriously.

He looked down and smiled lovingly. "Aye, that I will gladly do."

He kissed her, softly at first and then harder until she surrendered to his touch. He rolled her underneath him and pressed her into the bed as he went intently about his mission. Maggie felt the fogginess take over her mind, and all her worries slipped away, in the way that only Duncan could make happen.

Maggie and Duncan went in together to check on the babies the next morning. Cracking the door open, they could hear them giggling. They tiptoed closer to the crib to see what was making them laugh and stopped when they saw the reason. A trio of wooden animals that Joshua had carved for the babies, which normally rested on the table nearby, were in the crib with them...and floating about eight inches above their heads; the three little ones kicked their feet, and waved their hands in excitement.

Their parents watched in wide-eyed astonishment. The toys moved of their own accord, circling like a mobile.

Maggie held out her arms behind her and Duncan seized her hand; they inched silently toward the bed. As soon as the babies gaze went from what was above them to their parent's faces, the toys dropped harmlessly into the crib.

Maggie let out a little whimper and turned to Duncan, who's own face had gone rather pale. "How?" She squeaked.

"I am afraid to ask," he whispered to his wife before calling over his shoulder, his eyes still focused on the children.

"MOTHER!"

Lady Aurnia stepped into the nursery from the hall, tugging at a loose string on her gown. "Yes, dear?" she asked when she finally looked up.

Duncan shook his finger at the crib. "Could we make toys float in the air when we were babies?"

His mother looked at him strangely. "Of course not." She walked over and placed her hand on his forehead. "Are ye feverish, or have ye been in the whisky already this morning?"

"That would be an easier explanation," muttered Maggie under her breath, chewing on her finger.

She shook her head slowly in disbelief and picked up the three toys, examining them closer while the babies happily continued to kick and play.

Lady Aurnia moved next to her. "What on Earth is going on?"

Maggie held them up. "These were floating above the babies when we came in."

The older woman took one in her hand and gave it her own thorough examination. She looked down at the children, just as Cecile stuck her head in the doorway.

"Want us to take the babies downstairs?" Cecile asked.

"NO!" they all shouted in unison.

Cecile stepped back, surprised by the emphatic reply just as Maggie remembered herself.

"We have them this morning, Cecile. Thank you."

"Alright," the nursemaid mumbled, and she disappeared back out into the hall.

Each one picked up a baby and watched them closely.

"More of Finn's Fae fuckery, I assume?" asked Duncan.

"Duncan!" scolded his mother. "Watch your mouth around the bairns!"

"Mother!" Duncan retorted, "Our children are causing things to float in the air. I think my language is the least of our concerns at the moment."

Logan noticed them all gathered in the nursery and came inside. "Are we going down for breakfast?"

"Get Gabe and Quinn. We need to have a family meeting in the drawing room...*NOW!*" commanded Maggie.

Once they were all gathered and the doors were closed, they put the babies down on the floor on a blanket.

"What's the issue?" asked Quinn.

"It seems the babies are playing more now," said Duncan, pacing and wiping beads of sweat from his forehead.

"Isn't that normal?" asked Gabe.

"Not when their toys play by themselves," replied Maggie, still in a state of shock.

"What?" exclaimed Gabe, Quinn, and Logan, simultaneously.

Duncan folded his arms and pointed his index finger down at the children. "When Maggie and I went in this morning, their wooden toys were suspended in the air above them, moving around in a circle. The toys dropped as soon as the babies saw us."

Everyone turned to look at the babies, who were busy amusing themselves, seemingly laughing at the silliness of the adults around them.

Maggie rubbed the back of her neck where her muscles had tensed up. "Finn did say we may see some unusual things," she mumbled.

"Do ye think he is behind this?" asked Duncan.

She shrugged. "You're asking me? I know as much as you do, which is pretty much nothing."

"Well, they obviously get this from your side of the family," said Duncan, dryly, with a wave of his hand.

Maggie slowly turned to glare at him.

Lady Aurnia touched Maggie on the back reassuringly and shot her oldest son a look of warning. "I think all we need to do right now is just keep a keen eye out," she said. "There is not much else we *can* do."

Maggie stayed very close to the babies the rest of the day, afraid to leave them with any of the staff. She took them outside to sit and play on a blanket on the grass while she watched Gabe and Quinn play tag with Kat and Alastair.

Gabe came over and sat down next to her.

"Are they wearing you out?" asked Maggie.

"Damn! I am too old for this," he laughed, waving to Quinn. "It is a good thing I married a man twelve years younger than me to chase our children around."

Maggie rubbed him on the back. "Cheer up, it could be worse. They could be making inanimate objects dance all over the place. Want to trade?"

Gabe looked over at the babies happily playing among themselves. "I think I will stick to the ones I have," he grinned. "Anything else happen since this morning?"

Maggie shook her head.

He put his arm around her; he saw how bothered she was and had no idea what to say to comfort her. "Just another exciting day," he said, and kissed the side of her head.

"You have no idea how much I dream of having just one normal day around here." Maggie rolled her eyes.

"You would get bored," he teased.

"I would try my best," she quipped and then sighed. "How are things going with Alastair?"

"Much better than I expected." He watched them running across the lawn. "He is a very shy child, but he is starting to come around. Now that the initial shock has worn off, Quinn, well he is over the moon and Kat already has her new brother wrapped around her little finger, as she has all of us."

"What about you?" she asked.

"I am good. I am not rushing things because I do not want the boy to feel too overwhelmed. He has already had to deal with so much in his few short years of being in this world, but I feel like we will get where we need to be, given enough time."

"Sounds like a little bit of wisdom has come along with that age," smiled Maggie.

"Yes, well, *something* good should come along with it to make up for the body parts that start to ache and give out," he said and stretched out his left arm, a look of discomfort crossing his face.

"You okay?" she asked, concerned.

"I'm fine. I think I just slept in an odd way."

They noticed Duncan striding across the lawn.

"There ye are," he said and came over to join them, stopping in front of the babies. "No more floating things," he scolded mockingly and wagged his finger in jest.

They giggled back at their father and he waved his hand back at them jokingly.

"Ye three are hopeless."

"They are such happy babies," remarked Gabe.

"Thank goodness," said Maggie. "Can you imagine three unhappy ones at one time? And magical ones, at that? I shudder to think what we would be up against."

"Nay!" said Duncan. "I do not think we would survive." He kissed Maggie on the top of the head. "Hello, my love."

"Where have you been?" she asked.

"I was showing Mother and Logan around the estate. I think Mother has fallen in love with the children at the school, and I think Logan has fallen in love with Hettie's cooking."

"They say the way to a man's heart is through his stomach," smirked Maggie.

"Not mine," grinned Duncan, devilishly, and he sat down next to her.

Maggie pulled him closer to her by his collar and kissed him. "Oh, I *know* the way to your heart, and it is just a tad bit lower."

Gabe rolled his eyes. "For goodness sakes, your babies are right here."

"How do ye think they got here," chuckled Duncan.

Duncan looked down at his children. "Any more strange happenings?"

Maggie shook her head. "Fortunately, it has been very quiet."

He reached over and touched Maggie's face when he saw how concerned she was. "It will be alright, my love. We will figure things out."

"I know," she whispered and leaned her face into his hand.

Cecile and Cora came through the side door. "You ready to put the babies down for their nap?" asked Cecile.

"Yes!" said Maggie as she stood, smiling to Gabe and Duncan. "I will be right back."

The three women took the children inside and left Duncan and Gabe alone to talk.

"This business with the babies, on top of her concern for John, along with everything else that is going on, is wearing Maggie down," Gabe said.

"Aye, I know," Duncan replied. "I do not know how to calm her nerves."

Gabe thought for a moment. "You and Maggie have not had a break since the babies came. Why don't you take her somewhere, even if it is just for the day, just the two of you? You could use some time alone, and there are enough nursing mothers around here who are happy to pitch in."

"What if they start doing...other things?"

"Duncan, your mother is here, along with Quinn, Logan, and me. We can handle whatever may come up...literally. Besides, if your mother is anything like mine, she is itching to get them all to herself anyway. You and Maggie are nothing more than obstacles standing in her way."

Duncan laughed out loud. "Aye, ye are probably right." He looked back towards the house. "That is actually a wonderful idea. If I can get her away from all these distractions, even for a little while, it would do her some good." He smiled. "I have been working on a surprise for her for a while now and it has just been completed. The timing could not be more perfect."

Maggie laid on her side and faced Duncan in bed that night. "What do you think they will be able to do as they get older if they can already move toys like that before their first birthdays?" she whispered.

Duncan slid his hand down on her hip. "It does not matter what they can or cannot do. They will be who they are, and we will be here to deal with whatever the future brings, to love them, to teach them right from wrong, and to guide them on the right path because that is what parents do."

"What if they decide to turn on us? We are already outnumbered, and they *are* magical, apparently. The terrible twos should be interesting to say the least."

"Aye, ye have a point," he laughed. "Let's just hope they stay as happy as they are now."

Maggie moved her hand to his chest. "The teenage years will be approaching rapidly. Maybe we should start checking out some of those spell books downstairs to see if there is anything that can help us for when that time comes."

Duncan groaned. "Especially if our girls are anything like ye when they mature. God help us if ye all have your monthly courses at the same time; there may be no survivors."

Maggie smacked his rear as he laughed, and he wrapped his arms around her tightly.

The next morning, Duncan got up early to make some arrangements, while letting Maggie sleep in. When he was finished, he woke her with a kiss.

"Good morning, my love." He pushed the hair back from her face.

"Good morning. Are the babies awake?"

"The babies are already taken care of," said Duncan, "and I need ye to get dressed. Ye and I are taking the day off."

"What?" She sat up. "We can't just take a day off. We have children."

"Aye we can, and we are. The babies are in very capable hands, and I have a surprise for ye that is going to take up the entire day."

Maggie started to protest but he put his finger to her lips and shushed her.

"Trousers and top. The horses are saddled and waiting for us. No arguing."

She bobbed her head around. "Alright! Give me a few minutes to get ready."

An hour later, they were on horseback, riding slowly, enjoying the warmth of a beautiful day.

"Are we going to the waterfall?" she asked when she noticed the direction they were headed.

"Aye, your gift is there."

"My gift?" she asked. "What gift?"

"It's a surprise," he teased. "And, one I think ye will like."

As the waterfall came into sight, Maggie could not believe her eyes. She dismounted with a look of wonderment and a wide smile on her face.

"You did this?" she asked.

"I had some help. We talked about it, but never actually had a good place for it, so I figured this was the perfect spot—our own little personal escape."

"I love you so much." She turned and kissed him.

A Native American longhouse had been built into the landscape next to the waterfall—the place Maggie always rode to when she needed a break. She had brought Duncan to see it not long after they were married, but they had not been back for a long time. The longhouse was exactly like the one they had stayed in the night of the wolf moon ceremony when Powaw performed the marriage blessing over them.

Maggie went inside to get a better look. It only had one entrance, with a woven blanket hanging from the doorway for warmth and privacy. A bed, covered in deerskins, blankets, and pillows, was in the middle of the longhouse, along with a small table that had several clay pots on it. The fire ring was on the far wall with a small opening to let the smoke out.

"I don't know what to say," said Maggie.

Duncan pulled her close. "Say ye will spend the day here with me forgetting about everything outside of these walls."

"I will do my best," she purred and slipped her arms around him.

Her husband kissed her and led her over to the bed. "Ye did not ask me what was in the pots," he smirked.

"What's in the pots?" she asked excitedly.

"A nice supply of that wonderful oil that I intend to cover every single part of your body with."

"Oh!" exclaimed Maggie. "I can hardly wait!"

"No need to wait," he said, and he kissed her again.

Duncan took his time undressing her, before finally laying her face-down on the bed. He took out a handful of the oil and warmed it in his hands. He spread it over each part of the back of her body, before flipping her over, taking the time to massage every inch of her skin until Maggie was breathing heavily just from the touch of his hand. He then took another bit out, and using his fingers, he pressed it into her opening and gently rubbed it around inside of her, preparing the way.

When he replaced his fingers with his tongue, Maggie laughed, then cried out and shuddered with delight as he quickly pushed her over the edge. She lay panting as she pulled his face up to hers, biting his lips and ordering him inside of her.

He shed his own clothes before climbing atop her, whispering her name, and professing his love. He took a moment to cover his manhood with the oil before easily slipping inside of her in one fluid motion, slowly at first, taking the time to kiss her lips between each thrust, and only quickening the pace when she reached the edge once more and she begged him to join her. When his seed released, his fingers were intertwined with hers, his tongue was buried in her mouth, and their bodies throbbed from the sheer intensity of their act. He rolled her over on top of him, never separating, and they rested briefly.

They spent the next few hours entangled in each other's arms, repeating the performance. As the sun started to set, they moved their lovemaking to the water, and as the darkness was about to fall, they worked their way back to the bed. Maggie pulled him tightly against her as they lounged.

"I suppose we should go back," she whined, running her fingers through his unbound hair.

"Or we could stay the night," he suggested and nibbled on her neck. "There is firewood already chopped and we never got around to eating the food I packed, so we will be fine."

"What about the babies?" She placed her hand on the back of his head and gently urged him to move from her neck down to her right breast which was aching for his attention. He licked and teased, looking up to see the expression on her face as she closed her eyes and moaned with desire.

"They are being spoiled as we speak. As a matter of fact, it would be rude of us to take that time away from their grandmother who came all the way from Scotland to see them."

"Won't they be expecting us?" She hissed through her teeth as she grazed her nails across his back.

"I told Gabe not to wait up," he replied with a smirk before tracing a line with his tongue across her chest and to her left breast, which he took in his mouth and suckled mercilessly until he felt her back arch and she cried out for him dreamily. He then knew he had her right where he wanted her for the night.

"It *is* getting dark," whimpered Maggie, pulling his face back up to hers.

"Aye, it may be dangerous to travel so late," he growled and tugged on her bottom lip with his teeth.

"And it *would* be a shame to waste all that oil," she purred before she took his face in her hands and sank her tongue into his mouth forcefully.

He pinned her arms above her head and grinned. "Stay here!" he ordered, pressing himself against her for effect, "while I get a fire going. We are going nowhere until morning." He kissed her one more time before he rolled off the bed, gathered the wood and built the fire.

Maggie laid on her stomach and watched him, completely naked as he worked; his handsome, chiseled face and magnificent body illuminated by the flames from the fire, and wondered how she ever got lucky enough to have this wonderful man as her husband and the father of her children.

4 CHAPTER FOUR

Early the next morning, they reluctantly dressed and rode back to the house. Everyone was at the breakfast table when they arrived.

Maggie and Duncan stopped off at the drawing room to check on the babies, who were happily playing with Kat and Alastair as Cecile and Cora looked on, before they made their way into the dining room.

"Look what the cat dragged in," teased Quinn.

Maggie leaned down between Gabe and Quinn, kissing each one on the cheek. "If you two are good boys, I may tell you where the cat dragged us in from. You might appreciate going there yourselves one of these days."

"I take it you had a good time?" asked Gabe.

"We most certainly did and thank you all for giving us the chance. I needed that more than I realized."

Lady Aurnia smiled. "It was our pleasure! I enjoyed spending the day with the children very much, and the bairns were even gracious enough to sleep soundly throughout the entire night."

"*That* was another gift from Finn. He said as long as the sun was down, they would sleep straight through."

"That is a pretty useful gift!" remarked Lady Aurnia.

"Very!" replied Maggie. "Anything *unusual* happen while we were gone?"

"Nay! The babies were perfect angels."

Duncan noticed an all too familiar look of concern cross Maggie's face. He took her hand. "Nay! Stop it! I spent all day and night working to get *that* look off your face. It is far too soon to see it again."

"Oh, do not act like it was killing you," mumbled Maggie, rolling her eyes.

"I never said that I did not *enjoy* my work, my love." He winked and playfully tapped her on the rear. He pulled out a chair and helped her sit before taking the one next to her.

She smirked as he grabbed her leg under the table.

"How did Alastair make out yesterday?" asked Maggie.

"He seems to be adjusting well," said Quinn.

"He is already taking his big brother duties seriously," added Gabe. "He is very protective over Kat."

"He is of the babies, as well," noted Lady Aurnia.

"Well, that's a good thing," replied Maggie. "It means he is starting to feel like part of the family."

The following afternoon, while the babies were napping, and everyone was out, Maggie decided to check the books to see if there was anything that might help with John. She pulled one off the shelf, sat down, and started to flip through the pages.

"Maggie are ye down here?" called Quinn.

"Yes! I am!"

"There ye are," he said, reaching the bottom of the stairs. "I was looking everywhere for ye."

Maggie closed the book. "I was hoping to find something to help us with John. Where are Alastair and Kat?"

Quinn came over and took the seat next to her. "Kat went down for a nap, and Alastair is at the school playing with some of the children. Mother is keeping an eye on him. Gabe went to speak to David Percy on some legal matters, and I was hoping to speak to ye alone while he was gone."

Maggie leaned back. "What's on your mind?"

His face became very serious. "I am worried about Gabe. He is not sleeping, and when he does, he is having horrible nightmares."

She frowned. "Is it the same dream he had about Kat?"

"I do not know. He will not tell me, and that is not like him. Do ye have any idea what is going on? Is he more upset about Alastair than he is letting on to me? Because if he is, he needs to tell me."

Maggie shook her head. "No! I do not think the situation with Alastair troubles him. I know he has kept his distance a bit, but it is more out of concern for the boy than anything. He doesn't want to push too hard. I do know the nightmare about Kat shook him badly, but he has not mentioned it since that first time, so I assumed it no longer bothered him."

Quinn leaned forward, his face in his hands. "I do not know what to do, Maggie, and I am terribly concerned about him."

"Have you tried mixing up something for him to help him sleep?"

"Aye, I have offered, but he has refused it each time. He has never shut me out like this before. It's just not like him."

"I will talk to him and see if I can find out what is going on." Maggie leaned forward and touched his arm. "Gabe loves you and your relationship is more solid now than it has ever been, so do not worry yourself about that."

"Thank ye, Maggie."

"So, how are *you* doing with Alastair?"

Quinn's eyes widened and he blew out a long breath. "I think I am still a bit in shock. It is taking some time to adjust, but we are getting there."

"Well, you know, Duncan and I are always here for you if you need us."

"Aye, I know, and I am very grateful for that." Quinn looked around. "Want some help?"

"Please! I am a bit lost here."

Quinn grabbed a few books from the shelf, put them on the desk, and started going through them.

"Here is the recipe I had in mind," he finally said, and he placed an open book in front of Maggie. "It will slow the heartbeat and breathing to barely detectable, and cool and turn the skin gray to give the appearance of death. It only lasts for a very limited time, so he would have to ingest it just before he goes up on the gallows, and the measurements would have to be exact."

"Is it safe? What if something is a tad bit off?"

Quinn winced. "It will kill him, but there is a better chance with this than there is at the end of a hangman's noose."

"Well, we will have to take our chances," replied Maggie.

She continued to look through some of the books as Quinn pulled one other book from a top shelf.

"Ye might be interested in this one," he said.

"What is it?" she asked.

Quinn laid the book in front of her. "It was Danu's; your mother's."

Maggie dropped her gaze to the book, then looked back up at Quinn. "My mother's?"

"There are books here from the main gods and goddesses. Some of them contain musings, poetry, historical recordings, and some even have their most used spells."

"What is in hers?"

"I do not know. The oldest of the books are written in a language that no one else, including our family, is meant to read. That is one of them, but I suspect that ye will be able to understand each and every word without any difficulty."

Maggie stared down at it and lightly touched the cover...then slid it away. "I am not sure I am ready for that," she whispered. "I am not sure I ever will be."

Quinn squeezed her shoulder, comfortingly. "I understand. It will be here when ye are ready and so will I if ye need me to be."

She placed her hand over his. "Thank you!"

Gabe returned a little while later while Maggie sat at her desk and worked on some paperwork for the shipping company.

"Where is everyone?" he asked.

"Out and about. Quinn is down at the school with Kat and Alastair, letting them play, and Cecile and Cora took the babies outside so I could catch up on some things here that have been piling up over the past couple of weeks."

Maggie laid down her quill and leaned back as she watched him carefully. The lack of sleep and stress had started to show lines on his face and bags under his eyes.

"I am glad we are alone. I wanted to speak to you for a bit." she said.

"You sound so serious, Mags."

She got up and pulled the doors closed, then poured him a drink, motioning for him to sit.

Maggie sat down on the table in front of him. "Tell me what's going on with you."

He shrugged. "I don't know what you mean."

"Quinn says you are not sleeping and that you are having more nightmares."

Gabe set his drink down on the side table and looked rather flustered. "Quinn worries too much, and he had absolutely no business telling you that!" he snapped.

Maggie placed both her hands on the sides of his face and forced him to look at her. "I am not buying that for one minute. Tell me the truth. What's going on?"

He shook his head. "There is nothing to tell."

"Damn it, Gabe! It's me, Maggie. The one person who knows and understands you better than anyone. What in the hell is bothering you?"

Gabe closed his eyes and sat silent for a few moments as he gathered his thoughts before he said anything. "I am sure it is nothing," he finally said very softly.

"Tell me," she whispered.

"I am having nightmares, only it is not exactly like the first one I told you about. Now, it is different and the same one repeats each time I close my eyes." He picked his drink back up and took a large sip of it.

"It starts out the same. Kat is running away from me and I am chasing her to the edge of that cliff, but now when I try to save her, I go over the cliff instead of her and she is on the edge, reaching down for me, only she isn't alone. Now Quinn is next to her, with you, Duncan, and even Alastair. You are all reaching for me, but as I touch someone's fingers, I slip and fall away from all of you. When I am falling, that is when I wake up, but when I open my eyes, the fear is so strong that my heart feels like it is coming out of my chest."

Gabe looked at Maggie, a look of undeniable fear in his eyes. "I am afraid that it is an omen that I am going to lose all of you." A single tear slipped down the side of his face.

Maggie stood up and pulled him tightly to her breast and she kissed him on the top of his head. "You are not losing any of us and we are not losing you."

She took his face in her hands. "I promise, and you know better than anyone that I keep my word. Tonight, you need to let Quinn mix up one of his potions to help you sleep and then let him take you to bed. Trust him and let him do whatever he needs to do to settle your mind. Don't pretend, don't protest, just let him do what he deems fit. Tomorrow, things will be much better; you will see."

Maggie kissed him on the lips and then she wiped the wetness from his face with her fingers. She fished around in his pocket where he kept his handkerchiefs, pulled one out, and handed it to him to wipe his nose.

"You still know me a little too well, you know that?" he sniffled and laughed as he accepted the square of linen.

"Well, thank goodness we know each other so well, otherwise our spouses wouldn't know who to come to for advice when they are at a loss." Maggie took his hands. "Do you feel better now that you have told someone?"

"I do, but I will feel much better when they go away."

Maggie cupped his face again. "Let's see what we can do about that."

Maggie and Gabe walked down to the school after he regained his composure. As soon as Kat saw him, she came running into his arms. He scooped her up and covered her with kisses.

"Are you having fun, sweetheart?" he asked.

She happily nodded and hugged his neck. As soon as he put her down, she took his hand, and led him over to Quinn, where they had been playing.

Maggie came to stand next to a smiling Lady Aurnia, who watched over them. "They really are very happy together, aren't they?" she said.

"Yes, they are."

Maggie took Lady Aurnia by the arm and nudged her over to a bench away from where anyone could hear. "I need to ask you something. In the dealings you have had with the Fae world, how significant are dreams, more importantly, nightmares?"

"It depends," she replied. "Mostly dreams are just that, but if they are recurring or particularly disturbing, it can be some sort of warning, or it may be nothing at all. Why do ye ask? Are ye having some that are bothering ye?"

Maggie shook her head. "Not me," she looked back across the yard, "but Gabe is."

Lady Aurnia followed Maggie's gaze.

"I am more than a little concerned. There is just too much happening around here at once for it not to be connected."

"I agree," the older woman said. "The Fae have not been heard from in generations and all of a sudden, the one who happens to appear is the King of the Fae himself and he seems to have taken a great interest in all things surrounding ye, his granddaughter."

Duncan and Logan joined Quinn and Gabe with the children. Maggie smiled as the children from the school all ran up to greet Duncan; he took the time to greet each one and call them by name.

Maggie leaned toward Lady Aurnia, as she nodded in their direction. "When Duncan first arrived, all of the children here were terrified of him. They would go out of their way just to avoid him."

Lady Aurnia chuckled. "Well, he is large and can be rather intimidating."

"They can't seem to get enough of him now, and he loves every minute of it."

"I see why ye could not leave them, Maggie, to stay in Scotland. All of these people are very special, and what ye have created here is nothing short of astounding."

"They are family to me, and they give me far more joy than I give them."

Duncan was holding one of the children in his arms, when he caught sight of her and waved.

She sent him a message. *I need to speak to Quinn alone. Don't let Gabe know.*

He frowned. *Everything alright?*

I will tell you later.

Duncan leaned down and whispered into Kat's ear. Kat nodded, took Quinn by the hand, pulled on him, and marched straight to Maggie. Kat then crawled up onto Maggie's lap and rested her head against her chest as she sucked her thumb.

"Duncan has Kat doing his dirty work, I see," chuckled Maggie.

"Aye. She will do anything for him. We should get him to come over at bedtime and tell her to go to sleep; maybe she will listen to him."

Quinn looked at his mother. "May I have a moment to speak with Maggie alone?"

"Of course," she said, and she went to join the others.

Quinn sat down beside her. "Did ye speak to him?"

"I did. He is having disturbing nightmares where he is separated from all of us."

Quinn frowned.

"Mix him something to make him sleep tonight, preferably something to stop him from dreaming, if you can. Take him to bed and 'comfort' him as only his husband can, until we figure out what is going on here."

He waved at Gabe. "Ye think there is something more to this and that we need to be concerned about it, don't you?"

"I do, and we need to get to the bottom of it, sooner rather than later. I have not seen anything rattle him like this before and I don't care to ever see it again."

Kat slipped down and ran back to join the group, and Quinn chased after, making her laugh.

Duncan made his way over and took the seat next to Maggie. She leaned against him.

"What is going on with Gabe?" he asked.

"He has been having nightmares, only I think there may be something more to them. We need to stay close to him and make sure he is...protected."

Duncan slipped his arm around her. "I will speak with Quinn and Logan. We will make sure he is not alone at any time."

"Thank you," she whispered.

Cecile, Cora, and Hettie came around the corner with the babies. Maggie took Kendric and Morgan in her lap and Duncan took Alanna. Alastair came over to greet them and Gabe followed behind.

Gabe reached for Morgan. "Here, let me help you out there."

He picked her up and held her high in the air as she grinned and kicked her feet, happy as always to be in Gabe's arms. A slight noise caused Maggie to turn her head and look up. A crow had landed on a tree limb right next to Gabe. The crow began to make a loud cawing sound over and over, becoming louder each time. Maggie stared at the creature and could have sworn that crow looked her right in the eye before flying away. She couldn't help but think back to the legends she had heard as a child of crows being bad omens and harbingers of death and a cold shiver ran down her spine.

Maggie was wide awake that night. She silently slipped through the house, down to where the books were stored. She ran her hands along the spines and tried to decide where to start. This night, she had a different mission from her previous recent visits.

She pulled out book after book and thumbed through, looking for something to explain Gabe's nightmares and for a way to protect him from them. After two hours of searching, she had still had no luck. She went to put one back on the shelf and smacked it back into place, more out of frustration than anything. As she did, another book fell off the shelf and landed open. Maggie bent over, picked it up, and noticed that the page it was opened to had the image of a crow across the top. She took the book and sat back down at the table, closer to the light from the candle. She skimmed the text, and soon realized that this particular book contained information describing the different gods and goddesses and their respective abilities. The one on that page described a goddess, represented by a crow. She was a warrior, a shapeshifting foreteller of doom, who had domain over war, destiny, and fate. She would often transform into a crow to watch over soldiers on the battlefield and transport them from life into death.

Maggie leaned back in the chair, a sense of dread and fear filling her. Gabe was a soldier, and if anyone in the Fae world would come to escort him into death, it would be this one. The visit from the crow, coupled with Gabe's nightmares, had convinced Maggie that he was in extreme danger. She pushed the book away and was so lost in thought, that she never heard Duncan come into the room.

"Maggie, what are ye doing down here this time of night?"

Maggie stood up, went to him and buried her face against his chest.

He embraced her tightly when he physically felt the angst that rolled off her.

"I think death may be coming for Gabe."

Duncan took her by the shoulders to look her in the eye. "Ye think what? What makes ye believe that?"

Maggie explained everything that was happening and showed him the book page she had found.

He sat down slowly, and he looked over the text for himself. He leaned back against the chair and covered his mouth with his hand. "Ye could be reading more into this than there actually is Maggie. There are crows all over this place, and Gabe's nightmares may be because of some deep-rooted fear caused by all of the changes he and Quinn have been dealing with as of late."

Maggie folded her arms and leaned back against the table. "Or maybe not. I am not willing to take that chance with Gabe's life."

Duncan took her hands. "Fae have not involved themselves with the affairs of mankind for a long time."

She squeezed his hands. "They didn't...until I came along. Now, we are up to our eyeballs in this stuff. All you need to do is look at our children and their floating toys to know that."

He pulled her down onto his lap and knew he could not argue *that* point.

"I will not let him go," she whispered, pressing her forehead against his. "Finn has all of these supposed plans for me and the babies, but if he takes Gabe away from me, from us, this world can be damned to its own fate and I will not lift one finger to stop it."

Duncan pulled her tightly to him, not knowing what to say, so he didn't say anything.

They sat quiet for a long while, just holding each other until Duncan finally broke the silence. "It will be dawn soon, and the babies will be up. We should go back upstairs." He picked up the book and put it back on the shelf then noticed another one out on the table.

"Why is this one out?" he asked.

Maggie sighed. "Quinn thought I might want to look at it. It was my mother's book."

"Have ye?"

She shook her head. "I am not ready for that, not yet."

He left the book where it was and escorted her back to bed.

Maggie picked at her breakfast the next morning, remaining quiet as Duncan looked on with concern.

Gabe and Quinn came down after everyone was already seated.

Gabe kissed her on the cheek. "Good morning."

Maggie watched him as he took the chair across from her. "Did you sleep last night?" she asked.

He smiled and turned briefly to Quinn. "I did. Quinn fixed me right up with one of his drinks and it helped a great deal."

Quinn rubbed him on the back, lovingly.

Maggie pushed her plate away.

"Why so sullen this morning, Mags?" asked Gabe.

"I guess I am just tired," replied Maggie and she forced a smile.

Duncan slipped his hand over onto her leg under the table and gave her a reassuring squeeze.

Maggie laid her napkin down beside her plate and pushed her chair back. "I am going to the nursery to check on the little ones."

The babies were sleeping in that morning, while Maggie stood over the crib with her arms folded, keeping watch over them. She moved to the window to look outside.

"Hear me, Finn," she said firmly, "if you take him away from us, I will *never* forgive you. Quinn needs him, the children need him, and I need him most of all. If you care for me in the least, you will not let anything happen to him."

Silence was the only response she received in return.

5 CHAPTER FIVE

Over the next few days, everyone kept a close eye on Gabe, never leaving him completely alone. Quinn's nightly drinks were allowing him to rest while keeping the nightmares at bay, and he was slowly getting back to his usual self. Everyone started to relax a bit, except Maggie, who was overly mindful of everything in their surroundings. Each night, after Duncan fell asleep, she would slip down to the collection room to go through more books.

That night, she pulled out a book, took a seat and was getting ready to open it when Duncan came up behind her chair. He placed his hand over the cover and prevented her from opening it.

"Enough, my love," he said softly. "Ye are making yourself insane trying to figure out a way to protect Gabe from some danger that may not even exist. Sometimes, dreams are just dreams, Maggie, and ye need to let this go."

She leaned back and covered her face with her hands. "I know," she whispered. "I just hate feeling so helpless."

Duncan shifted to her side and leaned back against the table. "There is no spell in any of these books to keep someone from death if it is their time to go."

"Then what good are they?" She shoved the book away, frustrated.

"Maggie, these books were not meant for humans, not even for the ones of us that have *some* Fae blood. They are meant to be returned to the gods and goddesses to whom they belonged to, when and if, they ever choose to return. Yes, we have spells granted to us for everyday use, for the protection of the stronghold, herbal remedies for illnesses, and even for repairs to the house when needed, but none of these are really for us. We are simply the guardians."

Maggie blew out a breath. "So, what can I do?"

Duncan took her hands in his and he knelt before her. "Calm yourself for one thing, because making your own self ill will not help anyone. Spend some time with Gabe. If his time is indeed ending, and I seriously doubt that is the case, but *if* it is, cherish what time ye have with him. There is nothing more ye can do."

She closed her eyes, knowing that the words Duncan spoke were the simple truth of the matter, and that if it was his time to go, there would be nothing she could do to stop it.

She opened her eyes and smiled slightly as she touched his face. "When did you get so smart?"

"I have my moments," he replied before he kissed her hand.

She brushed her fingers through his hair. "I have been neglecting you the past few days, haven't I?"

"Aye, ye have, but I may be persuaded to let ye make it up to me," he winked with a sly grin.

She stood up, pushed him roughly back into a chair, and watched the amusement form in his eyes as he laughed softly.

"What do you say to defiling a sacred room?" she growled, dropping to her knees before him and running her hands over his thighs. Maggie pushed his robe away to expose him, and he watched with utter delight as she lowered her head, taking her time to lick and tease his member. As his desire rose, he fisted his hand in her hair and urged her to take his manhood into her mouth; she happily obeyed, enjoying the power she wielded over him in that moment. Just as he felt himself about to let go, he stopped her, pulled her to her feet, and carried her to the large altar table covered with plush, soft fabrics. He sat her on the edge of the table, it being the perfect height for their bodies to meet, tore off her robe and made her ready to receive him. He worked her up to the verge of her own desire with his fingers as he kissed her, and then entered her using slow, deliberate strokes, waiting for her to catch up so they could explode together.

They lay back on the table panting when they were done.

"How many sacred rules did we break tonight?" she asked breathily as she raked her tangled hair back.

Duncan laughed. "All of them, and I couldn't care less. As a matter of fact, I think we should do it again."

He bit his bottom lip, rolled her underneath him, and they broke the rules twice more that night.

The next day, Maggie rode over to Gabe and Quinn's house, and knocked on the door.

"Maggie! What a nice surprise!" Gabe kissed her on the cheek. "What are you doing here this fine morning?"

"I came for you," she said and stepped inside.

Kat ran over to greet her. Maggie picked her up and covered her with kisses before setting her back down on her feet.

"For me? Did you need something?" asked Gabe as he smiled down at his daughter.

"Yes! I need you to go with me into town today."

"For what?" he asked.

"I need some time with my best friend."

Quinn came into the room with Alastair. "Morning, Maggie!"

"Morning, you two. I am stealing Gabe for the day," she said and ruffled Alastair's hair.

"Are ye going to bring him back?" teased Quinn.

"We'll see," she grinned as Alastair hugged her around the waist and she kissed the top of his head.

Quinn turned to Gabe. "Go! Have some fun!"

"Are you sure?" he asked.

"Aye! Both of ye could use some time away."

"Alright," said Gabe. "Give me a few minutes to get ready."

Maggie sat down and Quinn came over to her.

"How's he doing?" she asked.

"I am still mixing potions for him to drink at night, but at least he is sleeping."

"That's good," she said.

Quinn sat down next to her and Kat crawled onto his lap to play peekaboo with Alastair over the back of the couch. Quinn took a good look at Maggie and frowned. "Are ye feeling unwell?"

She leaned forward and rested her elbow on her knee with her chin in her palm. "I just have a lot on my mind."

He nodded. "It will be good for the two of ye to spend the day together. Maybe ye both can relax a bit because Lord knows, ye both need it."

Two hours later, Maggie and Gabe walked through the streets of Williamsburg arm-in-arm, just like they used to do so often. It was market day, so the atmosphere in town was very light and merry. They stopped in at the shipping office to greet Captain Russell, who had everything well in hand. They moved on to the shops to pick up some new things for both their houses and some gifts for the children, while stopping to chat with people they knew.

When they passed by the Golden Ball, Maggie took Gabe by the arm, and pulled him inside.

"Good afternoon, Mr. Craig," said Maggie.

He looked up from his work. "Mistress MacGregor! Colonel Asheton! How good it is to see you both!" He came around the counter to greet them.

"Is my order ready?" she asked.

"It is," he replied and moved behind the counter. He took out a small box that contained two rings. He handed them over to her and watched her face for her reaction.

Maggie looked down and smiled. "You did a beautiful job," she said.

She handed the larger ring over to Gabe to show him. It was a gold ring, made for a man, with the same design as the one on their backs.

Gabe looked closer. "It's the MacGregor mark," he said in amazement.

Maggie slipped the other ring on her third finger and stretched out her hand to admire it. It was a smaller version of the one Gabe held.

"Perfect!" she said.

Mr. Craig was pleased. "I will get the rest of your order," he said and went into the back.

Maggie looked at Gabe. "Do you like it? I had it made as a surprise for Duncan."

Gabe looked at it again. "I do! He will love it!"

Mr. Craig returned with another box. "Here you are Mistress MacGregor," he said and wrapped up the two they were holding before handing both packages over to her.

"Thank you, Mr. Craig. I will see you soon."

She put the small bundles in her drawstring bag, took Gabe's arm, and they walked to the Raleigh Tavern, taking a small private table in the back. Maggie noticed that every woman in the place stopped what they were doing to turn and get a better look at Gabe.

The barmaid greeted them as they sat down. "Hello, Maggie! Colonel Asheton!"

"Hello, Gracie!"

"Rum punch?" she asked.

"You know me too well! Two to start and keep them coming," grinned Maggie.

"Did you leave the babies at home with that handsome husband of yours?" she asked when she brought their drinks.

"I did! I left them with him and his two brothers," she replied.

Gracie put her hands on her hips. "You're hiding another one out there?"

Maggie nodded. "Newly arrived for an extended stay."

"Make sure you bring him by. You can't keep all these attractive fellas to yourself," she said, winking at Gabe while pinching his cheek. "At least, I got to see this one."

"Oh Gracie! You will break my heart if you ever fall in love with another," he flirted.

Gracie blushed and went to get their food.

"You've still got it, Gabe," teased Maggie.

"Got what?" he asked.

"That sex appeal that drives women mad. Every woman in this place is trying to figure out how to get you in a dark alley alone."

Gabe almost spat out his drink when he laughed. "Yes, well, I am a happily married man."

"I know! I never officially got you a wedding gift, especially since you didn't invite me to your wedding!" she scolded with a wrinkle of her nose.

Maggie took out one of the boxes that Mr. Craig had given her. "So, allow me to do it now. When I had these rings made for Duncan and me..." she slid the box over, "I took the liberty of having ones made for you and Quinn, as well. I know you cannot have wedding rings, but these, you both can wear inconspicuously and out in public."

Gabe looked down, stunned. He opened the box to see two men's rings made just like the one he saw for Duncan.

"Mags," he said, "I don't know what to say." He looked up. "That was very thoughtful of you. Thank you." He leaned over and kissed her on the cheek.

"And, I *am* very sorry you were not there when we married."

"You're welcome. I thought that it would be nice to have something for the whole family to share, and when all the children are old enough, we can have them made for them as well."

Gabe smiled. "I love that idea."

Maggie took a big sip of her drink. "Quinn says you are sleeping better now."

"Yes! His nightly tonics have worked wonders."

"Are you two getting enough alone time together with Alastair there now?"

"Do couples ever get enough alone time after they have children?" he smirked.

Maggie bobbed her head around. "Duncan and I do our best." She grinned behind her glass.

"You two do have a healthy appetite for each other."

She shrugged. "I do not know why, but I cannot get enough of that man."

"So, I have noticed!" he snarked. "I do not know how you two find the time or the energy for all of that."

Maggie leaned closer to him. "We take it when and where we can get it."

Gabe chuckled. "Ah! And where might that be?"

"Last night, it was in the collection room." She sipped her drink.

Gabe set his own glass down, suddenly very curious. "What?"

Maggie rolled her eyes. "I have been neglecting Duncan the past few nights, and I needed to make it up to him. We were there, we were alone, there was the altar table..."

Gabe pointed at her. "You had better hope that our mother-in-law doesn't find out about this. You will be a dead woman."

She scoffed. "Oh please! Lady Aurnia would lock us in there herself if she thought it would get her a few more grandchildren."

"At the rate you two are going, I am sure it will not take long."

"I don't know, Gabe. I am not as young as I used to be."

"I seem to recall you saying that exact same thing before you got pregnant with the triplets."

Maggie grimaced. "Oh! You do have a point, and according to Finn, there will be siblings."

"How do you feel about that?"

Maggie downed her drink and waved Gracie for another. "I would be good with that, and I know Duncan would be too. Although, we may need a bigger house if this pattern continues. Speaking of close quarters, how are you and Quinn explaining your relationship to Alastair?"

"We really haven't. He is always asleep before we go to bed, and we are up before him. Honestly, I think he is young enough that he doesn't give it any thought."

"He is settling in well at the house?" she asked.

"He is. We are all still getting used to each other, and he is a little standoffish with me, but I think it will all work itself out. He already calls Kat his little sister, and he is fiercely protective of her."

"He is the same way with the babies," pointed out Maggie. "I mean, it is a good thing, but it is as if he feels it is his personal responsibility to watch over them."

"I think it is because he helped to take care of his mother when she was sick," said Gabe.

Gracie brought their food and they continued to chat. After they were finished eating, they continued to talk and drink. By the time they left, Maggie had so much to drink that Gabe had to help her stand up.

"It is a good thing we brought the carriage," snickered Gabe and helped her into the coach.

Maggie fell against the seat after she got in, breaking into laughter.

"You need to pull yourself together before we get home," he warned. "Duncan will have my hide for letting you have too much of that rum punch."

She waved him off. "I don't think the ride is long enough for me to sober up." She hugged him as she leaned against him.

He kissed the top of her head and wrapped his arm around her.

"Thank you for coming into my life," she whispered, pulling him tight.

"I should be the one thanking you, Mags."

When they arrived back at the house, Gabe stopped to have a conversation with Harm. While she waited, Maggie spotted Duncan, leaning forward against the fence at the stables. She quietly crept over to sneak up behind him, pressed her cheek flat against his back, and ran her hands around to caress his chest. "Hello, my love."

"Hello, sweetie," he said, and he turned around. Only it wasn't Duncan she was wound around...it was Logan.

"Oops!" giggled Maggie. "You are not my husband!"

Logan didn't even try to conceal his amusement. "Nay, but I can pretend if ye like," he grinned as he embraced her and kissed the side of her head.

Maggie noticed a very displeased Duncan and Quinn coming towards them at a rapid pace. "Shit! He looks pissed!" she whispered to Logan.

"What the hell do ye think ye are doing fondling my brother?" demanded Duncan.

"Maybe she decided to trade up," goaded Logan.

Maggie pointed at Logan who still had his arm around her. "I thought he was you."

"Logan and I do not look that much alike," he grumbled as he got closer.

"No, your faces don't, but your asses sure as hell do," she said and burst into laughter.

Duncan caught her just before she fell forward.

"There you are, my love," she said as she patted his chest.

"Rum punch at the Raleigh Tavern?" he asked, already knowing the answer to his question.

"Just a little," she said, pinching her fingers together to demonstrate.

Duncan turned to Gabe who had just walked up. "Ye brought my wife home drunk?" he asked in jest.

Gabe shrugged. "Like I could stop her! Besides, it is the first time she has had more than a sip since she got pregnant. She's earned it."

"Aye, she has," mumbled Duncan as he looked down at Maggie. "Let's find ye somewhere to lie down, shall we?"

"Oh!" exclaimed Maggie. "I like that idea."

He turned her entire body to face the house and, when she stumbled and almost fell backwards, he simply swept her off her feet, carried her inside and upstairs to their room. He placed her on the bed, crawled beside her, and propped himself up on his elbow.

"Did ye and Gabe have a good time?" he asked as he disentangled her bag from her wrist and tossed it on the table.

"We did. It was just like old times," she replied.

"Well, ye do seem a lot less tense now," he said and looked her over.

"That's not all I am," she growled and rolled over on top of him, straddling him.

He caught her by the hips as they kissed. He pulled away and held her hands in place to stop her. "Later, my love." He pushed her gently back over on her back.

Maggie looked confused. "What?"

Duncan kissed her nose. "Ye have had entirely too much to drink, and it would not be right for me to take advantage of ye like this."

"Aw, come on!" she whined and wrapped her arms around his neck. "I give you full permission to take advantage of me, several times over. In fact, I insist upon it."

"I am afraid the answer is nay, my love."

"You are no fun," she pouted and dropped her arms back on the bed.

"I will show ye how much fun I can be," he smirked, "but only when ye are fully awake to appreciate every moment of it."

Maggie wrinkled her nose at him, annoyed.

He winked, kissed her, rolled off the bed, and strode out of the room.

Maggie turned on her side, groaned, and dozed off to sleep.

When she woke up a few hours later, her head pounded, and she felt like she was going to be sick. She noticed Duncan leaned against the wall, his arms folded, smiling as he watched her.

He came over to her bedside, helped her to sit up, and handed her a glass. "Drink this!" he ordered.

"What is it?" Maggie asked suspiciously.

"It helps when ye have had too much to drink."

Maggie took a sip and promptly gagged. "Uh! Yuck! It tastes like ass...with a touch of mint." Maggie made a face and handed it back to him.

"Aye, it does...but it helps," he said and pushed it back to her. "Get some more of it down."

She rolled her eyes, pinched her nose with her fingers, and took a large gulp.

After a few minutes, Maggie did indeed start to feel better. She looked over at the drink.

"How did that work so fast?" she asked.

"It is a recipe from one of the books downstairs."

She scratched her head. "The Fae gave you hangover recipes?"

Duncan shrugged. "Well, Scots do like to drink.... not as much as ye, mind ye," he teased and kissed her.

Maggie took Duncan's hand. "I have something for you."

"For me?"

She nodded, reached for her bag on the table, took out the small box, and handed it to him. "I wanted to get you something, and I thought you might like this."

Duncan opened the box and took out the ring. He looked at it closely, then back up at Maggie. "Maggie, this is...I don't know what to say. How did ye do this?"

"I took a drawing of the symbol to Mr. Craig and he made it. Try it on," she urged.

Duncan slipped it on to his right hand and it was a perfect fit.

Maggie took out the one she had made for herself and slid it on her own right hand and showed it to him. "Do you like it?" she asked.

"I love it. Thank ye," he said, and he kissed her again. "This was very thoughtful of ye."

"I had a set made for Gabe and Quinn, as well. I thought maybe they could wear them in place of wedding rings."

Duncan held the ring up in the light. "It is magnificent and a wonderful gift, my love."

Maggie slipped her arms around him. "I love you Duncan...even if you won't take me to bed when I beg you to."

Her husband smirked. "Well, ye aren't drunk anymore, and there is nothing to stop me now since the wet nurses have the babies for the rest of the day, so ye are all mine," he said and he flipped her over on the bed, laughing. "Let me thank ye properly."

"Oh, I like the sound of that!"

Later, as they dressed for supper, Maggie stood at the window and caught sight of Gabe, Quinn, and Alastair on the back lawn. She watched Gabe kneel to speak to the boy, but when he tried to talk to him, Alastair ran over to Quinn, and clung to his father's leg. Gabe's head dropped, the disappointment apparent on his face as he slowly got up and smiled at him. They all turned and came inside the house.

"What are ye looking at?" asked Duncan as he pulled on his boots.

Maggie folded her arms and turned to him.

"I am concerned that Alastair and Gabe are not getting on well."

"What makes ye say that?"

Maggie moved next to him. "Just a feeling I get. I mean, Gabe is convinced things will work out, but I don't know. Alastair has taken to everyone else so well; everyone except Gabe. I don't understand."

Duncan pulled her down onto his lap. "This is all very new for them, Maggie. It is an adjustment for everyone here. Give it some time. The boy has lost his mother, been taken from his home, and now brought to another country. It is a shock for him as it would be for anyone, but even more so for a child."

"I suppose you are right."

A few days later, Maggie had just finished feeding the babies when Alastair appeared in the nursery doorway, peeking inside.

"You can come in," she said.

Alastair smiled shyly as he came over to look at Morgan, who was fast asleep in her arms. He touched her little finger and she grasped his in her sleep.

"Why aren't you playing with the other children?" Maggie asked, putting Morgan down with her brother and sister.

"I was looking in on Kat to make sure she was still napping," he replied.

Maggie took him by the shoulders and led him downstairs. "Hettie just made some sweets. What do you say we go try them out?"

He nodded excitedly.

They gathered a plate, filled it up, and went to the drawing room to snack where Alastair made himself comfortable and happily munched away.

"Alastair, you are a wonderful big brother and cousin. Why *are* you always checking up on Kat and the babies?"

He shrugged. "I just feel like I am supposed to."

Maggie leaned back against the chair. "How do you like it here, with your father?"

He swallowed his mouthful of food. "I like it a great deal. My father is a good man and he loves me. He tells me so every day."

Maggie sensed there was something he wasn't saying. "And, how do you feel about Gabe?"

The boy stopped eating and looked down.

She leaned over. "It's alright. You can tell me anything."

Alastair brushed the crumbs from his shirt. "He *says* he will teach me how to use a sword."

Maggie looked at him puzzled. "Oh well, you are a lucky little boy! Gabe was the one who taught me how to use the sword."

His eyes lit up. "Really?"

"Really! He is a very good teacher and I am sure you will be an expert in no time."

He looked down again, a look of sadness on his face. "Aunt Maggie, can I ask ye something?"

"You can ask me anything you like."

He sighed. "Will he go away?"

"Who? Gabe?" she asked, surprised.

"Yes."

"No, sweetheart! Why would you think that?"

Alastair suddenly looked very grave. "I got up the other night to make sure Kat was asleep and I saw the bedroom door open. My father and Gabe...were in the same bed...hugging and kissing."

Oh boy!

Maggie blew out a long breath. "How did you feel about that?" she asked, unsure of what else to do.

He frowned. "My mother used to have men that would come to her bed that would hug and kiss her like that, but they would always leave and never return." He looked up at Maggie with a lost look in his eye. "I like Gabe very much, and I don't want him to ever leave."

Maggie's heart melted and she pulled him into a hug. "Alastair, Gabe isn't going anywhere. He loves you, Kat, and your father very much. You are his family and he will never desert you."

Alastair wiped his face with his sleeve. "He wouldn't? Are ye certain?"

Maggie shook her head. "Never, ever in a million years would Gabe leave any of you on purpose!"

He seemed relieved, and very pleased. "I am confused about one thing," he said, suddenly.

Only one?

"What's that?"

"Why do he and Father sleep in the same bed?"

Oh, dear God in Heaven!

She shifted uncomfortably and tried to figure out exactly how to explain this to him. "Do you know how most children have a mother and a father?"

He nodded, completely focused on the conversation.

"And, how both parents sleep in the same bed?"

He nodded again. "So, they are both my parents?"

"Well, yes, but instead of having a mother and a father, you have two fathers."

He cocked his head at her, confused.

Maggie thought a moment, not wanting to confuse him anymore than he already was. "You know how your Uncle Duncan and I love each other? Well, your father and Gabe love each other in the same way, and they show that love by sharing a bed...that they hug and kiss in."

She felt like she was digging herself into a deep hole in a conversation that Quinn and Gabe should have been having with their son. She wiped the beads of sweat that had formed on her forehead with her palm.

"Are they married?" he asked.

Maggie shrugged. She was in too far now to lie to the boy.

Oh, what the hell?

"How would you feel if I said they were, but in their own way?"

He became quiet and lost in deep thought for a few moments.

Great! Now you have broken the kid.

A wide grin slowly spread across his face. "I would like that very much. I would be the luckiest boy in the world to have two fathers."

Maggie took his hands.

Whew!

"There is only one thing Alastair," she said and became very serious. "Some people don't like the kind of love your father and Gabe share."

"Why not?" he asked.

"I don't know. I wish I knew. You see, I know and you know that love is love and it does not matter, but these other people, if they knew about them and how they lived...they might try to hurt them, so you can never talk about it to anyone except to me, your uncles, and your grandmother. We all must work extra hard to keep them safe. Do you understand?"

He puffed out his little chest and grinned. "I will protect them, Aunt Maggie, I promise."

Maggie smiled back and hugged him tight.

"I have one more question though," he said.

Please don't be a sex question. Please don't be a sex question. Please don't be a sex question.

"Yes?" she asked.

"May I call Gabe 'Father', as well?"

It was Maggie's turn to get emotional. Tears welled up in her eyes. "I think that would make him very happy. Why don't you ask him yourself?"

"I will. Thank ye, Aunt Maggie."

Maggie patted his back. "Now go play. Aunt Maggie may need a drink or five."

He laughed and ran off.

Maggie collapsed back on the sofa as Duncan, Quinn, and Gabe came into the drawing room.

"What are ye up to?" asked Duncan.

She narrowed her eyes at Gabe and Quinn.

"Oh, I was thinking about going into town to buy a door lock for Gabe and Quinn's bedroom door."

"Why on Earth would you do that?" asked Gabe, pouring drinks.

"Because, apparently your bedroom door has a habit of not staying closed at night."

"What are ye talking about, Maggie?" Quinn took a glass from Gabe.

"Your son got up to check on Kat the other night and saw the two of you in bed...doing things that married people do." She wagged her finger at them.

Gabe and Quinn froze and turned to each other with horrific looks on their faces.

Duncan winced.

"Oh, God!" said Gabe as his hand flew to his mouth.

"What exactly did he see?" asked Quinn, the blood having drained from his face.

"He said he saw you hugging and kissing."

"And, that's all? Are you sure?" asked Gabe.

"That's all?" asked Quinn, looking to Gabe. "Isn't that plenty? Obviously, something upset him."

Quinn plopped down in a chair.

"He was afraid that Gabe was going to leave and never come back," answered Maggie.

"Why on Earth would he think something like that?" asked Gabe.

"Because his mother would have men over that slept in her bed, and they never stayed around for any length of time. He was worried that Gabe was going to be like one of them."

Quinn put his face in his hands. "Oh no! That poor child!"

"I explained to him that you two love each other, and him and Kat, very much, and that Gabe would never leave. He is actually pretty excited to have two fathers now."

"And you are sure he was not upset?" Gabe's face was as pale as Quinn's.

"No! He is a very smart and understanding boy for his age. I think you two should sit him down and talk to him some more, of course, but he is going to be just fine. He has a right to know, and the two of you should not have to tiptoe around in your own home."

Gabe placed his hand on Quinn's shoulder. "Maggie is right. It is past time that we sat him down and talked to him about many things."

Quinn laid his hand on Gabe's. "Aye, it is."

That night as Maggie climbed into bed, she noticed Duncan fiddling with the door.

"What are you doing, my love?"

"Checking our door lock," he grinned. "We do not need *our* bairns walking in on us while we are doing 'things'."

Maggie rolled her eyes. "Who are you kidding? That won't work. They will just wave their little hands and magically open it anyway."

Duncan looked back at the door. "Aye, ye may be right." He sighed and disrobed.

"I was so afraid I was going have to explain sex to Alastair. I think I will leave that little chat to his two fathers. I am already dreading having it with our own three."

Duncan looked at her oddly and climbed into bed. "Why would we tell them about that?"

Maggie looked back at Duncan strangely. "Did your parents not tell you about the birds and the bees?"

He scoffed. "The birds and the bees, aye. But, about things done in the bedroom...nay! And we will not be telling our children any such things either!"

"Well, how did you learn?" she asked, suddenly extremely curious.

Duncan slipped his arm around her and she leaned against his chest.

"The way all men should...at a whorehouse where their favorite uncle takes them when they are old enough," he grinned, "or in my case, my father's best friend, Dougal. It is better to learn from a woman who is experienced in such delicate matters, especially when ye are an inept young lad who hasn't the faintest idea what he is doing."

Maggie made a face. "What is it with men and whorehouses? Those places are filthy and disgusting."

"Aye, they are and that's why we like them," he teased with a wink.

She smacked his chest. "Well, *our* son will not be learning in one of those places. Thankfully, the only uncles he has in America have no need or desire to darken the doors of such establishments."

Duncan smirked at her. "I am sure someone will take pity on him."

Maggie gave him a dirty look. "And, what about our daughters?"

"They will learn from their husbands on their wedding nights, the way they are meant to."

"Talk about your double standards!" Maggie raised up. "Well, you were sorely disappointed, weren't you?" she said sarcastically.

He wrapped both arms around her. "That was different. I knew I would have ye for my wife and it did not matter."

"How did you know that?" she asked, lightheartedly.

He kissed her. "After I met ye, I knew there would never be another for me," he said sweetly.

Maggie eyed him. "We didn't wait until our wedding night. What makes you think our girls will?"

Duncan ran his hand down the curve of her hip. "I guess I will just have to keep them locked up until I find them suitable husbands."

"Good luck with that," she mumbled. Maggie brushed his hair back with her fingers. "What if my father had been here to lock me up?" she teased.

Duncan kissed her neck and growled. "I would have just broken down the door," he laughed. "Nothing would have or will ever keep me from ye."

Maggie watched Gabe and Alastair from the drawing room window. Gabe, true to his word, was teaching the boy how to use a sword. The soldier had found a smaller one, just the right size for a young boy, and the look on both of their faces said it all. The two of them were getting along wonderfully now that Alastair's fears had been allayed.

Quinn joined her to watch.

"Thank ye," he said to Maggie and kissed her cheek.

"For what?" she asked.

"For talking to Alastair. Gabe and I sat him down that same night, letting him know that he was safe and that we weren't going anywhere. He has been a much different, happier child since that night. He is now calling us both 'Father', and I know we have ye to thank for that."

"I am just glad that it is all working out." Maggie rubbed his arm. "Is Gabe still sleeping alright?"

"Aye. I have started backing down the dosage of the tonic I have been giving him and the nightmares have not returned, so that bodes well."

"Good!" Maggie sat down on the floor with the babies.

Quinn joined her. "Ye are still concerned though, aren't you, Maggie?"

"I am," she said, "but I am trying to be cautiously optimistic."

She decided to change the subject. "Duncan said that all of you are going on a hunting trip tomorrow."

"Aye! I am looking forward to it. It will be nice to be out with Duncan, Logan, and Gabe. Almost like old times back in Scotland; only then, we would go for days at a time."

Maggie grabbed Kendric's big toe, making him giggle. "Only now you have children to get back to."

"Aye, and I wouldn't have it any other way," he grinned.

"Are you taking Alastair?"

"Nay, not yet. We are hunting with bows and he needs to learn first. He was not raised with weapons in hand, the way we were, so he will have to work his way up." He looked around the room. "Where is Mother?"

"She and Kat are down at the school. Your mother spends every chance she gets with the children there. She loves it."

"She is happiest around little ones."

The side door flew open as Alastair raced in with Gabe on his heels.

"Father says I am doing well, Aunt Maggie!" he said excitedly, and he rushed over to hug her.

"That's wonderful." She smiled and squeezed him back.

"You are a natural," said Gabe before he collapsed in a chair.

"We are both very proud of ye," added Quinn as he stood, and ruffled his hair.

"I am going to tell Grandmother." He grinned and ran off.

"How is his father doing?" asked Maggie, seeing how exhausted Gabe looked.

"Either I am getting old or I have gone soft since I left the army," he said as he leaned back.

"Probably a little bit of both," she teased and handed him a drink.

"Oh, thanks." He gratefully accepted it.

Quinn sat down next to him. "Ye do look a little worn out," he said, touching his leg. "Are ye feeling poorly?"

"I'm fine. Someone kept me up late last night," he replied, playfully.

They exchanged a look; the kind that only lovers share after a special night of lovemaking.

Maggie went back over and sat down with the babies. "I hope you locked the door this time," she said sarcastically.

"Double checked it," Gabe said with a wink.

"Ye and Duncan will need to start doing that pretty soon," Quinn pointed out.

"Why bother?" asked Maggie. "When you have magical babies who can open them anyway, it seems kind of pointless."

"Has something else happened?"

"No," sighed Maggie, "not yet, but if they can float things now, I am more than a little concerned by what they will be able to do later."

She stood back up and eyed Gabe warily. She went to his side and touched his forehead with the back of her hand. "Are you sure you're feeling okay?"

"Yes! I am perfectly fine!" He brushed her hand away. "Stop being a mother hen."

She could not. Maggie's unsettled feeling would not go away.

The next morning, Duncan woke Maggie before dawn and kissed her goodbye before departing for the hunting trip.

She touched his face. "*PLEASE*, be careful," she begged.

"We will. I love ye and we will be back before ye know it!"

"I love you too," she said, watching him leave, her mind very uneasy.

6 CHAPTER SIX

It was late afternoon when Hettie and Askuwheteau came rushing into the drawing room to find her.

"Maggie, we need you to come to the village!"

Her stomach dropped; she knew something was terribly wrong. "What happened?"

"There was a hunting accident."

Maggie felt a little faint and she leaned against the desk to steady herself.

Askuwheteau caught her by the arm.

"Who? What happened?" she demanded.

"Gabe caught an arrow in his shoulder. They were close to the village when it happened, so they brought him there. Duncan sent me to get you."

"Hettie," she commanded, "get Cecile and Cora to help Lady Aurnia with the children. Do not tell Kat or Alastair about what has happened."

"We will take care of them," she said. "You go!"

Onyx was outside, pawing at the ground as he waited for Maggie. They rode hard to where Gabe had been taken, and Maggie slid off the big horse before he even stopped.

Duncan and Logan were standing just inside the longhouse when she arrived.

She rushed into Duncan's arms. "How is he?"

The sound of Gabe screaming in agony was her answer.

She jerked her head in that direction and dashed to his side to see that Powaw had just pulled the arrow through and was cauterizing the wound. Gabe was pale, breathing hard, with his eyes closed and his face contorted in pain.

Quinn sat next to him and held his hand; Quinn's own hand gone white from where Gabe beared down when the hot poker hit his shoulder.

Gabe passed out from the pain, shortly thereafter.

Once Powaw was finished, Wawetseka took his place and started cleaning out the wound with water.

"How is he?"

"It missed his heart and the bleeding is not very bad," answered Quinn, still visibly shaken and upset.

Wawetseka took Maggie's hand and squeezed it to comfort her. "Powaw knows what to do. We will take care of him, Maggie."

Maggie turned to Duncan who had come in behind her. "How did this even happen?"

"It was one of our young braves that had crossed off our land," answered Askuwheteau, his face guilt-ridden. "He shot his arrow into the movement in the woods, thinking it was a deer. He only saw Gabe after he was hit. He should have known better. I am so sorry, Maggie. The tribe bears this responsibility."

"It was an accident," said Duncan softly. "It was nobody's fault; it just happened."

Maggie went to stand behind Quinn. She wrapped her arms around him and laid her head on his shoulder. She could feel his body tremble, terrified at the thought of losing Gabe.

"Tell me what you need to make a potion for his pain. We will send someone to the house," she whispered.

"I know what he needs," Logan answered and turned. "I will go and get it."

Duncan touched Maggie on the back and inclined his head towards the outside.

"I will be right back," she told Quinn.

Mingan, Askuwheteau, and Powaw were standing outside, speaking among themselves, as Maggie and Duncan walked over to join them.

"Powaw says that we must watch for fever now. He will perform a prayer over Gabe after he gets cleaned up," said Askuwheteau.

Maggie touched Powaw's arm. "Thank you."

He nodded before walking away.

Mingan turned to Maggie. "I cannot tell you how sorry we are for this. It should not have happened." His gaze moved around to a young boy about eleven or twelve, who was standing near one of the longhouses, looking down.

Maggie recognized him from the school. "It was Kitchi?" she asked.

"Yes, and he will be punished," replied Mingan.

Maggie glanced over at the boy, who looked miserable.

"No!" said Maggie. "Please, don't! He did not do it on purpose, and Gabe would not want him to be disciplined because of an accident. Besides, he looks like he is suffering enough."

Mingan let out a deep sigh. "You are very kind, Maggie, but children must learn."

"What if he is only allowed to hunt with one of the parties from now on?" asked Askuwheteau. "Kitchi would consider that a punishment, and it might teach him to be more patient and cautious."

"Aye, that is an excellent idea," agreed Duncan, "and more than fitting."

"What do you say, Maggie?" asked Mingan, stroking his chin, pondering his decision.

"I think that is more than fair," she answered.

Mingan nodded slowly. "The final decision will be up to the one he wronged. We will care for Gabe until he is well."

"Thank you," she said.

Mingan and Askuwheteau left to go and speak with the boy.

Maggie leaned into Duncan's chest as he put his arms around her. "I had a sinking feeling that something bad was going to happen," she whispered. "I should have paid more attention to it."

"Ye could not have known and ye cannot blame yourself for it."

Gabe remained unconscious. Maggie and Quinn stayed by his side throughout the night and the entire next day. He would wake long enough to acknowledge them, then fall right back to sleep.

By the next evening, he had become restless and was in obvious pain, so Quinn mixed something for him and forced it down his throat. He settled as soon as it got into his system.

"He should sleep through the night," said Quinn, swaying a bit, so exhausted he was barely able to stand.

"Quinn, go get some rest and see to the children. They will be worried if both of you are gone for too long. I will stay with him tonight," said Maggie.

Quinn rubbed his eyes with the palms of his hands. "Ye have not slept either," he replied.

"Mingan said he would have another bed made up. I will catch a little nap and be right here next to him."

"I don't want to leave him," he whispered, looking over at Gabe.

"I know, but ye need to think about Kat and Alastair. They are asking for their fathers and they are becoming anxious," said Duncan, who hovered close by.

"Duncan is right. Go, and I will send for you if anything changes."

Quinn reluctantly stood, and hugged Maggie, before he touched Gabe's face and kissed him.

"I will stay, as well," said Duncan.

Maggie shook her head. "I need you at the house with the babies. I will come back when Quinn comes tomorrow."

"Are ye sure?" asked Duncan.

"Yes. I need you to rest tonight, so you can handle the babies while I sleep when I get back. Besides, it is quicker if I message you with my mind than if I have to send someone."

"Aye, that's true." He embraced and kissed her. "If ye need anything, just *think* the word," he smiled.

Make sure Quinn gets some rest.

"I will, my love."

Maggie sat down next to Gabe, wrung out a cloth she had soaked in water, and wiped his face with the rag. She pulled back the covers and peeled up his bandage slightly to take a closer look. The entry point was still red and inflamed, and that worried her to no end. Quinn had made a poultice to help with infection, but the skin was still hot to the touch.

"What I wouldn't give for a 21st-century hospital right now," she whispered, lightly stroking his face and pushing his hair away from it. She traced the tiny wrinkles that had started to form at his temples and the little laugh lines that everyone gets as they age and smiled to herself when she realized that they only made him look more handsome.

Wawetseka quietly came into the longhouse and touched her on the shoulder. "I brought you something to eat."

Maggie gratefully accepted the bowl offered to her. "Thank you."

"He is not as restless," said Wawetseka, touching Gabe's arm.

"Quinn has given him something for the pain and it makes him sleep."

Wawetseka smiled. "Quinn is good with using herbs to make medicine. Where did he learn so much about them?"

"In Scotland. It is across the ocean and it is where the whole family is from. They have passed down that knowledge for generations."

"Do you think he would teach me some of what he knows?" she asked.

"I expect he might. It never hurts to ask."

A few other women came inside next with their arms full of deerskins to make up a pallet for Maggie and with fresh bowls of water. A couple of them giggled as they looked over at Gabe and whispered to each other.

"What are they saying?" asked Maggie and she took a bite of the stew.

Wawetseka smiled and blushed ever so slightly. "They are saying he would make beautiful babies."

They both laughed.

"Yes, he certainly would," agreed Maggie.

"All of the unmarried women in the tribe are very happy when Duncan comes with Gabe, Quinn, and now Logan to visit. Even Sooleawa, who is eighty years old, now looks forward to seeing them."

Maggie chuckled. "In that case, I will send them down more often."

"You should get some rest Maggie," she said and patted her leg. "You look like you are barely holding up."

Maggie looked over at the pallet longingly. "Maybe I will close my eyes for a few minutes after I eat. It's been a long few days."

Maggie dozed for a couple of hours until the sound of Gabe groaning woke her. She got up to check on him, and found him soaked in sweat, burning with fever.

"Damn it!"

She stripped the covers off him, before bringing over a bowl of cool water with some rags to wipe down his face. He mumbled a few words, none that made any sense, and flopped around more than he should have; the movement threatening to reopen his wound.

His eyes suddenly flew wide open, but it was apparent that he was not focused on anything.

"I am afraid!" he called out in his delirium.

"Shhh Gabe! It's Maggie and I am here."

He started to cry. "Maggie doesn't know what is coming...he can't do that to her. It will kill her," he called out.

Maggie looked down at him and a nagging feeling in the back of her mind told her to pay close attention to the words that came out of his mouth.

She leaned close to his ear. "What's coming, Gabe?"

"The pain, the hurt ...Finn...he can't do that to her. She won't survive."

"Finn?"

He tried to raise himself up, but she gently pushed him back down.

Maggie crawled onto the bed next to him and she cradled his head against her breast, while she stroked his face and whispered in his ear.

"You are safe, and I am watching over you. I won't let anyone, or anything hurt you, I promise."

He settled down somewhat when he heard her voice, and only mumbled from that point on, but did occasionally call out to Jonathan, Penny, and Hannah, but none of his words made any sense. As she tried to shift, he became restless once again, almost throwing himself off the bed, so she stayed where she was, and he steadily tightened his hold upon her.

In less than an hour, he had wrapped his arms and legs completely around Maggie as if he were holding on for dear life and trying to protect her from some unseen force. Her limbs started to cramp so badly that she felt a tremendous amount of pain, unable to move in any direction. She was hot, sweaty, and having a hard time catching her breath because of the unholy grasp he had on her. Thankfully, Wawetseka came in to check on her a little before dawn and saw that Maggie was suffering greatly in her current circumstances.

"He is running a fever and every time I try to move, he becomes agitated. As long as I am in his death grip, he is quiet, but I can't lie here much longer."

Wawetseka thought for a moment. "I will be right back."

She returned a few moments later with two of the women from the tribe and instructed them in their native language. One of them slipped onto the bed on the other side of Gabe and laid down to hold him in place while Wawetseka helped Maggie up and the other woman took the spot that she just vacated. Gabe started to protest when they peeled his arms and legs from Maggie but settled back down once the other woman slid into her place. As she tried to stand, Maggie stumbled and fell to the floor because the blood flow had slowed to every part of her body. She managed to crawl over to the pallet and stretched out.

"Thank you!" she exhaled gratefully. "You just saved me."

"They will stay with him and make sure he is quiet."

Maggie sat up and rubbed her legs to get the circulation flowing when she noticed the pain in her arm. She rolled up her sleeve to see that Gabe had bruised her, leaving a black mark in the shape of his hand where he held on to her. Maggie watched as they bathed his forehead in cool water and wondered what had upset him so badly that he needed to hold on that desperately. She leaned her head on her knees and sent Duncan a message.

Gabe has spiked a fever. If Quinn has something for that, bring it as soon as you can.

We are on our way.

Maggie still sat on the pallet when they arrived. Quinn rushed in but stopped short when he saw the two women in bed with Gabe. He looked down at Maggie, somewhat startled and very confused.

"Leave them," she said, waving him off. "It is the only thing keeping him from tearing open his wound."

Quinn moved to the head of the bed and poured the mixture he brought into his mouth.

Gabe gagged and coughed but managed to get most of it down.

Maggie flinched as Duncan took her by the arm to help her up.

"Ow!"

He looked at her strangely and carefully pushed up her sleeve to examine what had caused the reaction. He frowned when he saw the bruising. "What happened to ye?" he demanded.

"It was a rough night," she replied with a sigh.

"Gabe did this to ye?"

"It's not like he did it intentionally. He was not himself."

Quinn came over to see what Duncan was talking about. "Christ, Maggie!" He knelt for a better look.

"He was delirious, and something terrified him. He was crushing me to death as if my very life depended on him."

"What would have frightened him that much?" asked Quinn.

Maggie scratched her forehead. "He *was* feverish...but...he mentioned Finn's name."

They all turned to look at Gabe, and Maggie explained what she had heard.

"More fuckery," whispered Duncan, anger in his voice.

"We don't know that," she said. Maggie tried to stand up, but her legs gave way. Duncan and Quinn reached for her at the same time and caught her before she fell.

"I need to move around."

They each took an arm and helped her walk around outside until the feeling came back to her legs.

"Let's get ye back to the house," said Duncan.

"I am not leaving while he is like this. I can't."

"Maggie!" Duncan protested. "Ye have not had any rest for two days and nights. Even ye have your limits."

"I'll rest here. Are all the children alright?"

He huffed. "The babies are being well cared for. Ye do not need to be concerned about them."

"I told Alastair and Kat that Gabe had to go on a little business trip and that he would be returning soon. Mother and Logan are keeping them busy," added Quinn as Mingan came over to join them.

"How is he this morning?" he asked.

"He spiked a fever in the night," answered Maggie. "He is having a rough go right now."

Mingan looked gravely concerned.

"I gave him something for the fever," said Quinn, as they moved back just inside the longhouse.

Mingan looked over to see Makkitotosimew and Nittawosew in bed with Gabe. "*They* won't help lower his fever," he whispered and chuckled.

"They were gracious enough to help me out. He becomes very upset when he does not have someone to hold on to," said Maggie.

Mingan's face became serious. "Sometimes, they do that when their spirit is clinging to one world while the next world tries to pull them away."

Maggie looked back over at Gabe and she thought about the other names he called out in his sleep; all names of people who had already passed...and she became even more concerned.

Mingan and Duncan walked outside while Quinn went with Wawetseka to get more of the herbs that he needed for Gabe's fever medicine. Maggie was drinking water from a ladle made from a gourd when she heard the two women still in bed with Gabe start to giggle loudly.

"Who are you?" she heard Gabe ask. "Where am I, and why are we in bed together?"

He was awake!

Thank you, God, for bringing him back to me!

Maggie dropped the ladle back into the bucket, folded her arms, and turned to grin at him.

"Good morning, sunshine!" she called enthusiastically.

"Maggie, what the hell is going on?" he croaked, completely astounded and confounded by the current predicament he found himself in. "Who are these women and where the hell are my clothes?"

One of the women ran her hand up and down his leg and winked at him.

The other one smiled, splayed her fingers over his bare chest, and caressed him lustfully.

Maggie looked down at the ground and used her hand to cover her mouth to conceal her amusement from the priceless expression that had appeared on Gabe's face.

She wasn't sure if it was a sense of relief, the severe lack of sleep, or just a mischievous streak that made her do it, but she found herself unable to resist the temptation of the perfect scene that played out before her.

She cleared her throat and forced the smile off her face. "You don't remember what happened?"

"Remember what?" he demanded, in a low, husky voice.

"Well, Mingan invited you to drink with him last night. He was concerned about you being all alone since you have not taken a wife, so he...offered you *two* wives...and you graciously accepted, because you didn't want to be rude or insult him by refusing his generous gift. Powaw performed the ceremony, which was lovely and very romantic by the way, and last night was your honeymoon."

What little color was left in Gabe's face, instantly drained. "Surely, you jest!"

Maggie shrugged. "Why else would you be in bed, completely naked, with two women from the tribe? I must admit, they both look *very* satisfied this morning. I can only assume your 'performance' exceeded their expectations."

Gabe shook his head. "That is not possible!" he said through gritted teeth.

"I should probably introduce you. This is Makkitotosimew, which translates to 'she has large breasts', and this is Nittawosew, which means 'she is *NOT* sterile'. You should probably keep that in mind, or Kat and Alastair may have to share their rooms with a little brother or sister."

Both ladies smiled and waved when they heard their names mentioned, having no idea what was being said about them.

Gabe slowly turned to look at one woman, and then the other. It just so happened that Makkitotosimew was the one who had taken Maggie's place holding his head, and, being true to her well-earned name, when Gabe turned, her breasts completely engulfed his entire face. At the same time, Nittawosew's hand, which was already on his thigh and very close to his manhood, steadily inched higher with each passing moment.

Maggie could no longer hold back, and she burst into a bout of laughter.

"You might need a bigger house, but I think you will all be very happy together," she laughed even harder and wrapped her arms around herself. "I am sure you will make Mathilda very proud using the tricks she taught you at the whorehouse all those years ago."

Gabe narrowed his eyes at her with a less-than-amused look on his face and glared.

Once she worked herself down to a snicker, she motioned the ladies out and sat down next to him.

"I am very glad to see you awake," she said as she grasped his hand.

Gabe tried to move his shoulder and winced as the pain shot through it.

"Now, will you tell me what is *really* going on?" he asked.

"You don't remember anything at all?"

"If I did, would I be asking?" he said dryly.

Oh, he's fine!

"The four of you were out hunting and one of the young braves mistook you for a deer. You caught an arrow in the shoulder. They brought you here and Powaw took it out, but you developed a high fever last night." She touched his forehead, "Which seems to have broken, thank goodness."

He closed his eyes. "I do seem to remember being hit now that you mention it. It is all very foggy though."

Maggie rubbed his hand. "Quinn has been giving you something for the pain and the fever and that may be clouding your mind. Don't stress yourself out over not being able to recall some of the details."

"Where is he?"

"Gathering herbs to make up some more medicine for you. He has been worried to death; we all have."

She kissed his hand.

"And, the women?"

"Oh!" she chuckled. "I was here last night when the fever hit, and in your delirium, you thought I was in danger. You wound yourself around me so tightly that I couldn't breathe and the blood flow to my body was cut off, but whenever I tried to move, you became agitated and unruly. I was afraid you would make your injury worse, and those ladies were kind enough to take my place this morning so I would not lose my own limbs."

"I'm sorry," he whispered.

"No worries. I am just glad to see you awake because you had me scared half to death." She kissed his head. "Let me take a look at your wound this morning."

She gently pulled back the bandages and noticed that it had started to look much better. "How do you feel?"

"Exhausted and everything hurts."

"Quinn will fix you up with something for that as soon as he returns."

He cut his eyes over at her. "You look like hell."

"I sit by your side for two days and two nights, and this is the thanks I get?" she teased.

"You should get some rest, Mags."

She turned when she heard Quinn and Duncan duck inside the longhouse.

"Look who I found." She rose and waved her hands in Gabe's direction.

Quinn went straight to him, obvious relief on his face and kissed him directly on the mouth. "Don't ever put me through that again!" he ordered and kissed him again.

Duncan came over to stand next to Maggie. "Welcome back," he said to Gabe.

"It is good to be back," he said.

Duncan caught Maggie around the waist as she fell back against him and her eyes closed of their own accord. "We are going to leave ye two alone; I'm taking this one to the house to get some sleep. If you need us, send for us."

Duncan led her outside, only leaving her long enough to get his horse.

Maggie noticed Kitchi outside the longhouse where he had been hanging around since all of this happened. She walked over to him and placed her hand on his shoulder.

"How is he?" he asked.

"He is going to be fine," she said.

Relief flooded the boy's face and he wrapped his arms around Maggie's waist as the tears spilled down his cheeks. "I am so sorry. I should have been more careful."

Maggie rubbed his back. "It was an accident. No one blames you, Kitchi. I know you would never do anything to hurt Gabe."

Duncan came over to join them. "Aye, she is right. Don't be so hard on yourself, just be more mindful of your surroundings next time."

He nodded. "I want to tell him how sorry I am."

"Let him rest for a while and you can tell him tomorrow," said Maggie.

"I will!" He wiped his face and went off to do his chores.

Duncan helped Maggie up on his horse and he climbed up behind her. She was asleep as soon as she leaned back against him and didn't even wake as he carried her up to their room and put her to bed.

Maggie woke up later that afternoon. She dressed, peeked in on the children, located Duncan, and went back to check on Gabe, who was resting comfortably when they arrived.

"I gave him something for the pain," whispered Quinn. "It seems to be helping."

He stood, and stepped outside, Maggie and Duncan following behind.

"I think he is going to be fine," he said and blew out a long breath.

"You should take a break," said Maggie. "Have you eaten?"

Two women walked by smiling, waving, and whispering to each other.

"Oh aye. Everyone has been so wonderful here. Nearly every hour, some dear woman has been bringing in food and drink and making sure that we have everything that we need."

Maggie kicked at the dirt with her shoe and looked down, chuckling.

"What's so funny?" asked Duncan.

She looked back and forth between them. "They aren't just being 'nice'. It seems the unmarried ladies of the village have an unhealthy infatuation with all of you, and they are more than happy to lend a helping hand. As a matter of fact, I think the two women who took my place this morning were sorely disappointed when I sent them away."

"Ye aren't serious, are ye?" asked Quinn.

Maggie looked at him incredulously. "Have any of you actually looked in a mirror? All of you are like walking gods especially compared to what the ladies of this country see on a daily basis. Of course, they are being nice! One look at any of you and their nether regions are lit afire, imagining how gorgeous their children would be with one of you as the father. Even Sooleawa, and she is an 80-year-old widow."

"Oh!" said Quinn. "That must have been the one who came in this morning to help wash Gabe. I thought she was being grandmotherly when she sent everyone else out and…" Quinn raised his hand to cover his mouth, remembering exactly how friendly she had been. "Oh, dear Lord in Heaven!" he exclaimed, shocked and appalled.

Maggie and Duncan burst into laughter.

"I wouldn't leave Gabe alone if I were you," said Maggie. "You may end up with another unexpected child on your doorstep, although if you want to enlarge the family..."

Quinn looked back at the longhouse. "Maybe I will stay here tonight just to keep an eye on him."

Duncan slapped him on the shoulder. "I can send Logan down to stand guard. I am sure he will be happy to handle all of them in your stead. He would be thrilled to wake up in bed with two women."

"You had better not let your mother hear that," giggled Maggie. "She will have him in a longhouse with a line forming outside. Nothing would please her more than to have an entire village of grandchildren running around here."

Duncan pointed at her and laughed. "Ye may be more right about that than ye know!"

"Quinn, if ye are staying tonight, ye should go see Kat and Alastair," said Duncan. "We will guard your husband for ye while ye are gone," he grinned.

"Aye, I think I will," said Quinn. "Gabe should be fine until I get back, but there is a mixture by the bedside if he wakes up in pain and needs it."

"We will take care of him," said Maggie and she leaned over and kissed his cheek.

Gabe was still asleep when Maggie and Duncan went back inside. Maggie sat down beside him, and lightly touched his face. He looked much calmer and his color was closer to where it should be. He reached up, took her hand and kissed it without opening his eyes.

"Hello, sweetheart," he whispered.

"How did you know it was me and not one of the ladies from this morning?" she asked.

The corners of his mouth twitched up. "I know your touch anywhere." His eyes slowly fluttered open.

"Are you in any pain?" she asked.

"No. I think Quinn has me sufficiently numb. I am extremely thirsty though."

Duncan handed Maggie a cup of water, then helped Gabe to sit up to drink as Maggie poured some into his mouth.

"Thank you," he said.

Maggie peeled back his bandages to check his wound. "I think you will live," she said and put it back in place. "Although, I wasn't completely convinced last night."

"I wasn't so sure I would live if my husband had caught me in bed with those two women," Gabe joked.

"Do you feel like you can eat something?" she asked. "The sooner you get your strength back, the sooner your virtue will be safe from all of these eligible ladies."

"Good point. Maybe, I *can* eat a little."

"I will see what I can find," said Duncan, and he kissed Maggie's head on his way out.

"Gabe, do you remember anything from the dreams you had while you were feverish?"

"No, why?"

"I was just curious. You were saying some things in your sleep and I was just wondering if anything in particular stuck with you?"

"What was I saying?"

Maggie hesitated, not wanting to upset him.

He noticed. "Tell me, Mags! Keeping secrets never goes well with us."

She chewed on her bottom lip. "You were calling out names...Jonathan, Penny, Hannah...and Finn."

"Finn?" he asked.

"And...you were worried about something that was coming. Something that would specifically hurt me." She could see that he focused his concentration on searching the memories from his dreams.

"I do not. I am sorry. I wish I could remember."

Maggie smiled. "I am sure it was just from the fever. You weren't exactly yourself."

He looked at her with sudden concern on his face. "Show me."

"Show you what?" she asked.

"Quinn said that I gripped you so hard that you were bruised. Let me see it."

She shook her head. "It's nothing to concern yourself with."

He grabbed her hand. "Show me!" he demanded.

Maggie paused, then begrudgingly rolled up her sleeve for him to see.

Gabe gently laid his hand over the bruise and saw that it was the perfect shape of his full handprint.

"Mags, I…" he choked out.

"You nothing!" She quickly rolled down her sleeve. "Forget it this instant. It was not your fault and it doesn't matter anyway. All that matters, is that you are awake, and you are going to be fine."

"That dream must have meant something for me to hold on to you that hard," he said softly.

Maggie wouldn't dare say it to him, but she was afraid he was right.

Duncan returned with a bowl of some sort of stew and Gabe managed to get most of it down.

"How are the children?" he asked as he ate.

"They are fine. Mother is keeping them busy. They think ye are away on a business trip," answered Duncan.

"Quinn has been going up to reassure them," added Maggie.

"So, what exactly did happen?" he asked Duncan.

"We were in a dense part of the woods. Ye crouched down to look at some tracks, and the arrow came out of nowhere. The boy fired on the movement, not on the sight of the animal. He made a costly mistake."

"What boy?" asked Gabe.

"It was Kitchi," answered Maggie.

"Kitchi?"

"He is beside himself," said Maggie.

"Aye. When he realized that he had hit ye, he was so upset that he fell to his knees and emptied his stomach on the spot. He has been outside this longhouse since we brought ye in. He has been waiting to tell ye how sorry he is."

"The poor boy. I do not want him to feel guilty about this."

Maggie shrugged. "You can tell him yourself if you are up for a visitor."

"Yes, I would like to tell him." Gabe handed the bowl back to Maggie.

"I will go get him," said Duncan.

A few minutes later, Kitchi's face appeared in the doorway.

"Come in," smiled Maggie.

He came across the longhouse to Gabe slowly.

"We will leave you two alone to talk," said Maggie. She took Duncan's hand and they stepped outside and once they were alone, Maggie slipped her arms around Duncan's waist. "I have missed you the past two nights," she said.

He buried his head in her neck. "And I have missed ye. I do not feel myself when I am away from ye." He accidentally brushed against her bruise, causing her to wince. Duncan took her arm and rolled up her sleeve. "That looks much worse now."

Maggie pushed her sleeve back down. "I am telling you, Duncan, he was terrified by something in that dream and then to hear him say Finn's name...my blood ran cold."

"Maggie," he took her hands, "he was ill, and fevers do strange things to people's minds. Let's just be grateful that he is going to be fine and not worry about things like that until we know there is something to be concerned about."

"I suppose you are right."

They stood there and held each other until they saw Kitchi leave the longhouse.

"How did it go?" asked Maggie, as they came back inside.

"I think he feels better now," said Gabe. "I promised we would take him hunting with us once I am recovered and he seemed happy about that."

"He has always looked up to you," said Maggie, sitting down. She turned to Duncan. "He lost his father a few years ago, and his mother has not taken another husband. The men here have taken him under their wing and try to fill the void when they can, but he always looks for Gabe when he is up at the house."

Gabe nodded. "Ever since his father passed, I have always made it a point to visit with him when I am here. He is a good boy and losing his father took a great toll on him."

"There aren't very many men here," said Duncan.

"Their numbers are slowly replenishing," replied Maggie. "They had lost a great many when the previous owners of the estate were here and starving them out, and they are still trying to recover."

Maggie winked at Duncan before she looked over at Gabe. "I think some of the women were hoping Gabe would help them out with some babies."

"Then they should be talking to the goddess of fertility," quipped Gabe.

"I can only do so much," Maggie retorted. "I am afraid I am not 'equipped' for what they *really* need."

"They need...what did you call them... 'sperm donors'?" chuckled Gabe.

"Wait!" said Duncan as he held up his hand. "I know I am going to regret asking this, but what exactly is a 'sperm donor'?"

Oh no! This should be interesting.

Maggie placed her hand on his shoulder. "It is a man who donates his seed to a woman, who wants a baby, without a husband, and who doesn't want to actually...do the deed...to get pregnant."

Duncan folded his arms and narrowed his eyes at his wife, blinking as he tried to picture it in his mind. "Then, how does it get where it needs to be?"

Gabe shook his head, amused by the expression on Duncan's face, and imagined that it must have been exactly how his face looked the first time he heard about it.

"Well, the men, take matters into their own hands, so to speak, 'servicing themselves', and when they finish, they do so into a cup. Then a doctor takes it and uses a medical instrument to put it inside the woman, so they don't have to have sex. They don't even have to meet because the man's seed can be stored for many years before they use it."

Duncan looked aghast. "Well, that takes all of the fun out of it and it sounds horrible!"

"I did not say it was fun. It is just a means to an end."

"What man would do that?" he asked.

Maggie shrugged. "Lots of them. They are paid a great deal of money for it."

It was Gabe's turn to speak up. "Wait! They get paid for it? And these women, they pay for the seed?"

"So, the men get paid to pleasure themselves, and the women pay to *not* have to be with a man." Duncan scratched his head. "What kind of sense does that make?"

He and Gabe shrugged at each other.

"Why wouldn't she just get a husband?" asked Duncan.

"Finding the right man is not always easy when there are six billion people on the planet. Some women have not found a suitable partner just before their childbearing years are done, and some women prefer other women in their beds. They don't like laying with men, just like Gabe and Quinn prefer men to women."

"No child of mine will ever come into this world like that!" scoffed Duncan.

"And, thank goodness for that," smirked Maggie and she kissed him. "I much prefer doing it the old-fashioned way with you."

He growled and kissed her back.

"You know, if you two could share a little bit of that lust that you have going on, this place would be overrun with children in no time," said Gabe dryly.

"We are not that bad," replied Maggie and she waved him off.

"Yes, you are!" he laughed, and the movement caused him to groan.

Maggie quickly moved to him. "You should be resting. Quinn left something for the pain, but it will put you to sleep."

"Maybe I will take it and take a little nap," he grunted.

She held the bottle to his lips, and he swallowed it. He was peacefully out in just a few moments.

Quinn arrived shortly after that and Maggie and Duncan went back to the house to spend some time with the babies. They took them outside with a blanket to let them play beneath a tree that was close to the house and in a private spot. They had just started crawling and always ended up in a pile, giggling.

"They are growing so fast," said Maggie.

"Aye, they are."

It was getting near time for them to eat and Morgan crawled over to her mother, indicating she was hungry by patting Maggie's chest. No one was around, so Maggie slipped off her top, situated herself cross-legged, and picked her up to nurse.

Duncan smiled, watching them. "I never tire of seeing ye like this," he said. "Ye were born to be a mother."

"These little sweethearts make it easy," she said, looking down into Morgan's eyes.

Maggie stroked her face, and Morgan locked on her mother's eyes.

The baby's gaze shifted to behind Maggie as she caught sight of something else. A black crow landed nearby, and Morgan seemed fascinated by it; she watched its every move intently and smiled. The crow hopped all around them, as if dancing a little jig just for Morgan and flew off.

"These crows are making themselves at home around here," said Duncan.

"Yes, they certainly are," replied Maggie, staring down at Morgan, and then looking off in the direction the crow flew.

They had a late supper that night, just the two of them since Lady Aurnia and Logan had left to check on Gabe and Quinn, leaving Cora to tend to the children.

Duncan took her by the hand and led her upstairs to the candlelight bath he had prepared for her.

"You are too good to me," she said as soon as she saw it.

"Ye have had a long couple of days and I thought you might want to relax for a bit." He kissed her. "Ye take a nice long bath, while I check on the babies, and I will be waiting in bed for ye when ye are done."

"That sounds perfect."

She soaked for a long time and when she was done, she dried off and slipped on her robe. Duncan was propped up against the headboard, wearing nothing but a smile when she came out. Maggie slipped off her robe and crawled in bed next to him. He spent the next two hours making love to her until she drifted peacefully off to sleep in his arms.

The next day, when Maggie went to check on Gabe, Mingan greeted her.

"Can we speak?" he asked.

"Of course," she replied, dismounting. Onyx wandered off toward Powaw, who waited for him.

"Do you know what they talk about?" she asked Mingan as he escorted her to his longhouse.

"No. Powaw never says."

"Don't you think it is strange that your medicine man has conversations with my horse?"

Mingan laughed as he watched Powaw and Onyx walk away. "I wish I could say speaking to your horse was the strangest thing he did. There are some things I believe I am better off not knowing."

Once inside, Mingan offered Maggie a seat and he took the one next to her. He asked everyone inside to leave them alone.

"I want to speak to you about our people. We need your help once again," he said.

Maggie looked at him inquisitively.

"The number of people in this tribe fell to only a few before you came here. We prayed for mercy and for our people. Our prayers were answered when The Great Spirit sent you to us, and we are grateful for all you have done for us."

Maggie took his hand. "I love all of you as if you are my family by blood."

"Maggie, we feel the same; you are one of our own," he replied. "Which is why we need you now."

Mingan turned his gaze to the people outside. "In the past, we lost a great many of our young men. By the time you came along, our village only had a very few young boys and many older men. Spirit has blessed us with children, but they have mostly been girls. There is now one man for every six women and those men are not as fertile as they once were."

Maggie was stunned. "I had no idea."

He nodded. "Soon, there will be no men left to help grow our tribe. We need boys to be born, and a great many of them for our people to survive."

She tilted her head. "I don't understand. What can I do to help?"

"Powaw tells me that you have the power to make women fertile by touching them."

Maggie shifted uncomfortably. "It seems I can indeed do that, and I am happy to lay hands on any woman who desires it."

"I am afraid that is only part of the problem," he sighed. "A few men cannot father all of the children or they will be forced to marry their own brothers and sisters."

Maggie winced. "I see your dilemma."

Mingan watched Maggie's face closely as he spoke. "If Gabe, Quinn, and Logan were to take wives here, to father children, it would help us grow. We would never ask anyone else outside of the tribe, but you and your menfolk are family to us. Powaw also says that your husband and his brothers carry a special blood that would be of great help to our people."

Maggie was taken aback by his words.

Maybe, I need to have a little powwow with Powaw. He seems to know a great deal more than he is letting on.

"I don't think any of them are interested in taking wives," she said, gently. "Logan will be returning home soon and Gabe and Quinn…. they have their hands full with their own children right now."

Mingan lowered his head in deep thought. "If any of them decided that they wanted to marry one of our women, and she wanted it too, would you allow it?"

Maggie laid her hand on his. "Of course, I would! Nothing would make me happier, but that decision is not mine to make. You are welcome to ask because I cannot speak for any of them, but I would not get my hopes up if I were you."

Mingan smiled at her. "We will see." The elder went to stand and Maggie helped him up. "We will plan a large feast and a fertility ceremony during the next full moon, and you can lay hands on our women who want to be mothers then. We will prepare longhouses for all of you so you can stay the night."

"We would be honored," said Maggie. "Especially, if it is anything like the last time we spent the night."

Mingan winked as he went to greet some of the children who were playing.

Maggie slowly made her way toward the house Gabe was in. He was sitting up and talking to Quinn when she entered.

"Good morning, you two," she said. "How is our patient today?"

"I am feeling a great deal better," he replied. "As a matter of fact, I am fairly certain I can make the ride back to the house."

She eyed him warily before looking to Quinn. "What do you think?"

"Let's have a look first," he said, taking off Gabe's bandage. "It is healing well."

"But, we do not want to reopen it," added Maggie.

"I can assure you that I will recover much faster when I am in my own bed next to my husband."

"I think you should stay at the main house until you are better. The children will be taken care of and you can rest comfortably," she suggested.

"Aye," agreed Quinn. "Besides, it is much closer."

"I can live with that," said Gabe. "Just bring me a horse."

Maggie and Quinn turned to each other, then back to Gabe.

"How about the wagon?" asked Maggie.

She sent a silent message to Duncan, and he was there within the hour. Quinn and Duncan helped him onto the back as half the village came out to bid him farewell.

"Thank you for everything," said Gabe to Mingan as they were ready to leave.

"You are all welcome here anytime."

Mingan turned to Maggie. "Remember what I said."

Maggie nodded. "We will see you soon." She climbed in the back next to Gabe and Quinn, as Duncan and Logan took them home.

"What did he mean by that?" asked Gabe.

"I will fill you in later. I don't think you are well enough for that kind of news."

When they arrived home, Quinn and Logan helped Gabe upstairs. Alastair ran up to greet him and Maggie stopped him. She pulled him off to the side and sat him down.

"Alastair, your father had a little accident while he was gone. He is perfectly fine, but he is very sore, and you and Kat need to be extremely careful around him. He is going to need to rest the next few days, but I know he is missing both of you terribly."

"Can I go see him?" he asked, impatiently.

"As soon as he is in bed. I think seeing you will make him feel a lot better."

Alastair thought for a moment. "Do you think he is hungry?"

Maggie smiled. "As a matter of fact, I bet he is. Why don't you go get Hettie to fix him something to eat and take it up to him?"

He ran off to the kitchen.

Maggie followed them up to find that they had settled Gabe in bed, and Quinn was giving him something for the pain.

"Alastair is coming up to see you, and we will bring Kat up after you have rested."

"I have missed them both so much."

"They have missed ye, as well," said Quinn.

"Do you need anything?" she asked.

"I am good," replied Gabe.

"Get some sleep," she said and kissed his cheek. Maggie took Duncan's hand and led him into their bedroom.

I need to speak with you in private.

Maggie closed the door and moved to the settee. She leaned forward and put her face in her hands.

Duncan came over, sat down next to her, and rubbed her back while he waited for her to speak.

"The tribe is in trouble. They have too many women, not enough men, and they need male children."

"Aye, they do. I have noticed it as well."

"Mingan asked me to grant fertility to the women who want it in a ceremony at the next full moon."

"Do ye not want to do it?" he asked.

"That's not it. I am happy to do that. You have seen the children there. They are healthy, well cared for, and loved."

"So, what's bothering ye about it?"

"They need more fathers, and a variety of them, so when the children grow up, they can marry someone besides their own brother or sister."

Duncan nodded. "That makes perfect sense."

Maggie grimaced. "Mingan mentioned that Gabe, Quinn, and Logan might be good prospects to fill that need."

Duncan chuckled until he saw the look on Maggie's face. "Oh, ye are serious? I thought ye were joking."

She shrugged.

"Oh my God! What did ye tell him?"

She put her hand on his thigh. "I told him that Logan would be leaving, and that Quinn and Gabe had their hands full now, without telling him that they were a couple."

Duncan leaned back.

"That's not all. Things are about to get even more interesting. Powaw told Mingan that the MacGregors carry a special blood that the tribe could really use in their people."

"How would he know that?"

Maggie pulled her legs up and turned to face him. "I guess Onyx told him? Who the hell knows? What I do know is that little piece of information just made all of you ten times more attractive."

Duncan laughed.

"I want to help them, Duncan, I really do, but I cannot find men for them."

"Nay, ye cannot. Ye can only do what ye can, and it will have to be enough."

Maggie laid her head over in his lap and groaned while he stroked her face. "Why does everything have to be so complicated around here?"

He kissed her. "Because life would be boring if it wasn't."

"On a brighter note, Mingan is preparing a place for us to stay on the night of the full moon."

"Oh!" said Duncan. "Well, that is something to look forward to."

7 CHAPTER SEVEN

Gabe recovered quickly and was back to his old self in no time.

The afternoon of the fertility ceremony arrived and the entire family, minus the children, was attending. Cora, Cecile, and a few of the other ladies volunteered to spend the night with all the children at the main house and planned on making a girl's night of it once they were in bed.

Maggie stood in front of the mirror and held up gowns, trying to decide which one was most appropriate for the occasion. "What does one wear for a fertility ceremony?"

"Nothing if ye want it to be successful!" laughed Duncan. "It *is* a fertility ceremony after all."

Maggie smacked at him playfully. "So, you want me to go there completely naked?"

He took the gown from her hands and tossed it on the bed. "It will just save us some time later on."

"Well, I can't let *you* go without any clothes on. Some woman may steal you away from me to make you her 'baby daddy'."

"Nay!" he said. "I am a one-woman man and I have no desire to even look at another, much less do anything else."

"Good answer," she said and kissed him.

An hour later, they were on their way. When they arrived, the entire village had been transformed by many lit torches and a large bonfire. Tables had been laid out with a bounty of food and everyone was in a lively mood.

Maggie had sent down a few casks of Mingan's favorite wine and it flowed freely.

Mingan greeted them as they arrived, along with Wawetseka and Askuwheteau. They laughed and talked, enjoying a wonderful meal, everyone completely relaxed, and Lady Aurnia, especially, enjoyed the festivities. When the full moon rose, all the children were sent to bed, and the adults cleared the area for the ceremony.

Mingan took his seat, and Lady Aurnia sat at his side in a place of honor.

He spoke first in Algonquin, then in English. "We gather here tonight to give thanks to The Great Spirit for our bountiful blessings, and to ask for our tribe to grow and prosper. We have been sent a great gift in Maggie MacGregor; she comes tonight to grant fertility to our women, and we are grateful."

Powaw stepped forward and spoke a blessing in words they did not understand. When he was done, the low rhythmic drums began to play in the background, the same ones that had worked Maggie and Duncan into such a fervor before. Powaw came to Maggie, took her hand, and led her into a circle constructed of stones, sticks, small branches interwoven with beautiful wildflowers, and illuminated by three torches. Maggie leaned forward on her knees as he laid his hands on her head and said a few words over her. Then, he moved to personally escort each woman to her and, as the first one stepped inside, a large group of fireflies descended around them, remaining there throughout the whole of the ceremony. The entire scene was nothing short of magical.

As each woman kneeled before Maggie, she laid her hands on them, wished for fertility, and felt the jolt that told her it had worked. She also tossed in a little extra wish for baby boys, even though she wasn't sure if it would mean anything. When she was done, fifteen women had come forward and received the gift from her.

Maggie had never done that many at one time, and the power that she used drained her of all her energy.

After the ceremony, Powaw took her hand and escorted her back to Duncan.

He caught her as she stumbled slightly into his arms. "Are ye alright?" he asked, worriedly.

"I am," she giggled, feeling a little giddy. "That just took way more out of me than I thought it would."

He gently helped her down onto the pile of skins they used as seats.

Maggie looked around. The drums and the wine were starting to have their effect as men and women started to couple off, laughing and talking. Two women had brought Logan more wine, pulling him close to whisper in his ear. Gabe and Quinn were surrounded, as well.

"I forgot to warn them about Mingan's idea," she whispered, stretching out.

"They will figure it out," he said as he ran his hand down the side of her body and traced her curves while looking at her longingly.

Maggie caught sight of Mingan watching over the whole scene with a big fat smile on his face. She laughed and he nodded to her. Maggie turned on her side, and Duncan leaned down to kiss her.

"Your eyes!" he said, stroking her chin with his thumb.

"What about them?" she asked, touching his face.

"They are glowing again!"

"That's nice," sighed Maggie.

"It does not concern ye?" he asked.

"I am too exhausted right now to care about anything," she softly laughed, "except how my husband is going to make me feel very shortly."

He picked her up and carried her to the longhouse that had been made ready for them. He set her down on her feet and caught her when she almost fell over.

Maggie leaned against the wall of the house while Duncan removed her dress, leaving her completely naked before him. He laid her down on the bed, so she could relax, and lost himself in pleasuring her as Maggie surrendered, letting him have complete control. He smiled devilishly when he felt her body jerk in blessed relief, and crawled up to kiss her lips, covering her body with his own, and burying himself deep inside of her.

"I could never live without you," she whimpered.

He kissed her neck as he let out a delighted cry of satisfaction. "I *will* never live without ye."

They did not leave each other's embrace the rest of the night.

Duncan pulled back the door entry and let in the sunlight the next morning to wake her.

She groaned and pulled the blanket over her head.

"Good morning, my love," he said and tried to uncover her.

She groaned again, only louder. "Go away!"

He peeled back a tiny corner of the deerskin and peered in. "Maggie, are ye not feeling well?"

"I feel like I have been hit by a bus."

"What's a bus?" he asked.

"It's a big thing that hurts like hell when it hits you. I think I need that hangover cure of Quinn's."

"Ye only had one cup of wine last night."

"Why do I feel like I had the whole cask?" she whined.

He managed to wrestle the blanket away from her after a little tug of war and was able to see her face.

"Your eyes aren't glowing this morning, well...no more than usual."

"Last night was so strange," she said. "The power surge was amazing while I was touching the women, but afterwards...it was like it sucked all of the life energy out of me."

"Ye used it more last night at one time than ye ever have tried to before."

"So, I do need a magical hangover cure?" she asked.

"Well, it's not like ye got much rest afterwards," he winked.

"Oh yeah...you may have a point there." She recalled their full night of lovemaking with a wickedly delighted smile on her face.

He kissed her on the top of the head. "Let's get ye home."

Gabe and Quinn knocked on the outside frame of the door. "Are you decent?" called Gabe as they came in.

Maggie pulled the blanket back over her head. "Never! And, stop letting the light in. It burns."

"Too much to drink?" asked Gabe.

"Too much fertility granting," she replied, poking her head out. "Apparently, there are unpleasant side effects."

"Well, the whole village was feeling those effects last night," he said dryly.

"Aye," said Quinn. "Gabe and I spent the better part of the evening fending off amorous women."

"Oh, I forgot to tell you. Mingan wants the two of you to assist with populating the tribe." She yanked the deerskin back over her head to cover her face.

"Huh?" asked Gabe. He crept closer to her and snatched the blanket from her face. "He wants us to what?"

"There is a shortage of males and they need more men to be… 'sperm donors'. He asked if the two of you and Logan would take wives."

"Ye are just now mentioning this?" asked a flustered Quinn.

"Oh relax. I told him not to get his hopes up, although I don't think that will stop the women from trying."

"Why didn't you just tell him 'no'?" demanded Gabe.

"Because I didn't," she said and covered her face with her hands. "They are like family to us and I didn't want to hurt his feelings by telling him that the women here do nothing for you and Quinn."

Maggie curled on her side and pulled the blanket tight around her.

"Have either of ye seen Logan or Mother this morning?" asked Duncan.

"Mother was out with some of the children earlier, but I have not seen our brother."

"Didn't he stay in the longhouse with the two of ye last night?"

"No," replied Gabe. "He never came in."

"Err…." Maggie winced. "You might want to figure out where he spent the night," she mumbled.

Duncan's eyes grew wide and he made a face. "Aye, we probably should."

They didn't have to look far, because Logan appeared in the doorway.

"Where have ye been all night?" asked Quinn.

"I stayed somewhere else so ye and Gabe could be alone. You're welcome, by the way."

"*Where* did ye stay?" asked Duncan.

"Not that it is any of your business," he said and folded his arms, "but I stayed in one of the houses with a few of the lovely ladies."

Maggie smacked her forehead with her palm. "Were any of them by chance ones that came up to me at the ceremony last night?"

"Nay, why?"

"It seems that the village women want you, me, and Quinn to give them babies," replied Gabe and he slapped him on the back.

Logan looked around. "What?"

"How many did you lay with?" demanded Duncan.

"None of them!" he said affronted. "Unlike the rest of ye in this house, I actually have some self-control."

Maggie blew out a breath. "It's good to know that one of us does," she mumbled sarcastically, looking down, and realizing that she had nothing on underneath the blanket.

"Why us?" asked Quinn,

"Apparently, Onyx told Powaw that you had special blood and because...well, look at you three. What woman in their right mind wouldn't want to fu-?"

"Hey!" shouted Duncan.

"Present company excluded," she said and squeezed his face. "You are the only one I ever want to fu-."

"Wait!" Logan held up his hand. "*Onyx* told him?"

Quinn shook his head. "Aye, they talk. Don't ask. It will only make your head hurt."

"Just be careful where ye lay your head down...or anything else for that matter," said Duncan. "We should probably gather Mother and go back to the house."

8 CHAPTER EIGHT

The following week, Maggie sat at her desk in the drawing room and made sketches on pieces of paper, then balled them up and threw them on the floor out of frustration.

Duncan and Gabe side-stepped the wads of trash when they came in.

"What are ye doing, Maggie?" asked Duncan.

Maggie blew a few loose strands of hair out of her face. "Trying to figure out how we can 'hang' John, without actually 'hanging' him. October will be here very soon."

Gabe reached down, picked up one of the crumpled pages, and smoothed it out for a better look. "What did you have in mind?"

She pointed to the paper in front of her. "If we can figure out some sort of harness that could be sewn into his coat, that hooks to the false noose... maybe?"

"What are all of these on the floor?" asked Duncan, kicking a few of them out of his way.

"Those are the ones that won't work. I just can't figure it out in my mind," she said, smacking her palm against the side of her head.

"Maybe ye should be talking to someone who puzzles these things out on a daily basis," suggested Duncan.

"Who do you mean?" she asked.

"Joshua! He makes all the building plans around here. Have ye thought to ask him?"

Maggie stood, took Duncan's face in her hands, and kissed him on the mouth. "That is a brilliant idea! Why didn't I think of it?"

She called out to Hettie to send for her builder.

"You wanted to see me, Maggie?" asked Joshua a few minutes later.

"Yes, come in." Maggie poured him a drink. "We need your help."

"What can I do for you?"

Maggie sat down next to him. "We need to find a way to hang a man without actually hanging him."

Joshua scratched his head. "You might want to explain that one to me."

"We have a friend who is going to be hanged, and we want to make it look like that is what happened, but we want to make sure he doesn't die," answered Gabe.

"I am not sure how I can help."

Maggie showed him one of her crude drawings and explained her idea for a harness inside a coat to connect to a hook within the noose.

"Can you take a look at this and see if you can figure out a way to make it work? I am having no luck, and you are the best one I know at figuring out the mechanics of things."

Joshua took the drawing. "I can sure give it a try," he said.

"Thank you," replied Maggie. "This is very important to me."

Joshua nodded and headed out.

Maggie leaned back against the couch and Duncan rubbed her shoulders from behind.

"Ye look tired, my love."

"I am," she replied.

"It seems to be taking you a while to get over that ceremony," Gabe pointed out.

"Must be that pesky human half of me," she said dryly. "Obviously, I am not cut out for the 'goddess' life."

One week later, they gathered around one of the large oak trees near the stables.

"Well, what do you think?" asked Joshua.

Maggie, Gabe, Logan, Duncan, and Joshua formed a circle around Quinn.

Quinn was rigged up in a leather harness; one piece went around each armhole where the sleeve of a coat met at the shoulder, and one long piece connected them across the back. A small metal ring was in the middle of the cross piece.

"Will it work?" asked Maggie, nervously.

"There is only one way to find out," said Logan and he grabbed a rope, with a hook on one end, and tossed it up and over a tree limb, then connected it to the ring on Quinn's back. They all watched anxiously as Logan and Joshua hoisted Quinn up until he was suspended a few feet off the ground. It held for a couple of minutes, before the eye hook pulled loose, tore the crosspiece, and caused Quinn to fall and land on his backside with an audible 'umph'. Gabe held out his hand and helped him to his feet.

"Are you alright, Quinn?" asked Maggie.

"Aye, I am fine," he said while he brushed the dirt off his clothes.

Joshua came over to Quinn and examined the part that had ripped.

"There was too much weight on that one spot," he pointed out.

Maggie frowned.

"Is there any way to distribute it?" asked Quinn.

"I could try spreading the loop out further, like when you hang a big picture on the wall, though I don't know if that will work," said Joshua. "Let me take it back and work on it some more."

"I will help ye," said Quinn and he slipped the harness off.

"Thank you both so much," said Maggie, wearily.

She started back towards the house with her shoulders slumped and her head hung down.

Gabe watched her go.

"This is eating her alive," whispered Duncan. "If we can't save John, I am not sure what it will do to her."

Duncan found her in their bedroom sitting on the bed.

"What are ye doing up here all alone?" he asked.

"Thinking."

He sat down next to her. "About what?"

Maggie turned to him. "Tell me again what my mother had domain over."

Her question disturbed him, and he regarded her cautiously. "Fertility, of course, good harvest, renewal and rebirth...Maggie, why do ye ask me this question?"

She laid her hand on his leg. "Could my mother...do something like...raise the dead?" she asked softly.

Duncan rubbed his face with his hand and stared back at her, more than a little concerned. "I suppose that could fall under rebirth, but I do not recall ever hearing of any stories or reading anywhere that she did." He took her hand. "Maggie, why are ye asking me something like this?"

She blew out a long breath. "If I have her abilities of fertility and good harvest, it would make sense that I would have the others, as well. If we cannot figure out how to save John any other way..." she trailed off.

Duncan saw the utter desperation on her face. He held up his hand to halt her. "Maggie, that would take a full-blooded goddess, at the very least, and even *if* that were possible, look what the fertility ceremony did to ye. It took ye days to recover. Ye might not survive something like that, and besides, we aren't even sure if your mother was capable of such a thing."

Maggie fell back upon the bed and curled on her side.

"We are running out of ideas and time," she whispered, on the verge of tears.

Duncan laid down beside her not knowing what to say to comfort her, so he just held her.

That night after everyone went to bed, Maggie slipped in to peek on the babies and found them fast asleep. She went down to the drawing room, closed the pocket doors, and poured two glasses of whisky. She sat one on the side table next to a chair and settled comfortably into the chair across from it with the other.

"Finn! If you can hear me, I need to speak with you. It's very important."

A small bit of fog blew in from underneath the pocket doors and he appeared in the chair across from her. "Hello, Maggie."

"Hello, Finn." She pointed to the glass on the table.

He turned and picked up the glass. "Thank ye," he said, took a sip and held it up. "Not bad for 18th century whisky...not good either mind ye, but not terrible."

He eyed her over the top of his glass. "What can I do for ye, my dear?"

"I need to know something," she said, and looked down while running her finger around the rim of her own glass. "Was my mother able to raise the dead?" she asked, softly.

Finn leaned back, crossed his legs, and gave her his full attention. "Why on Earth would ye want to know something like that?"

"Maybe I am writing a book," she said, sarcastically.

"Why don't ye just try *reading* a book?" he quipped mockingly. "Your mother's is downstairs on the table, chocked full of all sorts of handy tips and juicy tidbits, just waiting for ye to dig in, and ye have not even bothered to open it."

"I have my own personal reasons for that," she whispered and rubbed the spot between her eyes with her finger. "Can you just answer me, please?"

Finn tilted his head as he watched her intently. "Aye, she had the ability. It was within her power to bring back souls that had passed from this world into the next, but she never once used it."

"Do I have it within me as well?"

He set his drink down and leaned forward with his forearms resting on his knees. "Nay, ye do not!" he said. "At least, not as ye are now."

Maggie narrowed her eyes. "What do you mean by 'as I am'?"

Finn sighed. "Ye would be able to if ye were a full goddess, which obviously ye are not." He leaned back and steepled his fingers. "However, that *is* something that is within my own power to change."

She shook her head in disbelief. "You could make me a full goddess?"

"Aye! Ye could take your mother's place as Danu, the goddess of rebirth and renewal." He shrugged. "And to be perfectly honest with ye, nothing would make me happier than to have my granddaughter by my side."

Maggie had a strange feeling there was more to the story than he was letting on, as usual. "And what is the price for such a gift?" she asked.

Finn picked up the glass and sipped his drink, his gaze fixated on her. "Immortality."

"That's the cost?" she asked.

"Aye. Ye will live forever, or as long as this world does, watching everyone ye know and love grow old and die before your very eyes. Everyone ye come to care for will leave ye all alone in the end...even the ones ye raise from the dead will have to depart from ye eventually. That was one of the reasons your mother never used it. She would have only been prolonging the inevitable. What ye humans experience as years, we merely experience as minutes."

Maggie let that rather harsh reality soak in. "That is a pretty steep price," she replied.

"Aye, it is indeed, but the world would lie at your feet in return. Ye would never get sick, grow old, or die, and ye would be able to heal the very ground beneath your feet for future generations to come."

Maggie shook her head. "I will not live without Duncan, no matter what the cost," she whispered, "I could not watch him die, knowing that I would never see or feel him again. I would rather take my chances on being with him in the afterlife."

Finn nodded with a look of understanding. "The offer always stands, if ye ever change your mind, ye need only call out to me and I will come."

Finn waved his hand and their drinks replenished themselves.

"That's a handy little trick," said Maggie, astonished, holding up her glass to watch.

"It's very useful at parties," he smirked. "I am sure it will go over very well when I open that brothel...what did ye call it again? "Finn's- Fae- Fuckery?" He bobbed his head around. "I rather like the sound of it! I think it has a nice ring to it."

Maggie closed one eye and scratched her forehead. "You heard that, did you?"

"Oh, I hear a great deal, my dear," he said, and lifted his eyebrows. "Especially, when I visit the babies while ye and Duncan are 'otherwise engaged'."

Maggie was aghast and rather embarrassed. "You hear us?"

"Ye two *are* rather fond of each other," he laughed. "*Everyone* in the house hears ye, by the way."

Maggie covered her face with her hands. "Oh my God!"

"Everyone hears *that* particular phrase a great deal as well," he winked.

Maggie's face turned bright red.

"Oh, don't be embarrassed. Everyone who meets the two of ye are jealous of your love. It doesn't come around like that very often, but when it does, it is a thing of beauty. Besides, it provides a great deal of lively entertainment around here."

"How often do you come to see the babies?" asked Maggie in an attempt to change the subject.

"I pop in every now and then."

"Are you responsible for the floating toys?" she asked.

"Nay, that is all from the babies. I told ye to expect some unusual things."

"Unusual yes, but you left out the part about inanimate objects flying around the room," she snarked. "I don't suppose you would elaborate on what else we might expect?"

Finn chuckled. "Where is the fun in that?"

Maggie rolled her eyes. "At least answer this one question for me honestly. Is Kat a MacGregor?"

Finn nodded. "She is indeed. Her grandmother on her mother's side, Hannah and Penny's mother, was left in an orphanage in London when she was a baby. Her mother, Kat's great grandmother, was a MacGregor from the stronghold in Scotland. She fell in love and became with child by a man from a rival clan. When she told him that she carried his bairn, he spurned her and told her that he did not care for her. She fled Scotland, never telling her family what happened. She gave birth in London and left the child on the doorstep of a church."

"That's awful," replied Maggie. "What happened to her?"

"She never returned to Scotland. She changed her name and made a life in another country caring for the sick, before marrying and going on to have more children."

"I suppose it is just pure coincidence that my best friend Gabe ended up as her father?" asked Maggie with her eyebrows raised.

Finn smirked behind his glass. "Maybe not so much."

"Why do I have a feeling there are many things you are not telling me?" scoffed Maggie.

"Life is boring without a few surprises. Besides, Gabe and Quinn are good together and they are wonderful parents to Kat and Alastair."

"Yes, they are. Alastair was a pleasant surprise to both of them and a very welcome addition to the family."

Finn smiled. "He is a wonderful boy with a heart of gold."

"Yes, he is." Maggie set down her glass. "Want to see the babies while you are here?"

Finn stood. "I thought ye would never ask."

They quietly made their way up to the nursery, and Finn flicked his hand to illuminate a soft light that they could see by.

"You should teach me some of those tricks," said Maggie.

"Become a full goddess and I will gladly teach ye all of them," he winked.

They leaned over the edge of the crib. The three babies were fast asleep, holding hands as they always did.

"Look at these darlings," smiled Finn. "They are perfect."

"They really are good babies, thank goodness. I am not sure Duncan and I would have made it this far otherwise."

"Don't sell yourself short, Maggie. Ye are a wonderful mother to them. They are lucky to have ye." Finn reached down and touched each of them lightly on the face.

"You are welcome to come when they are awake, you know."

"I do not think your husband would like that. He isn't very fond of me."

Maggie turned to him. "That's not true. He is just very protective of me and the children...and his horse."

"As he should be," chuckled Finn, turning to her. "But I do hope *ye* know that I would never do anything to intentionally hurt ye or these little ones."

"I know that," she said, "even if you *do* leave a great many details out."

Finn laughed softly. "I should go. He is awake and wondering where ye are."

"Thank you for the talk," she said.

"It was my pleasure, my dear," he said as he leaned down, kissed Maggie on the cheek, and disappeared into the fog that trailed out of the window.

Maggie took one last look at the babies before she headed back to Duncan. He was indeed awake.

"I was just about to come looking for ye? Are ye not able to sleep?"

Maggie undressed and climbed in next to him. "I was having a chat with Finn."

Duncan sat straight up, alarmed. "Finn? What was he doing here?" he demanded, immediately alert and on guard.

"Relax," she said as she touched his chest. "I called him."

"Why would ye do something like that?"

"I had some questions about my mother, and he provided some answers. He also confirmed that Kat is, indeed, a MacGregor."

"Really? How did that come about?"

Maggie sighed. "Can I tell you in the morning? Right now, I need you to do something for me."

"What might that be?"

Maggie pulled him into a long kiss. "Guess," she teased.

"Now, who is trying to use their body as a distraction?" he asked.

"Is it working?"

"Aye," he growled and pulled her over onto him, "it is."

The next morning, when Maggie went into the nursery, she found a note on the dresser. She picked it up, read it, and smiled.

"Thank you, Finn," she said aloud. "I owe you one."

Maggie joined everyone at the breakfast table and handed Quinn the paper.

"What's this?" he asked as he set his cup down.

"I think it is the answer to our problem," she replied as she took a seat.

Quinn looked down to see a sketch, complete with dimensions and directions, for a harness like the ones used in theatrical performances on stage in the future.

"Is it doable?" asked Maggie.

"Aye, it is." Quinn looked up. "How did ye figure this out?"

"I didn't. I had a visit with Finn last night."

Everyone froze and turned to stare at her.

She explained what Finn had told her about Kat, and the news left the room silent for a few moments.

"It seems to me that I do remember my mother speaking of a sister once. Mary was her name, but Mother said that she was gone. I assumed she meant that she had died," said Lady Aurnia. "But, if she just up and left one day, that would explain why they never spoke of her more than they did."

Gabe took Quinn's hand. "Should we be concerned? About Kat?"

Maggie shook her head. "I do not think so. Finn seems very pleased by the fact that the two of you are Kat and Alastair's fathers, so I would not worry about that."

Gabe and Quinn exchanged uneasy looks; neither seeming overly reassured by her words.

After breakfast, Duncan pulled Maggie outside into the flower garden so they could speak alone. "What are ye not telling me about Finn's visit?"

Maggie sat down on the bench, pulled him down next to her, and filled him in on Finn's offer.

"He wants ye to become Danu?" he asked in disbelief.

"He also explained the cost… an eternity of being without the ones that I love... and living without you is not an option for *me*," she said and kissed him. "I cannot imagine living forever not being in your arms."

"On that we agree, my love," said Duncan as he pulled her tight and smothered her in kisses.

Three days later, Logan hoisted Quinn up a tree with the harness made by Joshua using the plans that Finn had left for them.

"It works!" said a delighted Maggie. "Can you figure out how to make the noose look real?"

"Already have," grinned Joshua. "It's almost done."

Maggie hugged him. "Thank you!"

Lady Aurnia and Hettie appeared from around the corner.

"What on Earth?" exclaimed Lady Aurnia, seeing Quinn swinging back and forth in the air. "What are ye doing up there, son?"

"We're having a hanging," laughed Logan.

"Hello, Mother!" waved a grinning Quinn from six feet off the ground.

"Lord have mercy!" said Hettie, shaking her head. "You never know what you are going to see around here. Nothing surprises me anymore."

"Well, we know the harness works," said Maggie. "Now, we just need to get it into a coat."

"You can use my uniform coat and adjust it to look like John's," said Gabe. "We are about the same size, and I can point out what needs to be added and taken away to make it identical to his."

"I have already talked to Cecile and she says she can do it, no problem," said Joshua.

Maggie breathed a huge sigh of relief. They had crossed the first, and one of the most difficult hurdles, in front of them, and exactly one week later, Cecile presented them with Gabe's coat that she had added the harness into and lined to conceal...it was perfect!

9 CHAPTER NINE

Maggie sat at her desk with David Percy in the chair in front of her looking over paperwork.

"The sale of the house has been finalized. You are now the proud owners of a new residence in New York City. Would you like me to put the deed with the other documents at my home?"

"Please!" replied Maggie. "I feel like everything is safer there."

David leaned back. "The shipping business is making a record profit. I am not sure how you do it, but you have the best business instincts of anyone I have ever seen in my entire life."

"I guess I am just lucky."

David's face turned serious and he looked down, trying to find the words he wanted to say. "There is something else I feel the need to bring to your attention, Maggie, but it is a very delicate matter and I am not sure exactly how to approach it."

Maggie folded her arms and rested them on the desk. "Surely, you have figured out by now that nothing shocks me, and the direct route is usually best, so just spit it out."

David watched her nervously and took in a deep breath. "There is some talk in town about Gabe and Quinn. People find it strange that they have not taken wives, and that the two men spend so much time together. Normally, all of you are in and out of Virginia so much that no one pays it any mind, but since you have been here for an extended time with the babies, it is being noticed more and it could potentially be a problem for them should certain assumptions be made, if you take my meaning. I thought you might want to know."

She nodded. "Thank you for telling me, David, and you are right, I did need to know. I will handle it."

He stood to go. "If there is anything I can do to assist, please do not hesitate to ask. Cora and I care for Gabe and Quinn very much, and we do not want to see any sort of trouble come to them." He picked up his hat from the desk and left.

Maggie rubbed her temples; a headache started to form. "Great! Let's add one more issue into the mix."

Maggie found the men down at the stables, working with some new horses they had purchased. Duncan and Logan were stripped to the waist trying to break in a new colt that was giving them a hard time while Gabe, Quinn, and Harm watched from the side. Maggie stopped to admire Duncan's sweat-covered body for a few moments, having all sorts of thoughts about being alone with him in the stable. She must have focused too hard and accidently let Duncan catch a glimpse. He turned to see where she was, caught sight of her, and lifted his eyebrows, intrigued.

Anytime my love.

Maggie laughed. *We have other things that take precedence, right now.*

She moved to join Gabe and Quinn. "I need to see you two inside when you are done here."

"Sounds serious," said Gabe.

"It is." Maggie turned and went back to the house to wait for them.

A short time later, they came into the drawing room.

"What's the problem now?" asked Duncan.

Maggie closed the pocket doors and took a seat. "There is some talk in town about Gabe and Quinn."

"What sort of talk?" demanded Quinn.

"It seems that since the two of you have not taken wives and that, coupled with the amount of time that you spend together, well, it is drawing some attention and causing some tongues to wag."

Gabe frowned. "I am afraid with everything that has been going on, I have slacked off on covering our lifestyle."

Quinn looked at him questioningly for clarification.

"Before you and I met," he explained, "I would attend events and make it a point to be seen more often out in public, spending time with the ladies in town. To everyone, I just seemed like I was someone...well, like John, who just loved women. Maggie and I would always be seen out together and people just assumed we were discreet lovers. But, since she has a husband now, and since you and I have wed, I have not been so diligent about covering our tracks."

"So, what do we need to do?" asked Duncan.

"Gabe and Quinn need to romance the ladies," shrugged Maggie. "Or, at least appear to. Gabe knows how to handle them better than anyone, and he can teach Quinn. Perhaps we should start with dinner and a show in town."

"Raleigh Tavern?" asked Gabe.

Maggie chewed on her thumb in thought. "Yes, and it might be a good idea to take Kat and Alastair with us."

"Why?" asked Gabe, "Not that I don't want to spend time with our children."

"If people see that you have children...by women...it might help. I know Kat isn't yours biologically, but most people do not know she is adopted. They will just assume you are her birth father. You can just say that her mother died in childbirth. And, Quinn can say that the mother of his child passed, so his own mother brought him to his father. None of these are lies."

"That makes a great deal of sense," agreed Duncan. "Will one trip to the tavern be enough?"

"No, it will not!" said Maggie and stood, walking to her desk to sift through the mail. "It's a good thing I received this yesterday." She held up an envelope. "An invitation to a supper party at the home of Charlotte White, the town's biggest source of gossip. It will be full of swooning women who will be excited to see such a handsome group of men walk through the door."

Gabe made a face and groaned, rubbing his forehead with his palm. "As much as I hate to admit it, Maggie is right. A performance there should buy us a good deal of time."

Logan, who leaned against the wall, broke into a wide grin. "Well, this should be interesting to watch."

Maggie walked over and patted him on the shoulder. "I am glad you feel that way because you get to do more than watch. You are the only actual single man here, and you will have to do your part as well."

The following day, the entire extended family, minus the babies, went into town for dinner. Maggie and Lady Aurnia rode in the carriage with Alastair and Kat.

"Remember our talk last night, Alastair. In public, you need to call your father, 'Uncle Gabe'. It is very important if we want to keep them safe."

"Don't worry, Aunt Maggie, I will remember. I will always protect them."

Maggie smiled and hugged him.

"Ye think this will really work?" asked Lady Aurnia, somewhat unsure.

"It will," replied Maggie. "Gabe has done this for so long, that he has perfected it. You will be amazed at his transformation when you see him at work. It was how he extracted information when he was in the army, and he was the best at what he did."

When they arrived, Duncan helped them out of the carriage, and kissed Maggie as she stepped out. The group made their way in the direction of the Raleigh Tavern.

"Make sure your wedding ring is visible," teased Maggie and took Duncan's arm.

"I have my dagger in my boot if I have to fight any women off," he grinned.

"I'll cover your backside," laughed Maggie.

"I would rather cover yours," he quipped, and kissed her cheek.

As they went inside, everyone stopped what they were doing to gawk at the new arrivals, especially the women.

Gracie came from the back to greet them, a wide smile on her face. "Well! Well! It is about time all of you came by for a visit."

Gabe leaned over and kissed her on the cheek. "You know I can't stay away from my Gracie," he smiled.

The woman blushed and almost melted into a puddle right there on the spot.

Maggie introduced her to the rest of the family, and they took a large table in the middle of the place.

"Who is this fine fellow?" asked Gracie.

"This is my son, Alastair," answered Quinn.

Gracie looked back and forth between them, a little surprised. "I should say. You two are the spitting image of each other."

"Allow me to introduce my daughter, Kat," added Gabe.

Gracie leaned down to Kat. "Well, hello young lady! I have heard all about you. Your father talks about you all the time."

Kat smiled and leaned against Gabe's chest with her thumb in her mouth.

"Rum punch all around?" she asked.

"You know it!" answered Maggie.

As they waited for their drinks, Maggie scanned the room. They were, indeed, the center of attention.

Lady Aurnia leaned close to Maggie and whispered. "Is it always like this?"

"Yes. Williamsburg loves Gabe and the MacGregor brothers."

They enjoyed a leisurely dinner and drinks, and afterwards, Maggie loudly announced, "Duncan, I think your mother and I will take Kat to do a little shopping. Why don't all of you stay here and enjoy your drinks?"

The men all stood as the ladies prepared to leave.

Duncan kissed Maggie on the cheek, and she whispered, "Good luck."

Maggie, Kat, and Lady Aurnia hadn't even made it to the front door before the good ladies in the tavern started inching their way closer to the table to say 'hello'.

Maggie pointed to the door as they stopped in front of Mr. Craig's shop. "I need to stop in here for just a moment," she said.

"Kat and I will sit here on the bench and keep an eye on the boys."

When Maggie came out, she took a seat next to her mother-in-law. "How's it going?"

Lady Aurnia grinned. "I thought Scottish women were forward, but these women…my goodness, they have no shame."

Maggie laughed. "These women have never seen anything like that group of men, and they are being reserved today. Wait until you see them at the party." She took out a box and handed it to Lady Aurnia.

"What's this?" the older woman asked as she accepted it.

"I had these rings made for the family as a symbol of our unity and love for each other. Of course, I had one made for you."

Lady Aurnia opened the box. "Oh Maggie, this is lovely! Thank ye." She slipped it on and hugged her.

Maggie handed her another box. "There are ones in here for Logan, Reade, and Evan, as well. I intend on having them made for all the children when they are old enough."

Lady Aurnia smiled and took Maggie's hand. "I could not have been blessed with a daughter any better than ye. I am so thankful that ye found your way to us."

"I am the lucky one," replied Maggie, squeezing her hand. "I have been gifted with an extraordinary family, and I am beyond grateful for all of you."

The men finally made their way onto the street.

"Work all the ladies into a tizzy?" asked Maggie.

"I think we are off to a good start," replied Gabe, picking up Kat.

"You and Quinn need to go make one more stop while we are here."

"Where might that be?" asked Gabe.

Maggie turned his body around and pointed down the street. "I think you two should personally visit Charlotte White and tell her how delighted we would all be to attend her party next week. While you are there, make sure you mention how much you have missed all the fair ladies of Williamsburg during your very lonely years in the army."

Gabe rolled his eyes and scoffed. "I don't think I've had enough to drink for this."

Maggie patted the lump in his coat pocket. "And that, my dear Gabe, is why you carry a flask!"

The evening of the soiree arrived, and Maggie was getting dressed while Duncan watched her.

"If you keep looking at me like that, we will never make it to the party," she said as she put on her necklace.

"I am perfectly fine with that," he said and grabbed her around the waist. "Maybe if everyone is focused on Gabe and Quinn, we can sneak out to the stables for some time alone," he growled, kissing her neck.

She adjusted his coat collar. "I have to admit, that does sound very tempting."

They took some time for a little pre-party foreplay for a bit making them the last two downstairs.

Lady Aurnia was dressed in a beautiful green gown that fit her perfectly and showed off her tiny figure. The men were all dressed to the hilt, wig free with their hair pulled back, looking sexier than ever.

Maggie stopped and smiled when she saw them standing in the drawing room having drinks. "Such a handsome group of fellows!"

"Are we sufficiently on display?" asked Gabe, dryly.

"I think the ladies of Williamsburg will be pleased," she replied.

Charlotte White greeted them when they entered her home. "Maggie! It is so good to see you."

"And you, Charlotte! Thank you for inviting us." Maggie made all the formal introductions.

"Maggie, I am so happy all of you came. We have missed you. Why, my guest list doubled when everyone found out that you were coming."

I am sure it did, and it wasn't because of me.

"Oh Charlotte, you flatter me."

They made their way inside and stopped to greet people they knew and to make introductions. It wasn't long before Gabe, Quinn, and Logan had been swept up by a group of women. Gabe must have given Quinn lessons, because he fell right into the same groove, dazzling the ladies with his winning smile and conversation. Logan was also enjoying the attention, since the women found him just as enticing—and he, for one, liked it.

Charlotte scooped Lady Aurnia up to get all the details on her boys while Maggie and Duncan hung back in a corner. Maggie stood in front of him, watching the crowd, as he discreetly rubbed her backside with his hand.

"We *will* give the town something to talk about if you keep that up," she said, over her shoulder with a smirk.

"I have no problem with that," he whispered before he planted a little kiss on the back of her neck and pressed his very 'ready' self against her.

Maggie whimpered, a surge of desire spreading throughout her body. "As much as I would really love to do that right now, I should probably go mingle with the ladies to find out what they are saying. Why don't you keep an eye on things over here?"

He groaned, slightly disappointed, then pinched her behind and winked as he slipped away.

Maggie found a seat next to Charlotte and Lady Aurnia.

"Oh Maggie! I was just enjoying getting to know your mother-in-law."

Maggie took Lady Aurnia's hand. "We are very happy to have her and Logan here for a visit."

"How many sons do you have?" Charlotte asked Lady Aurnia.

"I was blessed with five of them."

"How many are married?"

"Only Duncan, much to my chagrin. I would much prefer they settle down, but it seems they like chasing women more than they like marrying them."

"Maggie managed to catch one of them," said Charlotte.

"Those were special circumstances," smiled Maggie, knowing full well that she was digging for more information.

"How so?" she asked.

Maggie turned to look at Duncan. "That was love at first sight."

Duncan caught her gaze and smiled back at her.

Charlotte watched their exchange before looking in Gabe's direction. "I always thought you and Gabe would marry. You two have always been...inseparable."

Maggie sighed. "Gabe and I found we were better as friends and business partners than as anything else."

Their hostess focused her gaze directly on Maggie and sipped her drink. "I am curious. How did you find that out, my dear?"

Maggie remembered Gabe mentioning that Charlotte's daughter had tried to land him as a husband several years ago, but that he had extricated himself from the situation by using Maggie as the reason. Charlotte had not been pleased.

In that instant, Maggie knew exactly where all the gossip about Gabe and Quinn had been coming from, and she had an idea of how to squash it once and for all.

Making eye contact with the nosy woman, Maggie kept her voice low, "Gabe has always had a roving eye; as well as *other* roving body parts. He loves the ladies and he tends to have an affinity for…" She leaned in and waved Charlotte closer while whispering, as if she wanted no one else to hear, "...the whorehouses. I discovered that he has a favorite girl by the name of Mathilda that apparently does all sorts of things that proper young women would never do," she lied.

Charlotte almost dropped her drink in her own lap. Her eyes widened and she leaned in closer to hear every word. "Gabe Asheton?"

Maggie nodded.

Lady Aurnia caught on to Maggie's plan and decided to help it along a bit. "I blame Gabe for Quinn not taking a wife. They are the best of friends and they do everything together. It seems Quinn has also developed a taste for those disgusting places. They would spend days in Edinburgh, laid up with harlots of all sorts, before coming home reeking of alcohol and cheap perfume. I cannot tell ye how disappointed I am in Quinn."

Maggie nodded. "Gabe has a problem; he cannot stay out of them. That's why we are always gone for so long. It's darn near impossible to get him away from one. I love Gabe as family, but I was fortunate enough to find out about his 'perverse appetite' before we went any further. I have been spared a lifetime of heartache and misery because now I do not have to wonder about where he is and who he is with at all times."

Charlotte sat back in her chair as Maggie and Lady Aurnia exchanged glances.

"Of course," added Maggie for effect. "That is between us. He is still my business partner and I need him for that. I do try to keep him and Quinn on the estate and out of trouble...and well, since they both have children that have turned up unexpectedly, it is a little bit easier."

"Children, you say?" asked Charlotte, her curiosity burning a hole.

"Aye," said Lady Aurnia, "That is why Logan and I came. Quinn spent one night with a barmaid and got her with child some years ago. We only just found out about the boy and we brought him to his father. Lord only knows how many more are out there that we *don't* know about."

"Gabe has a daughter, whose mother died in childbirth that he was never married to. Although, he was involved with her sister many years ago. That sister and his son died in childbirth, as well, as I recall," added Maggie.

Maggie shot Duncan a silent message. *I am SO going to Hell after tonight.*

Duncan nearly choked on his drink and turned sideways to hide his laughter.

"Please, don't misunderstand me, Charlotte. Gabe and Quinn are both wonderful fathers when it comes to their children and both are very devoted to their love and care. They actually help each other out a great deal, and when they need to go out to...relieve their frustrations, as these two always need to do...they take turns watching the other's child."

Stick a fork in Charlotte White...she was done.

Their hostess had leaned back against the chair, pale as a ghost, fanning herself, trying to catch her breath.

"Pardon me, ladies, I think I need another drink," she said and stood.

Maggie and Lady Aurnia exchanged satisfied looks as Charlotte walked away.

"Nice plan," whispered Lady Aurnia. "I daresay this will never be an issue again."

Maggie tapped her fingers on the arm of the chair. "Let's make sure, shall we?"

Standing, she got Gabe and Quinn's attention by moving her head to indicate that she needed to see them outside. Duncan came to her side, and they slipped into the garden. She scanned the area to make sure they were alone before speaking.

"I am fairly certain that Charlotte is the one stirring up trouble for you and Quinn."

"Why would she do something like that?" asked Gabe.

"Don't you remember when her daughter wanted you to court her and you turned her down?"

Gabe smacked his forehead. "I had completely forgotten about that. But, why now, after all this time, would she start causing trouble?"

"People like that always bide their time until the moment is right. I think I have found a way to protect you and Quinn once and for all, but you need to drive it home."

"How do we do that?" asked Quinn.

Maggie winced. "I told her that the two of you are insatiable when it comes to women, and that you take a great deal of pleasure in the...whorehouses."

Duncan snorted while Gabe and Quinn gaped at her.

"Exactly, how does that help?" asked Gabe, rather annoyed.

"Think about it. If you have an affinity for the women at the whorehouses, then you aren't interested in each other. We told her that you are best friends and that is something you share a love of."

"We?" asked Quinn.

"Your mother may have helped me a bit," she said, scrunching up her nose and raising her brows.

"Oh God!" exclaimed Quinn. "Can this possibly get any worse?" He turned away and folded both hands behind his head, resting on his neck. "My mother is telling people that I like to frequent whorehouses!"

"What's the rest of this brilliant plan of yours?" asked a flustered Gabe.

"That's the hard part. You need to put the moves on Charlotte."

"You have got to be joking!" he cried out.

"Gabe! If she thinks you are basically a 'male whore' who wants every woman you can lay your hands on, what better way to convince her of that than to try it with her? If you do this tonight, by tomorrow morning, everyone in Williamsburg will think that Gabe Asheton is a cad...with the *ladies*...and there will be no question about where your true inclinations lie. Lady Aurnia and I laid all the groundwork; you just need to put the final nail in the coffin."

"It does sound like a good plan," said Duncan, trying to hide his amusement.

"Then, why don't you do it?" snapped Gabe.

"Because I am not the one married to my brother," retorted Duncan.

Gabe paled a little at the thought. "What do you think, Quinn?"

Quinn shrugged. "I don't know. It very well may be enough to keep people out of our business for a good long while to come."

Gabe shook his head. "What if she doesn't reject me?"

Maggie patted him on the chest. "You are a smart boy; you will figure it out."

"I am going to need a lot more alcohol for this," he groaned.

Quinn took him by the shoulders. "Well, come on lover! Let's get ye good and liquored up!"

After several shots of liquid courage and a great deal of coaxing and encouragement from the others, Gabe located Charlotte in the hall. He blew out a deep breath and mentally prepared himself. Squaring his shoulders, he called out, "Charlotte! Maggie sent me to find you. She is not feeling well and asked me to bring you to her."

"Oh?" said Charlotte seemingly concerned. "Where can I find her?"

"In the small room off the parlour. Come! I will show you." He escorted her inside, then closed the door behind them.

"Where is she?" asked Charlotte, looking around the room.

Gabe held his hand on the door. "I must confess, Charlotte, I lied." He rolled his eyes and mouthed curse words before he turned to face her with a wide smile on his face.

With a confused expression, Charlotte placed her hands on her hips and asked, "Why on Earth would you do that?"

Putting a lustful look on his face, Gabe eyed her up and down. "Isn't it obvious? I wanted to be alone with you. I have been watching you all night." He took a step closer to her and loosened the cravat around his neck. "You are a very lovely woman and I cannot stop thinking about you."

He moved until only a few inches separated them, then reached out to touch her face gently with the back of his hand. "I am afraid I am having wicked thoughts about you and all of the glorious things I can do to pleasure us both."

She narrowed her eyes at him and just as Gabe expected a hard slap across the cheek....

.... a wide, devilish smile slowly spread across her face.

She laid both her hands flat on his chest and bit her bottom lip seductively. "I have had a few thoughts about you, myself." She grabbed him by his coat and pulled him into a passionate kiss, shoving her tongue into his mouth and partially down his throat.

Gabe's eyes flew wide open and he tried to push her away, but she only gripped him tighter, before she took his hand and planted it firmly against her breast.

"We really shouldn't do this in here," said Gabe, when he finally broke from her grasp. He gasped for air while he tried to figure out the quickest way to extricate himself from his current predicament.

"I can lock the door," she purred. "No one will bother us in here."

She pulled him into another kiss, as one of her hands found its way a little further down, briskly rubbing against his member. The unexpected action caused Gabe to jump back a bit, and he moved quickly to gently free her hand from his private area, an action that only excited her even more.

Maggie, Quinn, and Duncan were listening on the other side of the door. Maggie's hand flew to cover her mouth, completely taken aback by the words that had come from Charlotte's lips.

Well, that didn't go as planned!

Maggie smacked Quinn on the back and pointed at the door.

"Get in there!" she whispered. "Gabe needs your help."

"What am I supposed to do?"

"Figure something out!" she commanded. Maggie pulled open the door and shoved Quinn inside the room before closing it behind him.

He stumbled in and looked back towards the hall, before turning to see Gabe, whose eyes were wide and pleading for assistance.

Quinn straightened up, as Charlotte eyed him suspiciously.

"What are ye doing, Gabe? I told ye...I was interested in her and, here ye are, sneaking off...to be alone with our hostess. I thought we were friends."

Gabe shrugged. "I... could not...control myself." He held out his hands. "Look at her. What man could resist such an enticing woman?"

"How could ye do this to me?" asked Quinn, hoping an argument would get them both out of the situation.

Charlotte looked back and forth between them, uncertain of what to think of the two men. She finally held up a hand to each of them in a 'stop' motion.

"Gentlemen! Gentlemen! There is no need to fight over me."

She grabbed Quinn's shirt with her right hand and Gabe's shirt with her left hand, pulling them both closer to her. "I would never forgive myself if I broke up such a wonderful friendship." She took in a deep breath and her face lit up.

"There is plenty of me to go around, and I am happy to let the two of you share me for the night. It's the least I can do to keep the two of you from quarrelling over little old me."

Maggie gasped in astonishment. *Fuckity fuck!*

Duncan placed his hands on Maggie's back, who was bent at the waist listening through the keyhole, and broke into boisterous laughter, unable to control himself or the tears streaming from his eyes. "This is the most entertaining supper party I have ever been to," he cried.

Logan came up behind them. "What's going on?" he whispered.

"Charlotte is about to take Quinn and Gabe to bed at the same time," snickered Duncan.

It was Logan's turn to break into a fit of laughter.

"Stop it, you two," Maggie whispered and shushed them. "This is not funny!"

Maggie needed to figure out something fast for Gabe and Quinn's sake. She straightened up and flung open the door just as Charlotte had a grip on Quinn's shirt while entrapping the poor man in a kiss.

"Quinn! Gabe! What are you doing? How dare you...accost our gracious hostess like this?"

Charlotte turned to Maggie and made a face, annoyed at the interruption. "I have this situation well in hand, my dear Maggie. I am... scolding them as we speak. I will make *sure* they learn their lesson tonight, even if it takes all night long."

Their hostess began to push Maggie backwards out of the room and Maggie clawed at the wall, trying to grasp onto something to stop her. *Damn, this woman is strong.*

She finally caught the doorframe and was able to get herself turned around. "Make sure you give them a stern talking to Charlotte." She wagged her finger. "The doctor says that they really shouldn't be with any women given those strange rashes that they picked up at their last visit to the whorehouse. It is some sort of infection and it seems to be very contagious."

Charlotte stopped and gave Maggie a horrified look. "An infection, you say? What sort of infection?"

Maggie nodded and whispered. "The doctor doesn't know exactly what it is, and he isn't sure if it can be cured either." Maggie heard the thump of Duncan falling against the wall in the hallway, now laughing even harder.

Charlotte looked back at Gabe and Quinn with a disgusted look on her face.

"Maggie, you should mind your own business," played along Gabe when he caught sight of Charlotte's reaction. "Charlotte and I were in the middle of discussing something and would very much like to get back to it."

"We all were actually. Ye should just leave us to what we were doing," added Quinn with a wink at Charlotte.

Charlotte grimaced, the thought of catching a horrible disease being far more than she had bargained for. She steeled her gaze and turned to face them as she wagged her finger at them. "Maggie is right. You two should be ashamed of yourselves. You should march yourselves right to the church, get on your knees, and beg for forgiveness for your sinful desires."

Maggie nodded at Charlotte. "You are absolutely right. As a matter of fact, I think we should leave and go there right now. I really see no other alternative. They must learn their lesson. Their eternal souls are at stake!"

Maggie held her hand towards the door. "Come on you two...off you go. Enough of bothering the poor women of Williamsburg just to satisfy your own selfish needs of the flesh for the evening."

Gabe and Quinn hung their heads, as if in shame, and shuffled their way to the door. Gabe winked at Maggie and let his hand lightly brush against Charlotte's backside as he passed by. She swatted at him, and he pursed his lips at her as if blowing her a kiss, but once they reached the doorway, neither him nor Quinn could get through it fast enough.

Maggie turned to Charlotte. "Charlotte, please forgive their inexcusable behavior. I will do my best to confine them to the estate from now on if you could see fit to not mention their filthy little problem to anyone else...after all, people may wonder exactly *how* you found out about those nasty little rashes they both have, and you *know* how people like to talk."

Charlotte's eyes widened at the thought of being the subject of the town gossip instead of the one spreading it. She patted Maggie on the back. "Of course, Maggie, and with any luck, maybe some of your good moral values will rub off on them."

Yeah! Let's go with that.

They rapidly bid everyone 'good night' and loaded into the carriage.

Gabe took out his flask, had a huge swig, and handed it to Quinn.

"An infection?" asked Gabe. "You couldn't come up with anything better than that?" he complained.

"It was that, or you and Quinn in a three way with Charlotte. Which would you have preferred?" replied Maggie.

"I'll take the infection," said Quinn, holding up his hand. "I am afraid we would not have survived a night with that woman. An infection would be easier to get rid of."

Duncan and Logan held their sides and leaned against each other as they continued to laugh.

Maggie turned to her husband with a scowl on her face. "Did you hurt yourself when you fell against the wall?"

"Ye heard that, did ye? I couldn't help it. I was laughing so hard that I lost my balance."

Taking the flask from Quinn, Maggie took a drink. "Well, I do not think anyone will give anymore thought to your preferences from now on, and I am pretty sure no women will be giving you any trouble either."

Gabe rolled his eyes.

"Ye two stop giving Maggie a hard time," scolded Lady Aurnia. "Ye should be grateful that ye have a woman as smart as her around and one that loves ye as much as she does to look after ye."

"You are right," said Gabe. "Thank you, Mags, for giving me an unexplained rash at the whorehouse," he said and kissed her cheek.

"You're welcome," she chuckled. "I am happy to give you an infection any time it comes in handy."

When they arrived home, Maggie and Duncan checked on the babies before they turned in.

"What a night!" said Maggie, falling back on the bed after stripping down to nothing.

"I rather enjoyed myself," chuckled Duncan, and he started to undress. "Usually, these things are so boring."

Maggie laughed. "I think this is one we will definitely remember."

Duncan removed the last of his clothing and laid down next to her.

Maggie fanned herself with her hand. "It is so hot in here. I need some air." She got up, walked over to the French doors leading out onto the balcony, and threw them wide open. "That's better," she sighed, and breathed in the cooler air.

She cautiously peeked over the balcony. No one was outside below them, so she stepped out onto the landing and braced her hands on the rail. Maggie closed her eyes as Duncan came up behind her and wrapped his arms around her waist.

He breathed in deeply and kissed the back of her neck. He slipped inside her from behind, moving slowly and taking his time until they were both pleasantly sated.

"How do we do that perfectly every time?" she asked, leaning back against him. "It's like we were made for each other."

Duncan turned her around, brushed the hair back from her face, and spoke gently, his sentiment heartfelt, "My love, we were a single soul split in half at creation, and this magic is what happens when we are brought together again, the way it was always meant to be. We are one, now and always, and now that we have found each other, nothing will ever separate us again, in this world or the next, this life or any other. I will never allow it, and on that, I give ye my word."

10 CHAPTER TEN

Over the next few weeks, they began to finalize their plans for John's rescue. Quinn perfected the potion needed to make John appear among the newly departed, which meant that they had cleared the second hurdle. The rest, however, was still up in the air and many of those details would depend on what they found when they arrived. It was decided that they would figure things out as they went.

Maggie was very uncomfortable with the thought but understood that she had no other choice.

Duncan did his best to prepare her for the worst, but each time he attempted to broach the delicate subject, she became upset to no end.

The time arrived for them to depart for New York. Logan insisted that he was going with them, while Lady Aurnia would remain behind to see to the children and the house while they were gone. Maggie and Duncan bid the babies a tearful 'goodbye' and promised to return to them as soon as possible. Gabe and Quinn left Alastair in charge as the 'man of the house', a title he proudly accepted and took to heart.

Soon, they were on their way and Maggie remained a complete bundle of nerves the entire trip despite Duncan's best efforts to settle her.

End of September 1780

They arrived in New York City a few days before what they knew would be John's execution date, and immediately made arrangements to get his coat with the harness to his servant, along with instructions to make sure that this was the one delivered to where he was being held prisoner. The recently hired servants at their newly purchased house had received word ahead of time and had everything ready for their arrival. After a late supper that night, they retired to the parlour.

"What do we do first?" asked Maggie.

Duncan paced the floor. "We need to scout the location. See who, and what sort of situation, we are dealing with. There are a great many details we have not figured out yet and time is running out."

"We will need to do it at night," added Gabe, "so as to not raise suspicion. If anyone recognizes us in that camp, we are dead in the water before we even begin."

"I can move around easier," offered Logan. "No one will know who I am."

"I have rented a house just on the edge of Tappan," said Maggie. "Our ship would be recognized if it sailed into port there, so we can ride there tomorrow and make our final preparations. I will instruct the servants here to be gone before our return with John on the 2nd."

"In the meantime, we all need to get some rest," said Quinn. "Tomorrow is going to be a long day."

Maggie couldn't sleep that night, so she went downstairs for a drink. She was sitting alone in the dark staring at the dying flames in the fireplace when Duncan found her.

"Come to bed, Maggie. Sitting here worrying is not doing ye any good."

She didn't move. "What are the chances we are going to pull this off?" she asked, quietly.

He knelt before her and cupped her face with his hand. "This plan will either work or it won't. We will do our best, but whatever the outcome, ye need to accept what fate deems fit."

Maggie's gaze shifted to the floor, and she slowly shook her head.

"Come to bed," he said, this time more insistent.

"I cannot sleep," she muttered.

"I will help ye," he said softly, taking the glass from her hand and setting it on the table. He rose and held out his hand. When she finally stood, he took her in his arms and kissed her slowly and deeply enough to cause her mind to dull. He carried her to bed and spent the rest of the night 'distracting' her.

The next morning, they rode into Tappan and picked up the keys to the private house on the edge of town that Maggie had rented. As the others went ahead, she and Duncan stopped at a local mercantile for some supplies they would need for the next few days and, as they loaded their purchases on the horses, Maggie felt an odd feeling that something wasn't quite right. A cold shiver ran down the length of her spine.

Onyx felt something as well, that caused him to balk and neigh when they prepared to ride off.

Maggie rubbed his mane and tried to soothe him as she attempted to figure out what was upsetting him.

Duncan looked back at Maggie when he sensed her uneasiness. *What is it?*

Maggie shook her head. *Nerves, that's all.*

But she wasn't entirely convinced of that herself; something else was getting her attention.

That night, Quinn and Logan slipped into the army encampment to get a better look at the situation. When they returned, they sketched out a layout of the entire camp, including where John was being held and where the gibbet would be constructed. While there, they learned that he had officially been convicted at trial that same day.

Maggie looked intently over the information in front of them. "I need to get in there myself," she finally said.

"Nay!" said Duncan resolutely. "That is far too dangerous!"

"Duncan is right," agreed Gabe. "There are too many people there who will recognize you if you are seen."

"That is precisely why I have to be the one to go," she said. "There may be someone there who can and will help us, but I do not know who that might be until I actually lay eyes upon them. We will not know unless I personally go."

"What if ye get caught?" demanded Duncan. "We have three bairns at home who need their mother."

Maggie folded her arms. "I will be in no danger if I am seen. Washington will not let any harm come to me, and if I do happen to come across any British soldiers, I can just say that I came to say my final goodbyes to John. I have friends on both sides in high places, so that will not be an issue."

"I don't like it," said Quinn.

Duncan shook his head firmly. "Nay! This is not part of the plan and it is not happening!"

Maggie laid her hands flat on the table and looked around at each of them. "Look! We will not succeed with this current plan and everyone at this table knows it. There are far too many unknowns and our details are sketchy at best. We need a better way to save John, and we will not find it standing around here looking at these damn drawings."

Duncan looked at Maggie with compassion in his eyes. "Or, maybe ye need to accept fate and let nature take its course," he said softly and gently touched her arm. "I know ye do not want to hear this, but maybe John's death *is* meant to be."

"How can you say that to me?" She jerked her arm free from him.

"Maggie..." he whispered.

"NO!" she shouted angrily before raking everything off the table and onto the floor out of frustration. "I will not accept that!"

She stormed out of the room and slammed the door behind her as she left the house.

Duncan turned to Gabe. "Please tell me how to get through to her!"

"You let her try," Gabe squeezed his shoulder and replied softly. "For her own sake and peace of mind, let her do what she feels the need to do. She will never forgive herself, or anyone here, if we attempt to dissuade her in anyway."

"She is not being reasonable," fretted Duncan, looking in the direction she had gone.

"I know, but when have you ever known Maggie to act on reason? She has always been led by her heart and to hell with the consequences. You know as well as I, that when it comes to someone she loves, she will stop at nothing."

"Aye," he sighed. "That's what I am afraid of." He left to go find her.

Maggie found herself outside on the porch, trying to clear her head. She knew there was no way they could save John at the rate they were going, but she had also vowed to herself to save him by whatever means necessary, even if that meant changing history. Washington already had all the information that he needed from John for the war effort and that included the name of the traitor from his inner circle. Maggie had an idea that she had been kicking around in her head for the past few months, although she had mentioned it to no one. Feeling like she was out of all other options, she decided that she had nothing to lose by going through with it.

Duncan found her looking out over the town, went to stand in front of her, and placed his hands on her shoulders. "We are not giving up, Maggie," he whispered.

Maggie leaned her cheek against his chest as he pulled her closer and rubbed her back. She looked over his shoulder and another chill went down her spine.

He felt her body shiver from what he assumed was the cold evening air. "Come inside and warm up."

She looked around one last time before she let him lead her inside, but still had the uncomfortable, eerie feeling that they were being watched.

The next morning before dawn, Maggie carefully slipped out of bed, dressed quietly, and went to the stables before anyone else was awake. She knew she wasn't the only one up at this ungodly hour.

Maggie pulled up her hood just before she arrived at the encampment, which was unnervingly quiet; hardly anyone was yet awake, save the one person she sought. She made her way to the building using the information Quinn and Logan had gathered the night before. Once she reached her intended destination, she dismounted from Onyx, nervously pulled herself together, and knocked on the front door. His personal servant answered.

"I need to speak with him," she said.

"Ma'am, it is very early, and he is not accepting visitors at this time. Come back at a decent hour."

Maggie caught the door as he tried to push it closed. "I know he is awake. He is the one person in this world who sleeps even less than I do. Tell him that 'a lady from Virginia' wishes to see him."

The servant looked at her oddly, as if he had just seen a ghost that had risen from the grave. It was obvious that the reference, if not the face, was familiar to him.

"Wait here," he finally said.

He returned a few moments later and pulled the door wide open.

"Please, come in," he said, tipping his head down slightly and stepping back for her to enter. He escorted her into the dining room, where she found the man she sought out holding a filled glass for her.

"What a pleasant surprise so early this morning," he said with a bow. "Please, allow me the pleasure of your company and join me for breakfast."

Maggie graciously accepted the proffered glass. "Thank you, and it is good to see you again, General Washington."

She accepted his offered hand and allowed him to show her to a chair that he adjusted once she was seated. "Please forgive the early hour, General. I knew you would be awake, and I needed to be somewhat discreet."

He moved around the table and occupied the spot directly across from her. "It is always a pleasure to see you no matter what the time of day. It gives me a chance to thank you for your information in Setauket. I, once again, find myself in your debt for saving my life. You, my dear lady, seem to have become my very own guardian angel."

Maggie smiled at him. "I was fortunate enough to be in the right place at the right time, once again."

"Well," said Washington, placing his napkin on his lap, "I am eternally grateful for your fortuitous timing."

Maggie sipped from her glass, and Washington pointed to her wedding ring.

"I understand 'congratulations' are in order on your marriage. Mistress MacGregor now, is it?"

She nodded. "It is…and thank you. We were married in Scotland two years ago on the last day of October…and we have been blessed with three babies since then."

"Three?" he asked, gloriously surprised.

"Triplets, one boy and two girls."

Washington's eyes flew open, wide with delight. "Oh, my goodness! You certainly have your hands full these days, don't you?"

"That would be an understatement," she laughed.

Washington set down his fork and gave her his full attention. "So, tell me. What brings you all the way from Virginia and away from your babies to Tappan?"

"I was hoping to redeem one of those favors you owe me."

Washington's face lit up and he looked intrigued. "Go on," he said with an anticipatory grin.

"I am here on behalf of Major André. He happens to be a very dear friend of mine, and I understand he is in your care."

"I see." Washington looked down at his plate, his face now solemn. "He was convicted yesterday," he said softly, half-apologetically.

"I am aware, General. I assume you already have all the information you can extract from him, and I know you understand that his death will serve no purpose to anyone. He was merely a soldier doing his job, not unlike your spies behind the lines doing theirs."

Washington nodded. "I agree with you completely, Mistress MacGregor. He does not deserve this, though I will deny I said that if I am asked. I have offered, nay pleaded, with the British army to exchange his life for Benedict Arnold's, but they refuse to give that traitorous wretch up. He is the one who should be swinging from the end of that rope, not Major André, and I cannot, for the life of me, understand why they would ever take that piss-poor excuse for a human being over someone as fine and loyal a soldier as the Major."

The General slammed his fist on the table and appeared to be genuinely angry. "I am giving them a few days in hopes that they will bring Arnold to me. The lines of communication are completely open and will remain so; they need only reach out and say the word."

"And, if they won't give you Arnold, will you still execute John?" she asked.

"As much as I loathe the idea, I am afraid I will have no other option, Mistress."

Maggie brushed a tear from her cheek. "Is there nothing I can say or do to change your mind?"

"I am truly sorry. I wish that I could help you; however, I have not given up hope that the British will change their minds and you should not either."

She looked over his shoulder, through the window overlooking the camp. "They will not," she assured him, disheartened and despondent.

He tilted his head. "You say that as if you know it for certain."

"I do," she whispered.

Washington sighed, knowing full well that she was probably right. "I can allow you to visit with him, if you would like," he spoke with compassion. "That *is* within my power and I will happily grant it. I owe you that much at the very least."

"Thank you, General, but I am afraid I would not be able to hold myself together, and I do not wish to cause John any further distress in his final days."

"I understand, but should you change your mind, the offer is still there." Washington watched Maggie thoughtfully. "Major Tallmadge is here, if you wish to say 'hello' to him."

Maggie forced a smile. "That might not be the best of ideas, either."

"I never got the chance to properly thank you for your letter that I received when we were in winter quarters at Valley Forge. Your advice to make Major Tallmadge spymaster was spot on, and without your urging, we would not be where we are now. Your timing was serendipitous to say the least."

He leaned back in his chair. "You seem to have a great ability for seeing the broader picture. It is a capability, I must admit, I am more than a little envious of. How is it that you are able to manage that when no one else can?"

Maggie smiled. "That is quite a story, and you would not believe me if I told you."

He smirked. "You might be surprised by what I would believe, Mistress MacGregor." Washington stroked his chin and watched her intently as he continued.

"My mother used to speak of women who were able to see visions of the future but were often too afraid to speak of them for fear of being accused of being a witch or worse. Personally, I think sometimes our Savior sees fit to send those visions to a select few, who may, in the right place and in the right time be able to use them for the benefit of a higher purpose, a greater good, if you will, to carry out His will. I am curious. Are you one of those people, Mistress MacGregor?"

As Maggie sat before him, for a split second, she seriously considered telling him the truth of the matter. The man before her had no idea what his tireless efforts on behalf of this fledgling country would create in the generations to come and would never be able to see it for himself. Instead, she remained silent as she carefully considered her words. "I am afraid I fall more on the side of sinners, than I do on that of the saints, General."

He looked amused. "I think that can be said for *all* of us these days, my dear."

She looked him square in the eye. "There seems to be a burning question on your mind, so ask if you wish, and if I have some knowledge of the answer, I will tell you the truth of the matter."

Washington studied her for a long moment, lost in his own thoughts, as he pondered her offer. "Will we be victorious? Will it all be worth it in the end?" he finally asked.

Maggie leaned forward. "You will, as long as you stay the course. What you have begun to build here, will become a nation greater and more powerful than you can ever imagine, and *you* will be known as the father of it all."

Washington's face was incredulous. "Me?" he scoffed. "I am but a farmer."

She nodded. "Yes, you are, and you will be amazed, and very proud of what springs from the seeds you sow, here and now. It all begins with you." She slid back her chair. "Thank you for breakfast, General, but I must be on my way."

He rose and went to her side. "One more question...a personal one, if I may be indulged? It is one that has weighed heavily upon my mind for quite some time," he said.

Maggie stopped. "I'm listening."

He hesitated slightly and folded his arms. "What was the reason Major Tallmadge wanted to leave Valley Forge so badly those years ago; the reason you asked me to keep him there instead?"

She blew out along breath and gathered herself before she answered. "He found out that I was carrying his child, and that the baby did not survive. He wanted to come to me, to comfort me, but I knew his destined path was with you. I had to let him go, so all the pieces would fall into place for you to win this war. The fate of this nation was something far more important than what I needed, or desired, at the time."

Washington's face clouded over, and he seemed genuinely taken aback by the revelation. He reached down and took hold of her hand; an expression of sorrow and regret crossed his face.

"My deepest condolences for both of your losses, but I am beyond grateful to you for your many sacrifices that have not gone unnoticed. Major Tallmadge has been invaluable to our cause, as have you."

Maggie laid her hand upon his and nodded sadly. "It seems rather ironic. John André saved my life, giving me the ability to save yours, yet I can do nothing for him in return."

Washington squeezed her hand. "I *am* truly sorry. I wish there was more that I could do for you."

And he was. Maggie could see on his face that denying her was the last thing he wanted to do. He was a man who liked to pay his debts and it devastated him that he could not do the one thing she asked of him. Maggie turned to go.

"She helped him get away, you know," she said as he escorted her to the door.

"Who are you speaking of?" he asked.

"Peggy Arnold."

Washington stopped dead in his tracks. "What do you know of the situation?"

Maggie shrugged "Only that she is no more mad than I am, and she faked her hysteria to give him the chance to escape. That is how he got away, is it not?"

Washington's jaw tightened and he simply nodded.

She sighed. "You will never get your hands on him, but if it is any comfort, history will mark him a traitor and he will have to live with that brand for the rest of his life. He will never know peace for his deeds while he remains in this world."

The General remain silent until he opened the door. "I hope to see you again soon, Mistress MacGregor."

Maggie smiled. "You will be in Williamsburg soon, and when you are, please come dine with us. I will introduce you to my family and show you around the estate."

He kissed her hand. "I look forward to that day."

She took her leave. Maggie went to Onyx, who was waiting outside the door, and laid her forehead against him.

"What now?" she whispered, aloud.

Maggie was about to climb on his back, when she caught sight of a familiar face. She thought her eyes were playing tricks on her at first, until she looked again. It *was* him. What was he doing here? She slipped on her hood and followed him to a nearby tent.

She knocked on the wooden frame of the one he had entered.

"Come in," he called out.

"Nathaniel Gardiner? Is that you?" she asked.

He looked up and it took a minute for him to recognize her.

"Mistress MacGregor? What are you doing here?"

She took his arm. "I was about to ask you the same question."

"I am the surgeon here at the encampment," he answered.

Maggie stared at him, his face suddenly becoming fuzzy and her eyes unable to focus. She started to feel a little lightheaded and her knees slightly buckled.

He caught her by the arm as she stumbled forward.

"Are you alright?" he asked. "You need to sit down."

He helped Maggie over to a makeshift cot that was used for patients.

She leaned forward and put her head in her hands, until the dizziness had passed.

He handed her a canteen of water.

"Thank you," she said as she accepted it.

"Are you feeling better?" he asked as he watched her closely. "You are very pale."

She sipped the water. "I am just surprised to see you here, of all places."

"Yes, well. I go where the army takes me."

"Have you seen John?"

He nodded; his expression grim. "I am afraid so. They convicted him yesterday and he will hang the day after tomorrow."

Nathaniel shook his head as he sat down next to her. "I wish more than anything that there was something I could do. It's wrong and everyone here knows it. He does not deserve to go out like this, not a man as good and honorable as he is."

Maggie had a thought. "What if there was something you could do to save him? Would you do it?"

"In a heartbeat," he answered. "John has saved me on more than one occasion. It is the least I could do."

She smiled and started to say something when someone knocked at the tent door and stepped inside.

Maggie rapidly twisted her body away and pulled up her hood as the person came closer.

"Oh, I am sorry. I did not know you had a patient," the man said.

Nathaniel looked over at Maggie and noticed that she had hidden her face.

"It's alright, Major Tallmadge." He stood and used his body to partially block Maggie. "Is there something I can do for you?"

Ben stared at the back of the figure who sat on the cot and felt oddly drawn to that person for some reason. He found himself unable to break his gaze and took a step towards Maggie, but Nathaniel blocked him.

"Major?" he asked firmly and a little louder. "May I help you with something?"

Ben shook his head, as if he had been in a trance that had just broken. "Forgive me. One of the men who came in late last night took a spill off his horse and has some injury to his leg. Can you see to him?"

Nathaniel glanced back in Maggie's direction. "I will be happy to as soon as I am done here. Please, allow me time to finish up with this patient and I will be right there."

Ben nodded. "Of course. Please, forgive my intrusion. We will be waiting for you."

He started out of the tent but turned back for one more look before he left.

"He's gone," said Nathaniel once he was out of sight.

Maggie lowered her hood and let out a sigh of relief.

"I take it you know the Major?" he asked

"A little too well," she replied. "It's best if he does not see me here right now."

Maggie stood. "Come to town tonight and meet us at the house we are staying at. We are working on a plan to save John and we need your help." She gave him directions and all the information he needed before she pulled her hood back up, and stealthily made her way back to Onyx. She mounted him and rode hard for the house.

Duncan was pacing the floor when she returned. "Where in the hell have you been?" he demanded, angrily.

Maggie smiled and pulled him into a long, deep kiss. "I went to plead with Washington for John's life, which he denied, but I think I found us some help on the inside while I was there."

He glared at her, unfazed by her kiss, seething.

Duncan sat rigid, still upset by her little trip out, as Maggie explained the morning's events at the breakfast table.

"I don't understand," said Logan. "What can this doctor do?"

Gabe looked around the table, his mind working out the details. "He can arrange to be the one to pronounce John dead, for one thing."

"He would do anything to help John," said Maggie, with some hope back in her voice. "Those two are like family.

As Gabe pointed out, if he can arrange to attend to John's 'body' after the execution, a great many holes in our plan just closed up. He will be here tonight, and we will have a better idea then of how things will work on that day. We can figure out a better plan when we have his guidance."

After they were done, Duncan took Maggie by the arm, and pulled her into their bedroom to scold her. "Ye cannot run off like that, half-cocked, without telling anyone where ye are going," he roared, infuriated.

"I was in no danger, Duncan." She took a step back. "I knew talking to Washington was a long shot, but I had to try. I had intended on being back before you even woke up."

"Nay, Maggie!" he fumed, as he took her by the shoulders, livid. "We have a family now! Ye are a mother, and our children and I cannot be without ye. Ye have to consider that before ye start making decisions that affect all of us."

Maggie put her hands on his chest. "I know, I'm sorry." She tried to kiss him, but he resisted.

"Don't be angry with me," she said softly and slipped her hands down and over his backside.

"Hmph!" he said and folded his arms.

Maggie then ran her hand down the front side of his body, until she reached her mark.

He narrowed his eyes at her, unyielding.

"Your face says 'no', but other parts of you say 'yes'," she teased.

Duncan shook his head. "I should turn ye over my knee and spank ye like a disobedient child," he said gruffly.

"If you insist," she purred, gently stroking him. "I will happily accept my punishment if you do it the right way."

He turned his head to the side.

"Your body is betraying you, my love," she said, playfully looking down...and it was; a large bulge emerged from the front of his breeches. He shifted uncomfortably where he stood and eyed her warily.

She moaned and whispered breathily, "There's that one part of you, that can already feel itself inside of me... moving in and out...in and out... in and out...until I am calling your name, tasting your lips, digging my nails into your back....clenching around your...."

Duncan could resist her no more; he rushed her, hard and fast, taking out his frustrations on her exactly the way Maggie had secretly hoped he would. The tension from the past few days had built to an explosive level, and they both needed a way to release the mounting pressure. He literally took her breath away as he fell upon her, his tongue forcefully claiming her mouth, demanding her unconditional surrender while he propelled her back against the bed. He furiously raised her skirts and undid his breeches, as she frantically bit at his shoulder and wrapped her legs around him. She tossed her head back and laughed as he slammed himself inside of her in a single, violent thrust much sooner than she had expected, but she was deliriously gratified to have him filling her completely. He let out a deep, primal growl as he buried himself all the way in, and she begged him not to stop. He pounded into her repeatedly, raising the bed from the floor as he did, both grunting and rutting like animals in heat during mating season. It was over in a matter of a few moments as he buried his seed deep within her, letting out a loud expressive sound of satisfaction as he did. His anger and her stress instantly dissolved as they faced each other, the sounds of heavy breathing the only noise to be heard. They gazed into each other's eyes and, in that moment, a look of knowing passed between them that said, 'all was forgiven'.

"I needed that," she laughed and touched his face.

"So did I, apparently," he replied and planted a chaste kiss on the end of her nose. He stood up, raked back his damp hair, and rid himself of his clothing,

Standing before her completely in the nude, he said softly, "Now, let me do this the right way." He removed her gown and tenderly made love to her.

Logan looked up at the ceiling. "Again?" he asked, exasperated. "How often do they go at it like this?"

"You don't want to know," replied Gabe as he glanced upwards. "It will only depress you."

"Aye," added Quinn, sitting down next to Gabe, "those two never stop. They're like rabbits."

"You should have seen them when she was carrying the babies," said Gabe. "Maggie was impossible to be around. I thought she was going to straddle Duncan in front of John when he was over for supper." Gabe sipped his tea. "Although, I got the impression that John would not have minded it."

"It's not even noon," said Logan, in disbelief.

"If they are at it like this now, we won't see them before dinnertime, especially as wound up as Maggie has been the past few days," said Gabe. "Duncan has a way of calming her when she gets like this. Maggie says he can somehow completely wipe her mind clear when she is troubled."

"I'm sure!" snarked Quinn.

Gabe shook his head. "It's more than that. They understand what the other needs unlike any couple I have ever seen before. It is almost uncanny."

Logan sat down. "Do ye think it has anything to do with Danu's fertility abilities that Maggie has inherited?"

"What do you mean?" asked Gabe.

"It makes sense that a fertility goddess would have a healthy desire, does it not?"

Gabe turned to Quinn, as he thought back. "He may be onto something there," he said. "Maggie went ten years without a man in her bed before Ben, and they were only together a handful of times, but since Finn came to her, and since she and Duncan wed, they do seem to...well, you know...to go at it quite a bit."

Quinn shrugged. "Aye? Maybe? Anything is possible."

Logan leaned back. "Duncan never kept a regular woman before Maggie. He would take one on occasion, when his mood became unbearable, but they were very few and far between. Maybe Maggie is affecting him as well."

"Finn did tell Maggie that he had a hand in their union," added Quinn. "There may be more to their relationship than any of us understand. Perhaps, we should mention it to them."

"Why don't you dash on up there and interrupt them to fill them in?" suggested Gabe, his words dripping sarcasm. "I am sure they will not mind at all."

"I think it can wait," chuckled Quinn, and he laid his hand over Gabe's.

Maggie lay propped against the headboard, sated and relaxed. Duncan was beside her, his arm lazily draped across her midsection.

"Ye seem calmer," he said, kissing her stomach.

Maggie ran one hand through his hair. "So, do you," she replied, with a wink.

"Ye do know how to quell my anger, don't ye?" He smirked and moved up higher.

"Just like you calm my mind when nothing else will," she said and smiled down at him. "As much as I would like to stay right here the rest of the day, we need to get dressed. We still have a great deal to do."

Nathaniel arrived later that evening.

"How will we save John?" he asked, as they all took their seats.

"First of all, Nathaniel, you need to understand something." Maggie kept her tone grave. "If we are caught, we may very well be the ones hanging from the end of a rope. If you do not wish to take the chance, no one here will fault you."

He shook his head. "John would not hesitate for me, and I will not for him. I am in, just tell me what to do."

She nodded at him. "Alright, let's make a plan!"

11 CHAPTER ELEVEN

By the end of the evening, they had a strategy in place. Not a perfect one, but one, nonetheless.

They all turned in early that night, knowing the next day would be all about planning the last-minute details.

Maggie was awake most of the night and only dozed off just before dawn. When she woke up, she found herself alone in the house. They had decided the previous night that Duncan would go gather some supplies while Gabe, Quinn, and Logan would leave before dawn and go to some of the nearby farms to secure more horses and a wagon. She slipped on her robe and went downstairs.

Entering the parlour, she had a strange feeling that she was not alone. She turned to scan the room, and when she did, someone grabbed her from behind and skillfully placed a sharp blade against her jugular vein, slightly piercing the skin.

"Scream, and I will kill you now," said a voice.

Maggie realized she could not move an inch, or she was dead. She could feel droplets of blood already forming on her neck where the knife punctured her skin. The man slid his arm, that was around her waist, further up so that he was in a better position to fondle her breasts as he buried his face against her neck and inhaled her scent deeply.

She was so repulsed that she felt like she was going to vomit.

"Don't worry. I won't let your husband miss all of the fun," the voice whispered, tauntingly. "I want him on his knees begging me to stop as I torture and beat you the way he did me...and just as you are about to leave this world, I will fuck you to death while he watches, just so I can see the misery and pain on his face. It will be the last thing he sees before I kill him."

The man shoved her to the floor, and it gave Maggie her first good look at who her assailant was: Captain Wilson, the man whom Duncan had beaten to a pulp for insulting her, and whom Ben had set up as a traitor to the Crown.

"You?" she spat.

He crouched down and dug the point of the knife into her chest with one hand while he pulled a pistol from his belt with the other.

"Yes, me! Imagine my surprise when I saw you and that husband of yours in town when I came to watch that bastard André swing. The three of you ruined my career and my life, but I will see the world rid of all of you in the next few days for what you did to me."

He raised his hand holding the gun.

"André will not save you now," were the last words she heard before he slammed her in the side of the face with the handle of the pistol and rendered her unconscious.

Maggie slowly came around; her head pounded, her vision blurred, and she found her hands and feet tied to a chair, her mouth covered with a gag. She blinked and was able to make out his outline across from her as he sat in a chair, the pistol laid across his lap.

"Good, you are awake. He should be home soon, and then we can begin the real fun." He looked around and laughed. "This was almost too easy. You and your husband here alone with no servants. I will be long gone before anyone even knows you're dead."

Maggie attempted to force the fogginess from her mind; the words he spoke finally registering. He did not know that Quinn, Gabe, and Logan were traveling with them, and he sure as hell didn't know that Maggie had her own way of warning Duncan.

She lowered her head and tried hard to clear it while she focused through the pain.

Duncan! Wilson has me at the house tied up and he has set a trap for you. He is armed with a pistol and a knife. He does not know the others are with us.

Her husband responded. *I am coming, my love.*

Wilson stood and walked over to Maggie; his eyes raking over her in a crude manner. He walked around behind her, ran his hand over her shoulder and pushed her hair away from her neck.

Maggie jerked and that made him laugh.

"You are going nowhere," he whispered and slid his hand down inside of her robe. He moaned, roughly grabbing her now exposed breast and leaning down to breathe heavily on her neck. "I can see what André saw in you."

He moved around in front of her, pulled up a chair so he could look her directly in the face, and sat down. He then scooched the chair as close to her as he could and ran his hand up the outside of her thigh, pushing her robe open to expose her leg.

Maggie turned her head away in disgust as he squeezed her thigh tightly and dug his nails into the skin.

"I really want to have a little taste before he gets here, but I want him to suffer as much as possible, so I guess I will have to settle for a tiny morsel."

She writhed against her restraints.

He pulled out the knife and made about a four-inch cut on her exposed chest, just above her breast.

Maggie screamed at him through the gag, blood pouring out.

He caught it with his finger, stuck it in his mouth, and closed his eyes, sucking every drop of the blood off the end of his finger. "Umm…" he moaned, as if in ecstasy. "So pure, so sweet, so tasty."

She looked at him with horrific abomination in her eyes. *What the hell kind of freak IS this guy?*

He opened his eyes to stare down at his now clean finger and spoke. "There is nothing quite like seeing the blood flow out of a person and the taste, well..." He let out a satisfied sigh and thoroughly examined his finger to make sure he had gotten it all. He looked back at her. "There is something about it that quenches as nothing else will."

He leaned closer to her, crushing her with his weight, to look her closely in the eyes. "Before I was stripped of my rank, life was good for me, for someone with unique needs such as mine."

He leaned back, lost in his own memories. "You see, while we were out scouting one day for the army, I came across a little cabin in the middle of nowhere belonging to the widow of a Continental soldier. You actually remind me of her a great deal." He pointed the knife at her. "She spoke to me with the same degree of contempt that you did when we first met. A week later, I paid her a visit. I caught her outside, dragged her back into her own house, tied her up, and had my way with her. When I was done, I told her to get on her knees and beg for her life. She did, and I let her think I was going to let her go, right before I slit her throat from end to end. You should have seen the look on her face as the blood spurted from her, and you cannot imagine the unexpected feeling of euphoria that it brought to me. I found myself unable to think about anything else, except doing it again. It was easy to take an occasional woman from the colonies, usually a girl off the street no one would miss or a whore that no one would look for, take her to that same cabin and do it all over again, watching the life leave their bodies, bringing me more satisfaction than fucking them ever did. I became bolder, more creative, planning out every detail in my mind beforehand, and I soon found out that I took much more satisfaction in bleeding them over time than in one fatal swipe. That's when I learned that each person's blood tasted a tiny bit different, and that I liked the flavor of it."

He paused to grab Maggie's face. "But that was before you and your husband stepped off that ship in Oyster Bay, ruining the one good thing that I had going in my life. You have no idea how much I am going to enjoy killing the both of you."

He stared at her for a moment, before pushing her away and getting up to walk behind her so he could regain his composure.

Maggie let out the breath she had been holding, repulsed and angered by the confession he had just made and even more annoyed by the bastard's timing.

Oh, for fuck's sake! Leave it to me to cross the path of the one serial killer in colonial New York on the worst possible day EVER.

He came back around in front of her, and put the chair back in place, before he sat down with the pistol; a malicious smile on his face as he looked her up and down. "I know exactly what I am going to do first. I have been planning this since I escaped that jail cell."

Leaning forward again, he gently took a few strands of her hair between his fingers and brushed the ends against his face. "I am getting excited just thinking about it," he growled with his eyes closed.

He fisted her hair tightly and jerked her head back as Maggie tried to pull free.

"On second thought," he wrapped a hand around her throat, "maybe we will start without him. I am not sure I can wait much longer."

A noise from the front door broke his concentration. He placed the pistol barrel against Maggie's forehead. "Oh good, he's here. Now, be a good girl and do as you are told."

But Gabe was the one who appeared in the doorway.

"Who the fuck are you?" demanded Wilson, visibly irate that things were not as he had envisioned in his mind.

Gabe held up his hands. "Easy there," Gabe took a step towards them and glanced over at Maggie.

Maggie could see that Wilson was thrown for a loop. He never expected anyone other than Duncan, and Gabe's appearance caused him to have to reconsider his plan. He pointed the gun at Gabe, trying to decide what he should do next.

"You are not MacGregor. There isn't supposed to be anyone else here. Who the hell are you?" he yelled.

Gabe could see the confusion on his face and decided to play into it. "I don't know who you are talking about. I only came by to make a delivery."

Wilson narrowed his eyes at him.

"No one else should be here! No one!" he screamed, shaking the gun at him.

He was starting to become unhinged in the way that all psychopaths do when things don't go exactly their way.

Maggie tugged at her bonds to no avail, afraid of what might happen to Gabe.

"I don't know who you are looking for, but I can help you find him," offered Gabe, attempting to appease him. "Why don't you let me give you a hand?"

Wilson cocked his head at Gabe in confusion. "You want to help me?"

Gabe nodded. "Sure. Tell me what he looks like. There was a man outside a few moments ago. Maybe it is him."

Wilson glanced at the window and started to look more desperate.

Gabe pointed at the window. "He is right out there. Go see for yourself. See if he is the man you are looking for."

Wilson's eyes looked wild as he held the gun on Gabe and moved to the window. He searched outside, taking his attention off Gabe for a few seconds, lowering the gun ever so slightly.

Gabe took the opportunity to step out of the line of fire and plant himself protectively between Wilson and Maggie. The next moment seemed to move in slow motion.

Maggie watched fearfully as Duncan and Logan, who had slipped in the back door during the commotion, silently rushed Wilson from the room beside them. They were on him before he turned back around. Logan grabbed the wrist of the hand that held the gun and pushed it downward. The pistol went off, but the shot went into the floor.

Wilson dropped the gun, and Duncan got his arm around Wilson's neck. They struggled only for a short while before Duncan got the upper hand, tightened his grip, and snapped the man's neck in one fluid motion.

"Rot in Hell, ye filthy beast," he spat, Wilson's lifeless body crumpling to the floor.

Maggie hung her head in relief.

Gabe rushed to her side and removed her gag. He looked down at her uneasily and pulled her robe closed before Duncan could see the state she was in. He mouthed to her so no one else could hear. "Did he?"

She shook her head, and Gabe let out a sigh of relief.

Quinn appeared beside them, took out his knife, and cut her hands and feet free.

Maggie leaned forward and laid her head on Gabe shoulder as her stomach lurched. "I am going to be sick," she whispered.

Quinn grabbed a basin bowl off a nearby table and handed it to Gabe just as Maggie vomited into it.

Duncan took Gabe's place in front of her and knelt. "Maggie, are ye alright?"

She nodded.

He pulled her as close and as tightly as he possibly could, and she wrapped her arms around him. He closed his eyes and thanked God she was alive.

When she pulled back, he pushed the hair from her face, and noticed the visible bruising from where Wilson had struck her, along with the blood from the cut on her chest.

His face contorted in hatred.

He moved her to the sofa, and wrapped a blanket around her, as Gabe brought her a drink.

She downed it in one gulp. "He was going to kill both of us," she muttered. "He told me that he had a system of raping and killing women in Oyster Bay and that he blamed us for ruining it."

"Multiple women?" asked a horrified Gabe.

"He felt the need to tell me all about it. He had a cabin set up where he took the ones who wouldn't be missed. It's no telling how many he did that to, and he...." Maggie looked down, sickened by the thought and another wave of nausea overcame her. "He developed a taste for human blood along the way."

Everyone exchanged stunned looks, then stared over at the dead body on the floor, revolted by the repulsive bastard.

"I'd say we did the world a favor," said Logan.

Quinn started towards the body. "We need to find a place to dump him that will not draw attention."

Gabe abruptly held out his arm to stop him. "Wait! I have a better idea." He pointed at Wilson. "An actual body for the coffin tomorrow would work much better than the bags of grain we were going to use, and I sure as hell would rather see that son of a bitch six feet under instead of John."

Duncan followed Gabe's gaze and line of thinking. "Aye! He and John are about the same size and they have a similar hair color. All we would have to do is switch them out."

"If they will not let Nathaniel seal the coffin, as long as the face cover is not removed, he very well could pass for John," agreed Gabe. "And since you snapped his neck, there will be no open wounds for anyone to question."

Quinn turned to Logan. "We can take blankets from upstairs, wrap him up, and store him in the stable. Onyx will keep anyone from getting in."

Logan and Quinn left to find the things they needed, and Duncan spoke to Gabe, "Will you see if ye can find some water and rags, so that I can clean Maggie up?"

"Of course," he said.

Duncan took Maggie's face in his hands; his own face strained with a look of wild panic in his eyes. "Maggie, I have to know," he said, before he paused to prepare himself for the answer, "did he…" he swallowed hard, "…rape ye?"

Maggie shook her head. "He wanted to wait for you, so you would have to watch him do it," she whispered before she choked up.

Duncan looked up at the ceiling and wrapped his arms around her so that she would not see that his bottom lip was quivering.

When Gabe returned to the room with the water, Duncan took the wet cloth, wrung it out, and carefully cleaned her wounds.

Gabe noticed that her face was starting to swell as he poured Maggie another drink. "Mags, that looks bad. Maybe we should get you checked over by a surgeon."

Maggie winced as Duncan touched it with the wet cloth.

"I have half a mind to find a way to bring the bastard back to life, so I can have the satisfaction of killing him again," muttered Duncan.

"We have other things to worry about today," Maggie reminded him. "Did you find the extra horses and a wagon?"

"Yes," answered Gabe. "We were just returning when Duncan found us to tell us what was happening."

"Nathaniel is coming back this evening. We will get him to look ye over then," said Duncan.

Quinn and Logan returned with quilts and were trying to figure out how to handle the body.

Maggie paled when she glanced in that direction.

"Let me take ye upstairs," said Duncan. "Ye do not need to be down here for this."

For once, Maggie did not argue.

Maggie crawled on the bed and curled onto her side. Duncan closed the door and came to sit next to her. He stroked her hair lightly, and asked, "Maggie, did he do something else to you? If he did, you need to tell me. As your husband, I need to know."

She wiped away a few tears with the sleeve of her robe.

"I had no idea," she choked out, "what a sick bastard he was. It was bad enough that he put his hands all over me...touching me the way that he did...but then he... made that cut across my chest with his knife just so he...could taste my blood! Duncan, what kind of fucking monster does something like that?"

Duncan swallowed hard and pulled her to him. "One that is burning in Hell right now, and one who will never touch ye, or any other woman, ever again."

He kissed her forehead, and Maggie forced a smile. "I should get cleaned up and dress," she said. "We still have a great deal to go over."

"Maggie, ye have been through an ordeal and ye have been injured. Ye need to rest."

"I will rest when John is safe."

She kissed him. "Give me a few minutes and I will be right down."

He squeezed her hand and reluctantly stood to go. "I love ye, Maggie."

"I love you too, Duncan."

After Duncan closed the door, Maggie went to the washstand and poured some water in the basin. She splashed her face with it, then looked in the mirror. Her face was swollen, bruised, and the cut on her chest was still oozing blood; the wound deeper than she first realized. She placed both hands flat on the stand and steadied herself as a wave of panic threatened to wash over her.

"Pull it together, Maggie," she said to herself. "You can have a breakdown when John is safe and sound. You do not have that luxury right now."

She wiped her face with a towel, took a deep breath, and dressed before heading down to the parlour.

The parlour had been straightened and there was no sign of the day's earlier events. No one said a word as she came in and sat down on the sofa.

"So, where do we stand?" she asked.

They went over each detail of the plan they had worked out. Now, all they had to do was wait for Nathaniel to come back that evening, to lead Quinn, Logan, and Gabe to the man who would be the executioner, who they intended on getting drunk at the local tavern before slipping something in his drink made from one of the Fae recipes that would make him sleep until well past the execution time. They had rented a room there to leave him in while Quinn took his place in the tent back at the encampment.

If everything went well, they would be riding back to New York City with John the following evening, and for the ship to Virginia that night, and if not, they would all be prisoners themselves.

Only time would tell.

They had a late dinner at the tavern, picked up some last-minute food supplies, and went back to the house to wait.

Nathaniel arrived around sunset.

"Maggie, what happened to you?" he asked as soon as he saw her.

"It is a very long story," she replied.

"She was attacked this morning. Can ye check her over please, for my own peace of mind?" asked Duncan, still concerned.

"Certainly," said Nathaniel as he went to her.

He grimaced as he examined her bruised face, and the lump that had formed on the side of her head.

"Did you lose consciousness?" he asked.

"Yes," she mumbled.

"What?" asked Duncan, surprised. "Ye did not mention that."

"I daresay there is a lot I haven't mentioned," she replied dryly, her fatigue washing over her like a tidal wave.

"Do you know how long you were out?" asked Nathaniel.

"No," she said.

"Any headache, dizziness, blurry vision, nausea, vomiting?"

"All of the above?"

Duncan folded his arms and paced the floor, his hatred for a dead man growing by leaps and bounds.

"You should be resting until all of these symptoms are completely gone."

Maggie sighed. "I will rest when John is safe."

He examined the cut on her chest. "That is pretty deep. You need to keep it clean and covered to keep infection out."

When he was done, Gabe handed him a glass.

"So, how confident are we in this plan?" asked Nathaniel, somewhat nervously.

The room went so quiet that you could hear a pin drop.

"That good, huh?" he asked sarcastically.

"There is just one thing we need to be clear on," said Maggie, "and this is *NOT* up for discussion." She looked around the room. "If this goes terribly wrong tomorrow, I will be taking the full blame for it and no one else."

Duncan scoffed. "Nay, ye will not."

Maggie stood. "Yes, Duncan, I will! And the rest of you will keep your mouths shut! I can work my way out of any situation that arises from this, but not if I have to get everyone in this room out of it as well."

Gabe shook his head. "You don't know that for sure, Maggie."

She sighed. "I know Washington owes me, and he repays his debts."

"He didn't repay his debt when ye asked him to spare John's life." Duncan reminded her, not even trying to keep his anger in check.

Maggie rubbed her forehead, the headache she had been nursing since the attack becoming worse. "I need everyone's word on this," she said softly.

The room remained silent.

She shook her head, which made her a little off balance. Duncan caught her before she fell against the chair.

"Take her to bed," ordered Nathaniel. "She needs all the rest she can get."

Duncan picked her up, carried her to their bedroom, and sat her down. He pulled back the covers, helped her undress, and put her to bed.

"Sleep, my love!" he said and kissed her forehead. "I will be right back."

Duncan went back to the parlour, looking very worried. "Will Maggie be alright?" he asked Nathaniel.

"If she rests and avoids upset, physically, she should be fine in a few days, but she really needs to be in bed."

"I expect this has shaken her far worse than she is letting on," said Gabe.

"Aye, it has," replied Duncan, the concern on his face growing.

Gabe stood. "You should be up there with her, especially with everything she has been through today. We will handle the tavern end of things and, once Quinn is safely entrenched in the camp, Logan and I will be back."

They all moved to head out the door, and Gabe turned to Duncan, looking up toward the bedroom. "Look after her and trust your instincts. You will know what she needs."

Maggie was already asleep, so Duncan moved to the window, and stared outside. He thought about how close he had come to losing her that day, and his emotions overcame him as he wiped the wetness from his cheek. In that moment, he knew that he would never be able to live without her. He heard her stir slightly, and as he turned, she began to cry in her sleep. He moved to her side and upon seeing her eyes still closed, he slipped into bed, and wrapped his arms around her.

"I am here my love," he whispered. "Ye are safe in my arms, and I will not let anyone harm ye."

He shushed her until she finally settled back down for a while, but she continued to be restless, and upset, until she finally opened her eyes a couple of hours later, only to see Duncan staring at the ceiling.

She snuggled in close to him and he shifted, which caused her to raise her head.

"You are awake?" she asked.

"I am, my love," he replied. "I am having a hard time sleeping tonight."

"I see his face every time I close my eyes," she whispered. "The image just won't go away."

He leaned over and softly brushed his lips against hers. Turning on his side, he looked her in the eyes and kissed her harder, never breaking their gaze, the entire time he made love to her. It was simple, it was silent, it was pure...and it was exactly what she needed to ease her mind.

Maggie fell asleep with him still inside her, and she stirred no more the rest of the night.

The next morning, they woke up early, packed their things, and readied to leave. Duncan, Gabe, and Logan unloaded the big bags of grain they had originally planned to use for John's coffin, and instead used them to cover up Wilson's body to transport it to where it needed to be.

Maggie and Duncan rode Onyx together to the edge of the encampment about an hour ahead of the appointed time so they could prepare. He kept his arm around her protectively the entire time. When they got close, he kissed her, told her he loved her, and dismounted to take his place on the wagon with Logan. They all pulled up their hoods and headed to their preplanned places.

It was getting close to the time, and Maggie's stomach was tied up in knots, not to mention her head still throbbed from the day before. She dropped Onyx's reins at the hitch, knowing that tying him was pointless, and looked around. The entire place was packed with people from all walks of life, all come to see a man hang.

And this is what passes for entertainment in the 18th century.

"Stay close," she said to Onyx.

He dipped his head in response.

Maggie pushed through the crowd and to the side closest to the medical tent. She caught sight of Nathaniel, who nodded an acknowledgment her way. She moved to a position where she could have a good look at the gibbet, praying that they could, somehow, miraculously pull this off.

She took a closer look at the crowd. Several high-ranking British officers, in addition to Washington's men, were in attendance, not to mention a great many women, dressed in mourning and all looking very downtrodden and distraught.

Oh John, please tell me you didn't hook up with ALL these women.

Maggie shook her head as she received a silent message from Duncan.

Are you alright, my love?

As good as I can be right now.

Be safe...I love ye so much!

I love you too, Duncan! You are my world!

Movement from the gibbet caught Maggie's eye. It was the executioner and, thank goodness, it was Quinn, fiddling with the rope and pretending to inspect it. He had replaced it last night with the dummy one after the camp had gone quiet. She looked toward the building that John was being held in. She scanned the crowd for Gabe but was unable to find him. She was getting nervous when she finally saw him about to knock on the door of the building that held John.

Now, all she could do was wait.

12 CHAPTER TWELVE

"Are those your sketches?"

John looked down. "Yes, a collection of my favorites."

Ben motioned, "May I?"

John handed him the book. "Please."

Ben turned the page carefully admiring his work. It was unfortunate that such a creative soul had ended up in the army and was now facing such a death. Ben liked the man, there wasn't anything *not* to like about him; he could even see them being great, life-long friends if dwindling time were not the issue. Turning the page, upon seeing a very familiar face, he softly whispered, "Maggie."

John looked back from the window he was looking out of and saw the stunned look on the other man's face and asked. "You know Maggie?"

Ben nodded. "Yes. I met her a few years ago in Philadelphia. We were…" The pain in his eyes helped John to make the connection.

John finished his sentence for him. "You were in love." Looking at him and the truth in his face, John realized, "*You* were the one she was in love with, the one who fathered her child that she lost."

Ben swallowed hard, "I didn't know until the baby was gone, and she asked me not to come. I had caused her so much pain and put her in so much danger…she had already almost died once for me."

Another awareness came to John. "*She* was the woman on the back of the horse in Germantown, the night she came back with a bullet in her."

There was no harm in telling a man about to hang the truth, and truthfully, Ben needed to unburden his soul. "She had brought us information before; I guess you could say she was our very first female agent, but that night, I just wanted to see her, to be with her, before we left for Valley Forge for the winter. It was my fault she was shot. That's why I insisted she go back to Virginia. If I had known she carried my child, I never would have sent her away. I would have quit the army, on the spot, just to be with her."

John saw the same degree of pain on his face that he had seen on Maggie's all those years before.

Ben looked at the images again. "How do you know her?"

John took in a deep breath. "I was the one that found her at the checkpoint that night. She recovered under my roof and we became close friends." He left out the rest not wanting to cause the man any more grief since he had already lost so much in losing Maggie.

"She spoke of her great love for a man that she could not be with. She was very much in love with you."

Ben whispered, "Not nearly as much as I was with her, and, truthfully, still am. After she wrote me and told me not to come, I was out of my mind with grief. Thankfully, General Washington, at that very same time, put me in charge of his spy ring. The work was long and tedious, but in the end, focusing on that was the only thing that got me through."

John leaned forward. "If I may ask a favor, Major Tallmadge? If you reveal your contacts after the war, please protect Maggie's name. She has a great deal to lose if the Crown finds out what she did. Even in the years to come, they may send someone after her in retribution."

Ben replied, "I would do anything to protect her, still to this day."

Patting him on the back, John nodded. It was a small way of comforting the poor man, a man he had grown very fond of. John knew that the loss of a woman like Maggie was a hard thing to accept, he himself feeling the same way about her.

A knock came at the door.

John sighed. "It seems my date with destiny has arrived." He remembered something.

He slipped the St. Michael from around his neck and motioned for Ben to lean forward. Slipping it over the other man's head, he said, "Maggie gave this to me, and I have never taken it off. It is a St. Michael, the protector of soldiers. I am sure she would be happy to know that I passed it on to you. Treasure it as I have...and keep the sketches, as well. I hope they bring back the good memories of the love that the two of you shared, and if you do ever see her again, please give her my love. Tell her I thought of her until the very end."

Ben stood. "I will. Thank you." He reached out to shake his hand. "Major André, it has been a pleasure. You have been a formidable foe, and it has been my deepest honor to have known you."

John gripped Ben's arm firmly, smiling, resolved to his fate. "Major Tallmadge, the pleasure has been all mine."

Ben looked back at the condemned man, then answered the door, and was astonished to see a face he had not seen in many years. "Colonel Asheton?"

"Hello, Major Tallmadge." Gabe took off his hat. "I was hoping you might be gracious enough to grant me a moment to say goodbye to my old friend, that is, if you would be so kind as to allow it, you know, for old time's sake."

Ben didn't move for a full moment, as he pondered the request. Glancing back at John, who seemed grateful for a friendly face, he turned back and nodded to Gabe. "Of course, but it must be brief."

"Thank you, Major Tallmadge."

"I will wait outside and give you two a moment of privacy." Ben slipped past Gabe.

Gabe stepped inside as John greeted him with an embrace, as he always did.

"I am beyond pleased to see you one last time, Gabe."

Gabe smiled sadly. "John, I do not know what to say to you, my dear old friend."

John nodded. "Our friendship has meant the world to me. I hope you will remember our time together fondly in the years to come."

"I will always treasure it," replied Gabe, cupping John's cheek with his hand. "I have something for you." He reached in his pocket and pulled out a small, corked vial. "Maggie asked me to bring this to you. She doesn't want you to suffer needlessly… none of us do."

John looked down at Gabe's hand, with a curious look on his face. "What is it?"

"It is one of Quinn's concoctions. It will save you from the pain if you take it now."

Chewing on the inside of his cheek, John sighed; the cold reality of his dire circumstance had started to sink in. "That was very thoughtful of her," he murmured.

Gabe noticed a tinge of disappointment in his voice. "She wanted to come," he explained, "but she is beside herself, John. She did not want you to see her upset for fear it would only make things worse on you. She sends you all of her love, and she wants you to know how much you mean to her."

"She is right. I could never bear to see her in any pain. Tell her…" John wiped away a single tear that had escaped his eye, ones that he had been adamant that he would not shed in the face of his fate. "Just, give her my love," he whispered.

Ben knocked on the door.

John popped off the top of the bottle, took a hard look at it, and downed it in one shot.

"Thank you, old friend." He pressed the empty bottle into Gabe's hand. They embraced one last time, before John composed himself.

Gabe straightened his coat for him and made sure to expose the hook of the harness without his knowledge.

"My coat seems to have become a little snug. I suppose it does not matter now," said John.

Gabe patted him on the back; he walked him to the door, and they shook hands as gentlemen. "I will see you on the other side, my friend," said Gabe and opened the door.

"I will be waiting for you." John raised his head, let out a deep breath, and stepped outside.

Two officers joined John, one on each side, for his painfully short walk to the pre-appointed place, Ben following close behind. He stopped to bow to his fellow officers as he made his way along the route, both sides showing a great deal of distress on their faces.

John was visibly taken aback when he saw the gibbet. He had requested a firing squad, an execution befitting an officer, but that request had obviously been denied. As he got closer, he stopped to look down at the ground, appearing to gather his courage, but instead devoted his full attention to turning over a rock with the toe of his boot; a simple distraction to take his mind off the fact that in a few mere moments, he would no longer be of this world and on to the next. He swallowed hard. The drink that Gabe had given him was starting to take effect and for that, he was grateful.

One of the officers next to him asked him, "Why this emotion, sir?"

"I am reconciled to my death, but I detest the mode," he answered, looking back up from the rock that had blissfully distracted him, if only for a few seconds.

John steeled his resolve and made his way up onto the wagon. He raised his chin. "It will be but a momentary pang," he said aloud to reassure himself, the drink beginning to fully affect him. He took out two white handkerchiefs and handed one to the Provost Marshal to tie his arms with when the time came. John looked out over the sea of people who had gathered to see him meet his fate. His eyes fell upon one hooded figure, that he somehow knew, without seeing a face, was Maggie. He tied the other handkerchief around his eyes, stepped forward, and slipped the noose over his own neck, wanting to do that much at least, of his own accord.

Quinn pretended to check the rope around John's neck, but actually hooked the harness to the back of John's coat.

The colonel that stood before him asked for his last words. John lifted the cover from his face and spoke. "I pray you to bear me witness that I meet my fate like a brave man."

The colonel nodded.

Darkness overcame John just before he felt the wagon go from beneath his feet…

…his old journey now ended, and his new journey now begun.

Maggie watched with bated breath and prayed in her mind that this would work. She gasped, and looked away, the instant John's body dropped down. She turned her gaze back towards the scene, unsure of what to expect, afraid of what she might see. A single tear streamed down her cheek, her mind trying to come to grips with what had just unfolded before her eyes.

13 CHAPTER THIRTEEN

Fuck! It worked.

Quinn, still dressed as the executioner, let John swing for an appropriate amount of time before he cut him down. People around them started to make their way to John's body to get one final look at the beloved man.

Maggie pushed through the crowd towards Ben. When she reached him, she took him by the arm and pulled him to the side.

"May I help you, ma'am?" he asked.

"I hope so," she said and pushed back her hood.

"Maggie?"

"Hello, Ben."

He slowly shook his head. "I should have known that if Gabe was here, you were as well." He noticed her face and became upset. "Maggie, what the hell happened to you?" he asked, greatly concerned as he gently touched her face.

She flinched as he touched her bruise. "It is a long story." Maggie grabbed his arm. "I need a favor Ben, and it's a big one."

Ben sighed. "What do you need, Maggie?" His voice was soft.

Maggie looked at him with torment in her eyes. "I want to say a final 'goodbye' to John. I need to unburden my soul of the guilt for some of the things that I have done."

Ben looked down at the ground. "He was the one you took information from in Philadelphia and in Oyster Bay...for our side," whispered Ben.

"How did you know?" she asked, surprised.

"I didn't, until I saw his sketches a short while ago."

He held up John's sketchbook. "He told me that he was the one that found you the night you were shot. That he took you in and you became friends."

"Then, you know that I owe him an enormous apology and, since I could not tell him while he was alive for fear of *your* safety, and because of my own shame, I beg you, please grant me that opportunity now."

"What exactly are you asking?"

Maggie took his hand.

He looked down at it longingly.

"A few moments alone with him, that's all. The things I need to say are best not said out in the open for all to hear." Maggie looked around until she caught Nathaniel's eye.

Nathaniel moved quickly to Ben's side. "Major Tallmadge, sir, I need the body taken into the medical tent to declare him officially deceased. If you have him and the coffin brought in, I will witness and seal it for immediate burial...before his body is...defiled, given the current circumstances."

Ben's face was unreadable. He did not speak for a full moment, before he turned to Nathaniel. "I will have his remains and his coffin brought to your tent at once."

Maggie pleaded with Ben using her eyes.

"Damn it!" he mumbled to himself. "Mistress MacGregor will be needing a few private moments alone with Major André's body to say her final goodbyes. Please allow her that time, but do not seal his coffin just yet."

"Yes, Major Tallmadge." Nathaniel turned to go.

Maggie squeezed Ben's hand. "Thank you."

Ben blew out a deep breath and turned to look the other way. "I would have let you see him before if you had come to me and asked me," he whispered.

She hung her head. "I know, but how could I have faced the man I called such a close friend after all I did for the side that just sentenced him to death. John was a good man, a loyal soldier, and he did not deserve this. I betrayed the trust of the one person who saved me in more ways than I could count on multiple occasions... and I did it all for you and Washington."

Maggie looked up at Ben with tears in her eyes. "He didn't just save my body the night I was shot. He saved my soul after I lost our child, and I would not have survived either without him. He took care of me and brought me back from a very dark place. I owe him more than you will ever know."

Ben's bottom lip started to quiver as her words tore at his heart. "Take as long as you need," he choked out. Ben wiped his nose with his sleeve and walked away so that she would not see the wetness on his own cheek.

After brushing the tears from her face, she pulled her hood back on and walked to the medical tent. She waited outside of it as they brought John in, looking back toward the gibbet to see that they had already started digging the grave. After they left, Maggie ducked in.

"How is he?" she asked.

"Are you sure he is not dead?" asked Nathaniel, checking him over and looking for any signs of life.

John's color had gone gray, his pulse barely being felt without searching hard, and his breathing so shallow that it was almost undetectable.

Maggie moved to John's side and started rubbing his chest with her fist. "Come on John! We have come too far to lose you now. You cannot leave me. I will not let you."

Quinn slipped in the tent, and pushed back his hood, having shed the executioner's garb.

"He is not waking up!" exclaimed Maggie.

Quinn reached into his pocket, pulled out another vial, and poured it into John's mouth.

"What is that?" asked Maggie.

"A heart stimulant. I packed it just in case we needed it."

They watched John nervously for several minutes until his color slowly started to return and his breathing picked up.

"Oh, thank God," said a relieved Maggie.

"You need to work fast," said Nathaniel. "I will stand guard outside and give you as much time as I can."

Maggie sent a silent message to Duncan. *Come.*

A few moments later, the back of the tent canvas lifted slightly, and Wilson's burlap-wrapped body rolled inside, Duncan and Logan pushing it with their feet. The smell made Maggie's stomach roll and bile rise in the back of her throat causing her to gag.

"Och! This dirty bastard stinks," groaned Logan.

Duncan cut loose the ropes that he was tied with and unwrapped him.

John had started breathing in deeper and was starting to stir.

"Help me get his coat off, Quinn," ordered Maggie.

Her brother-in-law held him up, while Maggie pulled the jacket free, and Quinn untied the handkerchiefs from his arms and face. As soon as Wilson's body was free, Maggie tossed John's coat to Logan to put on the cadaver. He and Duncan wrestled it on to the stiff corpse as best they could, having to snap a few bones to make it happen.

"Ben told Nathaniel not to seal it, so make sure his face is covered," said Maggie.

John had started to groan, and his body began to tremble.

Quinn patted his face to help bring him around and when his eyes finally fluttered open, Maggie's smiling face was the first thing he saw.

"I must be in Heaven," he stuttered.

"More like the other place," teased Maggie and she winked at him.

Quinn took him by the arm and helped him to sit up while Maggie grabbed a blanket and wrapped it around him.

"What is happening?" he asked as he looked around.

Maggie touched his face. "Long story short, we faked your hanging. You are still alive, although Quinn's potion did put you very close to death. You need to do exactly what we say so we can get you to safety."

They helped him out of the coffin and to a seat as Logan and Duncan put Wilson's body in his place.

Maggie took a flask from her pocket and gave it to John to drink. His color was still off, and he was disoriented. She grabbed a cloak that they had brought along and helped John to get it on, while Logan and Duncan adjusted the body to look as much like John as possible.

"Nathaniel needs to get them to seal that coffin quickly," said Duncan.

"Nathaniel?" asked John.

"He was gracious enough to declare you officially dead. It's a good thing he was here to help us," explained Maggie as she cupped his cheek.

Nathaniel ducked his head in with a grin on his face. "I figured I owed you a few lives, and I am happy to repay you with this one." The surgeon came over and hugged him. "Take care of yourself, old friend."

Maggie took John's hand. "Quinn and Logan will take you to our house and I will be along as soon as I can. Gabe will meet you along the way. We have my ship to get you out of New York as soon as it is safe. Do exactly what they say; they will take care of you."

John nodded and Maggie kissed his forehead.

"Thank you," he said.

They pulled on his hood and Quinn and Logan checked outside, then slipped out with him as Duncan took Maggie in his arms and kissed her.

"It may take me a little bit of time to get out of here, but I will be there as soon as I can."

"I do not want to leave ye," said Duncan.

"If they see you here, we will have too much to explain. I am among friends, so do not worry about me. I will keep in touch." She kissed him hard. "I love you and thank you!"

"I love ye too. Stay safe." Duncan slipped out the same way he came in and was gone.

Maggie stepped to the front opening of the tent once everyone had cleared out and sucked in some fresh air because the smell was so overwhelming.

"Ugh!" Nathaniel wrinkled his nose and made a face. "This one is ripe. Where did you find him?"

"Don't ask," replied Maggie. "Do you think he will pass for John?"

He nodded. "I don't see why not. They will not pull back the handkerchief to check, and any other discrepancies, I can blame on rapid decomposition. Since I knew John, they will take my word for it."

Maggie hugged him. "Thank you for all your help. We could not have done this without you."

He smiled. "Tell John to find a way to keep in touch with me. I am going to miss that man!"

"I will see to it myself."

"And, you get some rest," he ordered. "You need it, and you have definitely earned it."

Maggie smiled and touched his arm just as Ben stuck his head in the tent.

"Is he ready?" Ben asked.

Nathaniel forced a grim look on his face and nodded.

Maggie looked down at the ground and attempted to appear mournful.

Ben caught a whiff of the odor coming from the body and it caused him to step back. "What the hell?" He took out two handkerchiefs from his coat pocket, handing one to Maggie, using the other to cover his own face.

"Rapid decomposition. It happens sometimes," said Nathaniel. "That coffin needs to be sealed right away."

"Understood and agreed," replied Ben.

Ben gave the 'body' of Major John André one final, heavy-hearted, and regretful look of respect, before he ordered the men to take the coffin back outside and place it on display for a brief time before it was to be buried. Ben placed his hand on Maggie's back as they watched the wooden box being carried away. He seemed as miserable as Maggie was attempting to appear.

"I need a drink, and you are coming with me," he commanded and escorted her out of the tent.

They located their horses and rode to the nearest tavern. After they went inside, they took a small table in the corner and ordered.

"Today's execution was a travesty of justice," whispered Ben, lost in his own thoughts. "Major André did not deserve to meet his maker that way."

"No, he did not," Maggie said, softly.

"He and I spent a great deal of time together these past few weeks and, I have to say, I became quite fond of the man."

Maggie smiled. "John was very easy to love. There will never be another one quite like him."

Ben slammed his fist on the table. "You have no idea how much I wish that Benedict Arnold was the one up there at the end of the rope today instead of the Major."

"I think we are all in agreement there," said Maggie.

He looked down at his tankard and sighed.

"We talked about you," he smiled, slyly. "He told me that if I ever saw you again, to let you know that you were in his thoughts until the very end. It was obvious that he cared for you a great deal."

Maggie nodded. "The feeling was mutual."

Ben reached inside his shirt and produced the St Michael that John had given him.

Maggie leaned across the table and touched the charm hanging from his neck. "It's the one I gave him years ago, after he saved me."

"He gave it to me, just before. He didn't think you would mind, but it really should go back to you." He started to take it off, but Maggie caught his hand and stopped him.

"Leave it! I cannot think of a better place for it than where it is now."

Ben squeezed her hand and gingerly touched her bruised face with the other. "What happened? Who did this to you?"

"Our old friend Captain Wilson, who was in town for John's hanging. It seems he blamed me and Duncan for ruining his life and wanted to make us pay the price."

The blood drained from Ben's face. "Here? He is here?"

"Not anymore. Let's just say that, Duncan 'handled it', and leave it at that."

"I am so sorry, Maggie," he said, guilt-ridden. "That culpability falls solely on me. I was the one who arranged his demise, not you."

"No!" she said firmly, shaking her head. "None of us will bear that burden. Ben, while that bastard was holding me hostage, he confessed to me that he had raped and murdered several women while at that post in Oyster Bay…and that he had…" she stopped to close her eyes, his voice echoing in her mind, "….developed a taste for human blood."

Ben gasped, his eyes widened, too stunned to know what to think or how to respond.

Maggie took a large drink of her ale. "Let's just say, the world is a little bit safer on this day," her voice was low, cold.

Ben swallowed a lump in his throat as he watched her. "Maggie, did he…" he choked out, unable to say the words.

She shook her head. "Duncan got to me in time."

"Oh, thank God!" He let out the breath he had been holding. Ben wiped his mouth with his hand, his gaze remaining fixed on Maggie, who sat quietly with her eyes downcast. He decided that it was a good time to change the subject.

"How long will you be in New York?"

"I will be leaving soon. I have the babies to get back to," she replied.

Ben tilted his head. "Babies? What babies?"

"Oh!" Maggie's face lit up and she cracked a grin. "That's right, I have not seen you to tell you and the post probably hasn't caught up with you. I gave birth to triplets last December."

Ben leaned back, his mouth agape. "Triplets?"

"Yes! One boy and two girls and they are my world-Kendric, Morgan and Alanna."

"Maggie, that's wonderful news! Congratulations. I am very happy for you." His words were sincere, but also a tad bit sad.

Maggie took his hand in a comforting way. "Your time will come, and you will have more children than you know what to do with, Ben."

"You think so?" he asked.

Maggie felt a familiar jolt shoot throughout her body. "I know so!" *Especially now.*

She finished her drink. "I have to go, Ben. Thank you for what you did for me today. It really meant a great deal and I am in your debt."

They both stood and she hugged him.

"Maggie, I would do anything for you," he whispered in her ear.

She kissed him on the cheek. "I am not sure when I will see you again," she said, holding both his hands.

"We tend to cross each other's paths, hopefully even more so and under better circumstances when all of this is over," he smiled.

"I hope so."

Just as she was about to go, a loud, burly voice boomed from behind them.

"Well! Well! Well! Look who it is! You weren't going to leave without saying 'hello' to your favorite kidnapper, were you?"

Maggie laughed, recognizing the voice before she saw the face. Turning, she placed her hands on her hips. "Well, if you have come to kidnap me again, I hope you have arranged for better accommodations this time. I am not as young as I used to be, and I need more comfortable restraints."

"Of course! Only the best for Ben's Maggie." The man winked. "It is good to see you!" he said, embracing her tightly.

"It is good to see you too, Caleb," she grinned.

Caleb looked back and forth between the two of them, a mischievous glint in his eye. "You know, Maggie. I have been begging my oldest and dearest friend in the world here to tell me the story about you two, but he will not do it. It is the only secret he has ever kept from me since I have known him."

Ben shook his head with an annoyed look on his face.

"Maybe *you* could tell me the story about how you ended up turning our little boy into a man?" Caleb leaned close and whispered, "Did he know what to do, or did you have to show him, because I had tried to explain it to him, but I don't think he ever really understood? He has always been such a slow learner."

Caleb slapped him on the back as Ben buried his face in his hands, his cheeks turning bright red.

"Why, in God's name, did you ever tell him that?" asked Ben. "I have not had one day's peace since then."

"I am telling you, Maggie," Caleb continued to goad, "You have ruined him for all other women. I can't even get him to take one at the whorehouse, when I'm the one buying. Who turns down a free ride? You have spoiled our boy."

"Alright, I think that's enough," said Ben, clenching his teeth in a smile. He forcefully patted Caleb on the chest. "Maggie has to go."

Caleb gave her another hug. "Take care, Maggie and don't be a stranger. Things are so much more entertaining when you are around."

"Look after him," she whispered in his ear and kissed his cheek.

"Always!" he whispered back with a wink.

Ben escorted her outside and went over to greet Onyx as he always did.

"You are one of the few people Onyx doesn't try to bite, do you know that?"

"He and I understand each other," said Ben, rubbing the big horse's mane.

Onyx appeared to smile at him.

Ben shuffled a bit. "I am...um... sorry about Caleb."

"Don't apologize, Ben. Just be grateful you have a friend that loves you enough to give you such a hard time." Maggie hugged him once more. "Take care of yourself, Ben."

"You too, Maggie." He helped her up on Onyx, and waved, as she rode off.

Maggie got about a mile out of town when Duncan, riding on Gavina, fell in beside her. "I thought you were going on ahead."

Duncan shrugged. "I thought I would wait for the next beautiful woman to come along."

"Well, lucky for me that I got here first! Let's get out of here before she shows up," she grinned.

"Too late." He laughed and they spurred their horses forward.

14 CHAPTER FOURTEEN

John sat on the sofa and soaked down a whisky, staring into the fireplace after the long, hard ride back to the safehouse.

Gabe sat across from him, watching him intently, while waiting for Logan and Quinn to tend the horses. "How are you feeling?" he asked.

"My mind is still a little foggy," John said quietly. "I seem to be having a difficult time reconciling exactly what happened today."

Gabe got up and refilled his glass. "That is understandable. The mixture that Quinn cooked up had you on the verge of death without actually...well, you know. He said that it would be normal for you to be dazed and confused until it wore completely off."

"Did you know?" asked John softly, trying to piece things together in his mind, "that Maggie was taking information to the other side while we were in Philadelphia?"

Gabe hesitated slightly before answering. "I did," he replied gently, "and I found out later that it was because of me."

John slowly turned to Gabe, his eyes narrowed, his face full of confusion.

Gabe sat back down across from him. "Maggie met Major Tallmadge before I even knew she was in town. She had come to Philadelphia strictly to get some of the men in her employ out of some nasty trouble they had inadvertently gotten themselves into, and she had no intentions of staying more than a day or two. But then she met Ben, and they began a love affair. I knew she was seeing someone, but she never spoke of any details, so I had no idea who he was, much less that he was part of the opposing army. Do you remember when I was taken by Washington's army, right before you came to Philadelphia?"

John nodded. "I do."

"When Maggie found out, she was terrified for me, afraid that I was going to be tortured to death. She rode straight for their camp, and against Ben's better judgement and heartfelt pleas, made a deal with General Washington to exchange information that she did not have for my release. I did not find out about the whole thing until she was shot that night, and when I did, Major

Tallmadge and I together agreed to put an immediate end to it. I resigned my commission to take her back to Virginia, determined to keep her safe the way she had done for me." Gabe shook his head. "She was out of the spy business, with no intentions of getting dragged back in, until we returned from London and received word from you that General Clinton planned to recall me back into service. So, in true Maggie form, she turned right around and made yet another deal, this time with the other side, to hand over Benedict Arnold in return for my unconditional release from the army."

Gabe leaned forward. "And John, when she found out that you were going to be executed for the matter that she had a hand in, she would not rest until we found a way to save you."

John stared at Gabe in disbelief.

"As you found out today, when Maggie makes up her mind, there is no stopping her. Everything that she does is to protect those she loves the most."

Leaning back, John closed his eyes and swallowed hard.

Gabe stood and placed his hand on his shoulder. "Welcome to the exclusive club, old friend."

Quinn and Logan came into the room.

"We are all set. We can board the ship tonight, provided Maggie and Duncan are not held up for too long," said Quinn.

Gabe poured glasses for the two of them, which they accepted gratefully.

"How far behind do ye think they will be?" asked Logan.

"That depends on Maggie. I am sure Ben held her up for a bit, and Duncan will not come back without her. After everything that happened yesterday, they are probably riding rather slow, as well," said Gabe, sitting back down.

"Well, ye look much better," Quinn said to John.

"For someone who should be dead, I actually feel fairly decent," John replied and looked around. "How in the world did you pull this off?"

"It was a carefully planned group effort." replied Quinn, taking a seat. "The mixture Gabe gave to ye was a tonic made to imitate death. We had to get the timing just right so it would not hit ye too fast, and Maggie knew that Ben would allow Gabe in to say 'goodbye' to ye."

Gabe pointed to Quinn. "Meet your executioner. Quinn managed to get to the noose and switch it out for one we brought with us that was rigged with a hook that connected to a harness that we had sewn into your coat, or rather *my* old coat; the one we had your servant bring to you," said Gabe.

"Am I to understand that young Nathaniel helped, as well?" asked John.

"Yes," replied Gabe. "We had not quite figured out that part, but Maggie saw him when she went to Washington to plead for your release and recognized him as a dear friend of yours. He was able to convince Major Tallmadge to have you and the coffin brought into the medical tent to declare you dead and give us the time we needed to make a trade."

"That is when we rolled the dead body in to replace ye and made a quick exchange. I am Logan, by the way, Quinn and Duncan's brother."

John raised his glass. "It is very nice to meet you and allow me to offer my heartfelt gratitude for your assistance. Wait," he held up his hand, "whose body is in that coffin?"

"A chap I believe you know," said Gabe. "Captain Wilson."

"Wilson?" asked John with bitter contempt in his voice.

"He came after Maggie yesterday and Duncan dealt with him."

"Did he hurt her?" he asked, suddenly very concerned.

"He left his mark, but she is alright," replied Gabe.

"That bastard!"

"Ye have no idea," said Logan. "He confessed to raping and murdering women over a long period of time at his post."

"What?" John gritted his teeth. "I should have killed that son of a bitch with my bare hands when I had the chance!" he spat.

"If ye had, we wouldn't have had his body to pull this off, so be glad ye didn't," shrugged Quinn.

"This is so unbelievable," whispered John and shook his head. "I am amazed, still confused on many levels, and extremely humbled that all of you did this...for me."

At that moment, Maggie and Duncan came through the door, smiling.

Maggie went straight to John's side. "Hello, John," she said, cupping his face.

John placed his hand over hers. "Hello, beautiful!" He lightly touched the bruise on her cheek. "I am sorry that monster got anywhere near you."

She kissed the top of his head. "I am fine, John. Don't worry about me."

"Any trouble?" asked Gabe, offering Maggie his seat and getting up to pour drinks for her and Duncan.

"For once? No!" she replied and gratefully accepted the glass. "Everything went smoothly." She took a sip. "How are you doing, John?"

John shrugged. "I am alive, which is far more than I expected at the end of this particular day."

Duncan patted John's shoulder on his way to sit on the arm of Maggie's chair.

Maggie leaned over to John. "There is only one thing; Major John André died today, and I am afraid that cannot change." She laid her hand over on his. "You will not be able to contact your family or anyone else that you know, or you will put them in danger. You will have to start a new life, with a new identity, away from here for a while. If anyone finds out that you survived, we will all be in jeopardy."

John nodded. "I understand. It is for the best anyway. If the Crown believes me dead, my mother and sisters will be well-cared for."

John remained in front of the fireplace as everyone scattered to ready for their departure.

Maggie came halfway into the room and stopped, a grim look on her face. "John, there is something I wish to speak to you about."

"I have nothing but time, my dear Maggie," and he waved to the chair across from him.

She cautiously made her way over, wringing her hands as she sat down. "I understand that Major Tallmadge told you some things about me that I feel the need to explain. I do not want you thinking badly of me for what I have done, even though you have every right to be angry."

John reached across, took her hand and kissed it. "I already know. Gabe explained everything to me and none of it matters, Maggie. I understand why you did the things you did, and I know it was always done for the ones that you love. There is no explanation necessary."

A few tears slipped down her cheek.

He wiped them away. "Thank you for saving my life, and I am very honored to be considered among those you love the most."

Around midnight, under the cover of darkness, they made their way to the ship, boarded, and set sail for Virginia. Once underway, Maggie leaned over the rail of the deck and Duncan came up behind her.

He slipped his arms around her waist and pressed his chin to her shoulder. "We did it. I have to say I had a great many doubts, but we somehow managed to pull it off."

"You doubted me?" she teased and turned to face him. "That will teach you."

Duncan groaned. "Why don't ye 'teach me' a few things downstairs in our room?" he purred and bent his head.

"Maybe I will," she laughed softly as he kissed her neck, "but there is one thing that I need to do first. I will meet you in our room in a bit. I won't be long."

She kissed him and headed below deck.

Maggie knocked on John's door.

"Come in."

She opened it and stepped inside. "We are underway, and I think it is safe for you on the top deck. Would you like to take some fresh air with me? It's a beautiful night."

John stood. "Nothing would please me more," he smiled.

Maggie and John leaned against the ship rail and gazed up at the stars.

"How are you feeling?" she asked.

John smiled as he took in a deep breath of the salty air, taking time to savor it. "Like a new man."

"Good thing!" teased Maggie and leaned over against him. "What will you do?"

"I really don't know," he said and wrapped his arm around her shoulders. "This morning I was preparing to meet my maker, but now…"

"You will have a little more time to figure out how to explain all of those distraught women when you are standing at the pearly gates, trying to get in," she said dryly.

"What women?" he asked, feigning ignorance.

"The ones who came to see you off today. I expect you and St. Peter will be having a good long talk when your time comes."

John burst into laughter. "Yes, I suppose we will."

Maggie put her hands on her hips. "All of those women at your execution… did you… with *all* of them?"

He grinned devilishly. "Do you *really* want to know the answer to that question?"

She held up her hand and laughed. "No, I do not."

John caught sight of Gabe and Quinn on the other side of the ship and stopped to watch them closely.

"They are a couple, aren't they?" he whispered.

Maggie cleared her throat and looked back out over the water.

John looked down. "I would never put them in danger. Gabe is as dear friend to me as you are."

She nodded. "They have been very happy together since they met, and now, they are fathers to two wonderful children." Maggie laid her hand over on John's. "I am afraid none of us live what you would call a 'conventional' life in Virginia."

"Thank goodness, or I have a feeling I wouldn't be here right now," he replied.

"That was a nice thing you did," said Maggie.

He looked at her questioningly.

"You gave Ben the St. Michael I gave you."

"Oh, that. If I had known you were coming to save me, I would have kept it."

"I know. I am sorry that you had to go through all of that, but if you had known, it would not have gone off the way it did. Besides, I would have felt really bad if I told you we were there to rescue you and then failed."

"As would have I," he chuckled. "I thought it might please you if I passed it on to him. He and I spent a great deal of pleasant time together over the past few weeks, and I can see why you fell in love with him. He is a good and honorable man...and he is still very much in love with you."

Maggie bent over, laid her forehead down on the rail, and groaned. "I know, and what happened was all my fault. I began an affair with him that I knew I would never be able to see through...all because I was lonely. I hurt him so much, and I will carry that guilt for the rest of my life."

John placed his hand on her back. "Let me ask you this, Maggie. Would you have rather not had that time with him? Would you be right where you are at this very moment if you had not been with him all those years ago?"

Maggie straightened up and looked at John as she searched his face, trying to understand exactly what he was asking.

"Think about it. Your affair with him caused Gabe to leave the army, giving him the time he would have never had otherwise to go see his ailing mother, that led him to young Katherine and Quinn, and you to Duncan. Do not look at your time with Ben as some cross that needs bearing, but rather as a necessary stepping-stone to where you are now."

"I just never wanted to hurt him."

John sighed. "His pain from losing you made him a better soldier; a master spy. He told me that he threw himself into his work after you—and look at all their army accomplished from Major Tallmadge's endeavors because of that one broken heart. He told me if he had known about his child beforehand, he would have quit on the spot, and none of the work he has done would have ever happened. Maggie, he will move on, and when he does find someone else, he will treasure her a great deal more because he will know what he stands to lose if he does not."

Maggie's eyes welled up. John's words had a ring of truth, and she needed to hear them. She had told herself that she had let it all go, but, a tiny part was still buried deep down inside and continued to gnaw at her soul.

John took her by the shoulders. "I know for a fact that he would not want you to feel like this."

Maggie leaned against his chest. "You are right."

John pulled her into an embrace.

"I just probably shouldn't have taken his virginity," she said.

He pushed her back slightly to look at her. "You what? You didn't?" he asked, amused.

Maggie nodded. "Oh, I did!"

"Well, I won't be the only one doing some explaining at the pearly gates, will I?" he laughed.

She shrugged. "The rest of us already have a lovely spot picked out in Hell. It's actually quite nice. It does get a little warm in the summer, but the winters are very toasty. We will be happy to make room for you."

John wound his arm around her waist, and they both laughed as they looked out over the water.

Maggie made her way to their room below deck. She found Duncan in a chair, with his feet propped up on the table, smiling.

"There's my girl."

He planted his feet on the floor as Maggie went to him, took a seat in his lap, and kissed him.

"Have I told you how much I love you lately?" she asked.

"Aye, but I never get tired of hearing it."

She leaned closer to him and traced the contour of his face with her finger. "John is safe, everyone is well, and we have no babies to care for on the way home. Whatever shall we do with all this free time?"

"I know exactly what we will be doing." Duncan kissed her nose. "Ye will be going to bed to rest with that head injury...doctor's orders, remember?"

Maggie wrinkled her nose at him. "How about we *both* stay in bed? Is that close enough?" she teased in an attempt to change his mind.

He scooped her up in his arms. "Ye will stay in bed, and if ye are a good girl, I might join ye when ye are feeling better."

She shook her head. "I will just get right back up. I think you are going to have to hold me down if you want me to remain there."

Laying her down gently, he smirked. "I will do whatever it takes."

That night, Maggie woke up in a cold sweat with her heart pounding in her ears. The events of the past few days, along with the trauma from her time with Wilson, hit her all at once, and the emotion was overwhelming. She sat up on the edge of the bed with her head in her hands and the tears started to flow.

Duncan felt her as soon as she moved. He took her in his arms and pulled her back to him as she curled against him and broke into a heart-wrenching sob. This was what he had been waiting for since the day Wilson attacked her. He held her tightly and tried to soothe her, telling her that she was safe.

She cried until she had no tears left. When she had finally gotten it all out of her system, he reached over to the table beside of the bed, pulled a bottle of rum from the cabinet underneath, and made her take slow sips until she was thoroughly numb. Then he laid her back down on the bed and lightly stroked her face until she drifted off to sleep.

By the time they arrived home, Maggie was feeling much better. They managed to sneak John into the house without incident and instructed everyone to keep his presence a secret until they figured out what to do with him. After a few days, John started to become restless, so Maggie asked him to take a ride with her.

"Have you given any thought as to where you want to go from here?" she asked, their horses ambling at a slow pace.

"I honestly have no idea, Maggie. Truthfully, I think I am still in a bit of shock over all of this, and I am having a difficult time sorting out things in my mind. I do, however, know that I will hate to leave all of you."

"We do not want to see you go, either, but I need you safely out of harm's way."

He rode closer to her and reached out to take her hand. "I am not sure I have properly thanked you for giving me back my life."

"Just repaying the favor," she smiled and squeezed his hand.

It wasn't long before the Native American village came into sight.

"Maggie, what is this?" he asked nervously, as they approached. "We should not be riding so near the Indians."

"This is a safe place," she assured him. "We have built in plans all over the estate in case soldiers come, to protect everyone here, and *this* is yours. If we get unexpected company while you are still here with us, you need to ride as fast as you can, straight to these people, and they will hide you and keep you safe."

John looked at her, eyes wide, mouth agape. "But they are Indians! Why would they do something like that?"

"Things are different here, John," she explained. "We have found a better way to live in harmony with those around us and it works." Maggie smiled. "These people are as much family to me as the ones who are under my roof."

As they rode into the village, John was astonished to see that they were quickly surrounded by children, all cheerfully coming out to greet Maggie. She called them each by name as she dismounted and embraced them. They even made over Onyx, who appeared delighted by the attention. He watched the scene unfold, bewildered.

Mingan and Askuwheteau waved and approached the new arrivals.

"John, I would like you to meet Mingan, the chief here, and this is Askuwheteau, who is the protector of the tribe."

John nodded to the two men. "It is nice to meet you."

Mingan smiled. "Any friend of Maggie's is always welcome here."

They gave John a tour of the village and stopped to introduce him to several key members of the tribe.

"If you need to come here for safety, we will protect you," said Askuwheteau, as they walked.

"This place is unlike anything I have ever seen," smiled John, looking around. "Everyone is so happy and friendly, unlike the tribes we encountered further up north with the army. I cannot believe things are so much different here."

"No one is threatening their people or their way of life here," replied Maggie. "Make no mistake, things are not like this in other parts of Virginia, only here on this estate. Here, we all take care of each other, and it is a much better way to live. I just wish the rest of the colonies could see things the way we do."

Mingan nodded in agreement and smiled. "Maggie saved our tribe," he explained to John. "She fed us when we went hungry, helped us to grow when we had lost so much, and even now, she educates our children while seeing to our welfare. She is very special to us."

"You all mean the world to me," said Maggie and took his hand. "Would you believe that Mingan here did not speak a word of English when we first met?"

"It is true. I came to the school with the children one day and found that I enjoyed learning as much as they did, so I kept going back."

"That is amazing," said John.

Maggie noticed some of the women had popped their heads out of the longhouses and were craning their necks to get a better look at John. He saw them, as well, and looked back rather amused.

"Why are they all staring at me?" he whispered to her.

Maggie grinned. "You are an unmarried man. They are checking you out."

John smiled and waved at a few of the ladies, who waved back, and giggled, much to his delight. "What an extraordinarily beautiful group of women," he muttered, a happy expression on his face.

Maggie and Mingan exchanged looks as they noticed John's interest in the ladies of the tribe.

"Askuwheteau," said Mingan, "take John to meet Powaw. I need a few moments to speak to Maggie."

He nodded and led John away.

"Is your friend in need of a wife?" asked Mingan, grinning hopefully.

"I am pretty sure he doesn't want a wife," replied Maggie, "but John does love women and he now has nothing but time on his hands. He may just be willing to 'assist' you with your problem, if you have any women who are interested in him, as long as they understand that he will not be around long-term. He is not a one-woman man."

"I don't see that as a problem," Mingan smiled. "There is a full moon coming up soon. We need to celebrate the harvest and I think you should bring your friend, along with the rest of the family, that night."

Maggie could see that Mingan's wheels were already turning.

That same night, they all retired to the drawing room after supper. Maggie took John by the hand and sat him down in a chair.

"Have you decided where you want to go?" she asked. "Money is no object because we have you covered."

"I cannot accept your money," he argued. "You have already given me my life."

"Nonsense, John," she said and waved him off. "We have more than enough here, and we are happy to help you."

"Well," he said, thoughtfully, "I was thinking perhaps Paris for a bit to work on some of my artwork, until this war is finished. It is big enough for me to go around unnoticed."

Duncan handed him a drink.

"When the war is over, and after you have changed your look a bit, you should be able to slip back here for a while, if you like," said Maggie.

"Nothing would make me happier," he replied.

"We have all been talking John," she looked around at the others, "and you will need a new identity for your new life."

"Yes, I haven't been able to come up with anything yet," said John and sipped his drink.

"We had a thought," said Gabe, and he smiled and squeezed his shoulder.

Duncan stepped forward, handed him a small box, and said, "Well, since ye are already like part of the family, ye may as well make it official and let us give ye the name to go with it. We were thinking 'John MacGregor' might be a good choice."

John slowly looked down, set down his drink on the table, and opened the box. It contained one of the MacGregor symbol rings they all wore. He was completely stunned and overcome.

"I don't know what to say," he choked out.

"We all wear those as a symbol of our family unity," said Quinn, "and we would be honored to have ye as a part of it."

John slipped the ring on his right hand; a perfect fit. His face lit up in a smile.

"John speechless? I never thought I would see that day," teased Gabe.

"What do you say?" asked Maggie, taking his hand. "Want to be one of us?"

"I would be honored," he whispered, his eyes watery, and he stood to hug Maggie. "You are more family to me than my own, and I love you all. Thank you for letting me be a part of something so wonderful."

They all raised a toast to the newest member of the MacGregor clan.

The night of the full moon, they all rode down to the village together. A large feast had been prepared for their arrival and to celebrate the harvest.

"Do you join these ceremonies often?" asked John.

"A couple of times a year," replied Maggie and smirked at Duncan. "We have some fond memories we try to recreate."

Duncan laughed. "Aye, we do our best."

John looked over at Gabe.

"Don't ask," his friend scoffed.

"These ceremonies are truly something to behold," said Quinn, and snickered. "I think ye will enjoy yourself."

That night, after they feasted, the rhythmic pounding of the drums began, and the wine flowed freely. John found himself surrounded by women who wanted to get to know him better, and he was more than happy to accommodate them.

Mingan made it a point to have a private longhouse made up just for John, and anyone who desired to spend time with him, which he put to good use the entire night.

When Maggie and Duncan left to retire to their own longhouse for the night, they noticed that several women were going into John's abode, all looking very excited.

"Do you think I should have warned him about the women?" she asked.

"Would it have mattered?" chuckled Duncan.

"Probably not," she grinned.

Duncan pushed back her hair; she had worn it down loose for the evening. "John shouldn't be the only one having a little fun tonight. Of course, I only need one woman to make me happy."

"That is good to know," she said and kissed him.

He greedily returned her kisses, slowly backing her into their house for the night. By the time they reached the bed of deerskins, they were already free of their clothes, and more than ready for each other. They made love until dawn.

Maggie and Duncan emerged the next morning, just as the village started to come to life.

Gabe and Quinn came over to join them.

"How was your night?" asked Maggie.

"Refreshing," smiled Gabe, kissing her cheek. "Thank you for having Wawetseka leave a pot of that oil for us last night. You were right about that stuff," he whispered in her ear.

"I didn't."

Gabe looked at her strangely. "I thought you asked her too."

Maggie shook her head, then snapped her fingers. "I bet she probably left it in all of them in hopes that each of you would take a woman to bed. Sounds like something Mingan would have suggested."

Gabe's face relaxed a bit. "You are probably right."

Maggie smiled, but made a mental note to speak with Wawetseka.

"Anyone seen John this morning?" asked Maggie.

"Nay, but we saw him last night," replied Logan, coming over to join them. "He looked very 'occupied'."

"Think we should go check on him?" asked Quinn.

"I am sure John is just fine," mumbled Maggie, dryly.

John appeared a short time later from inside the longhouse, his hair loose and tangled, and his clothes askew with a big fat smile on his face.

"Have a good night?" asked Maggie, as she shot him a scolding look.

"I had a lovely night," he said dreamily and kissed her on the cheek. Maggie could tell he was still a little drunk off the wine and women from the previous night's activities.

"We should probably be getting home," Duncan pointed out.

John sighed as he looked back at the longhouse. "I was hoping to stay a little longer."

Mingan came over to join them and smirked at Maggie.

"You are welcome to stay as long as you like," said Mingan. "I will have some more of the women bring 'food' to you."

"That is very kind of you. Thank you. I must say, I have never felt such a warm reception anywhere else before in my entire life."

Maggie rolled her eyes. "Think you can find your way home later, or do we need to leave a trail of breadcrumbs for you?"

"Oh," replied John. "I will find my way along...eventually," he said and ducked back in where he came from.

"Ready to go," Duncan asked Maggie.

She smiled and kissed him. "I, um, left something in the longhouse. Why don't all of you get the horses saddled while I get it?"

He gave her a questioning look.

I need to take care of something.

"Alright," he nodded.

Maggie watched them go as she turned to go find Wawetseka. She found her outside of her home, grinding some herbs.

"Wawetseka! Good morning."

"Hello, Maggie!" she called and stopped to brush her hands together. "I was just preparing some of the plants to store the way Quinn showed me."

"He has been teaching you, then?"

"Yes, he has," she smiled. "He has been very kind to share what he knows. He is a good man."

"Maybe, you could return the favor and teach Quinn how to make some of that special oil that Duncan and I are very fond of."

"Yes!" she nodded. "I would be happy to."

Maggie looked down at the ground, trying to find the words. "Gabe said he enjoyed the pot you left in his room, as well. I suppose Mingan asked you to leave that for all the men last night, in case they took a woman back with them?"

"No, he did not," she replied and fiddled with some of the things on her makeshift table. "I left it as a gift for the two of them."

Maggie felt her chest tighten. "You know about Gabe and Quinn?"

Wawetseka laughed softly. "It is hard not to know. I saw how they were with each other when Gabe was hurt. It is clear how much they love each other." She looked up to see Maggie's face had gone pale. "Are you alright?" she asked and took her arm.

"I'm fine," said Maggie and waved her off. "I just wasn't expecting to hear that you knew."

Wawetseka handed Maggie a ladle of water from the bucket on the table where she was working. "They are meant for each other."

Maggie sipped it gratefully. "Yes, they are. Unfortunately, the rest of the world doesn't see things that way. They would be in a great amount of danger if anyone else knew."

"Their secret is safe here."

Maggie hugged Wawetseka. "Thank you. I'm sure Mingan will be disappointed."

Wawetseka chuckled. "Mingan has renewed hope with your friend, John."

"Well, if anyone is 'up' for the job, I am sure it is him," laughed Maggie.

15 CHAPTER FIFTEEN

John found his way back early that afternoon to find Maggie in the drawing room on the floor with the babies and came over to join them. Alanna crawled over to him, so he picked her up, and sat her on his lap.

"Hello, beautiful," he said to her, making her laugh.

"I am surprised at how good you are with babies," said Maggie.

"I love them, as long as they are someone else's."

Maggie scrunched up her face.

"What was that look?" he asked.

"I don't know what you mean," she said, and shifted her attention the other way.

"That!" he pointed.

Maggie turned to him with her lips pursed. "John, how many women were you with last night?"

"Why would you ask me something like that?" he asked, affronted.

"Just curious...for future reference."

"I think it is better if I do not answer that question," he grinned.

"Do you think you will ever want kids, John?"

"Maybe, someday. Truthfully, I thought about a great many things of that nature while I was waiting for my execution. I think facing death changes your perspective on life."

Maggie touched his shoulder. "You have a second chance to do everything you never thought you would be able to, and you should make the most of it. Do what makes you happy."

"Honestly, I am just treasuring every moment I have here. This place you have… there is something very special about it, and I have never felt more at home anywhere else in the world. I really do not want to leave, but I will not put my new family in danger by being selfish."

Kendric picked up a wooden toy bird that was in a pile of ones that Joshua had carved for them and was playing with it. Morgan, who had crawled over next to John, decided that she wanted it, so she held up her hand, and the toy lifted straight up in the air, hovering several seconds, before it moved from side to side as if imitating the wing movement of a real bird, straight into Morgan's hand.

Maggie froze and hoped that John did not see it, but the look on his face was undeniable...he had seen the whole thing.

Fuckity Fuck!

Houston, we have a problem.

John looked at Morgan, then back at Kendric, and finally to Maggie. All the blood had drained from his face.

Maggie covered her mouth with both hands as she sent Duncan a silent message. *Drawing room...NOW!*

John slowly sat Alanna on the floor, before he scooched himself backwards. "What the hell was that?" he whispered and crossed himself.

She held up her hands. "Please, let me explain."

"You have an explanation for that?" he asked while pointing at the toy.

Duncan slid into the room sideways, a panicked look on his face. "What's wrong?" he demanded.

"You have toys that are flying around the room by themselves," shouted John.

"Damn it!" said Duncan, as he moved to Maggie and helped her up.

"You are not surprised by this?" asked John. "Neither of you are?"

Maggie turned to Duncan. "We need to tell him everything."

"Aye," he agreed. "Let me get the others."

He left the room while Maggie went to the liquor cabinet, took out a full bottle of whisky, and handed it to John. "Here, you are going to need this."

John accepted the bottle, popped off the cork, and took a straight shot.

Maggie called for Hettie. "I need Cora and Cecile to take the babies."

"I will get them," replied Hettie.

Maggie knelt on the floor. "Behave yourselves," she ordered, pointing at them, before the ladies came in and took them out of the room.

John was still sitting on the floor, watching her intently.

She held out her hand and helped him to his feet, then pointed at the chair. "Sit...please," she said. "And drink."

He took another swig as the rest of the family appeared.

"We are all in agreement," said Duncan. "He should be told."

"I should be told what?" demanded John.

"John, you know we don't live a normal life here," she said and leaned against the arm of a chair, "you just don't know how abnormal it is. Please listen, with an open mind, and know that everything we tell you is true, but we need your word that you will never breathe a word of this to anyone else. It will endanger us all and everything we have created here."

He looked down. "I would never do anything to put any of you in danger...on my life."

Maggie pulled the chair around to sit in front of him. "Fifteen years ago, I fell asleep in the year 2018, and I woke up in the year 1765."

John's eyes widened with fear as Maggie told him her entire story. When she was done, Lady Aurnia told him the same story she had told Maggie in Scotland.

When they were done telling him everything, John looked around the room.

"You all believe this?" he asked.

"We live it," said Duncan.

"How is any of this possible?" John asked, setting down the bottle and raking his hands through his hair.

"You would not be here otherwise," replied Maggie. "If I did not know what I had learned about the history of this country, we would not have had the details we needed to know about your execution ahead of time. It is how I have walked the fine line I have during this war— and protected everyone here from it."

Gabe came over and laid his hand on John's shoulder. "I know it is hard to believe. I felt the same way when Maggie told me. It's a great deal to take in, but every word is true, I assure you."

"Does everyone on this estate know?"

"No! Only the people in this room and the two brothers in Scotland. It *MUST* remain that way."

John looked on the verge of passing out.

Maggie handed him the bottle he had set down. "Drink! It helps!"

"She's right," said Gabe. "It does help."

John chugged almost half the bottle.

"We are the protectors of all of this," said Duncan, "and now, as part of this family, ye are as well."

John blew out a long breath.

"Maybe John and I should have some time alone to talk," shrugged Maggie, looking around at the others.

"Aye," said Duncan. He kissed her before leaving. "We will be close by."

After they all left, Maggie turned to John. "I know you have questions, so let me have them."

"Maggie, I have so many questions that I do not know where to begin."

"I know. You wouldn't believe the questions I had when I woke up in 1765, next to one very strange horse...only I didn't have anyone to tell me what was going on. I had to figure it out alone. Everyone that I knew and loved was gone, replaced with a bunch of strangers and an entirely different world. Gabe was the first one I ever told, and it wasn't until after he left the army for me and we were back here."

"You went all that time, never telling another soul? How in the world did you bear it?"

Maggie took his hands. "I had no other choice. It was a matter of survival for me. If I had told anyone, I would have been locked away as a lunatic. I half thought Gabe was going to have me put away when I told him." She squeezed his hand.

"I am sorry that I had to burden you with this, and I wouldn't have if my children had not started making toys fly in front of you. Duncan and I have told them over and over not to do that, but do they listen? The teenage years should be interesting."

John burst into laughter at the absurdity of her statement, and he continued until tears were rolling out of his eyes. He hugged Maggie. "If I ever get over the shock of this, I am certain that I will be grateful that you trusted me enough to tell me your secret, and I will guard it with my life."

"I am very glad to hear you say that, John. You don't know how many times I have wished for a little of your wisdom in all this chaos. I am sure we will be having many late-night conversations about the questions you have."

"I look forward to them."

Maggie sighed. "Want to see what you are protecting? Half of it anyway."

"Why not?"

Everyone was outside the door, waiting in the foyer, when they came out.

"Let's show him what he is a part of."

Maggie led him down the secret stairs, the rest of the family right behind them.

John's eyes widened with amazement at what lay before him.

"I remember that feeling," said Gabe, "only the collection in Scotland was a great deal bigger."

Quinn and Gabe showed him around as Maggie whispered to Lady Aurnia. "I am sorry that this happened like this. Under normal circumstances, I would have consulted you first."

Lady Aurnia reached down and took her hand. "My dear, ye do not need my permission. Ye and Duncan are the keepers of this collection, and all decisions regarding it belong to ye."

Maggie leaned over on her. "Please, tell me there are spells here to control these babies when they are older."

Her mother-in-law laughed. "I am afraid ye are on your own. Trust me, I searched every blessed book in this collection at least ten times, to no avail."

"Damn!"

"What do ye think?" asked Duncan.

"This is...something else!" replied John.

Logan took him by the shoulders. "If ye are going to truly be one of us, ye need to take the mark."

"The mark?"

He lifted his shirt, and showed it to John, as did Duncan, Quinn, and finally, a reluctant Gabe.

"In my defense," said Gabe, dryly, "I was drunk, and it was Duncan's bachelor party."

"You all have it?"

"Even Lady Aurnia and I, but we are not hiking our skirts to show you," added Maggie. "The choice is yours if you want it."

John thought a minute. "I think I would like that."

"We can do it tonight after everyone leaves the house for the evening," offered Quinn.

"Maggie and Duncan may want to," Gabe cleared his throat, "'clean' the altar table before then."

"Oh, come on...seriously? Do ye two ever take a break?" asked Logan folding his arms in disgust.

Maggie narrowed her eyes at Gabe, while Duncan smirked and shook his head.

Lady Aurnia looked back and forth between them. She opened her mouth to say something, then closed it before she raised her finger at Duncan and waved it.

"Oh, I don't want to know, unless I get more grandchildren out of it, in which case, all is forgiven."

Maggie shook her head at Gabe, grinning. "You see, I told you so!"

Once the house was settled for the night, everyone met downstairs.

"Who do ye wish to do it?" asked Lady Aurnia. "The choice is entirely yours."

"Except Gabe and I do not know how," added Maggie.

"It is about time ye learned," said Duncan.

"No offense, but I prefer the ladies," winked John.

"Alright, Maggie and I will do it together," said Lady Aurnia.

Logan and Duncan helped John get ready on the table while Lady Aurnia and Maggie prepared the ink.

"Will it hurt?" he asked.

"Not a bit," said Maggie. "You may actually go to sleep."

Lady Aurnia showed Maggie what to do and instructed her as she took over. When they were finished, Maggie laid her hand over the mark and said the words.

"You are all done," she said and kissed the top of his head. "Welcome to the family."

They were cleaning up, and about to go back upstairs, when Gabe caught Maggie's arm. "We need to have one more ceremony tonight, if Lady Aurnia would be kind enough to indulge us."

"What are you talking about?" asked Maggie.

He squeezed her hand. "I got married without my best friend, and Quinn without his brothers, so I think it is time we correct that with another ceremony."

"Really?" asked Maggie.

"Really!" replied Quinn, smiling, his arm around Gabe.

Maggie hugged Gabe, tears rolling down her face. "I love you, Gabe."

"I love you too, Mags."

She wiped her face before embracing Quinn. "And, I love you, Quinn!"

"I love ye too."

"The children should be here!" Maggie said, suddenly.

"That is a wonderful idea!" said Quinn.

"Aye," said Lady Aurnia, "it is. I will go wake them."

An hour later, the small group stood as Lady Aurnia presided over the intimate ceremony. They used the MacGregor rings as wedding rings, and finally had the family together as they had wanted.

The children, while sleepy, were thrilled to be a part of it, and at the end of the night, Maggie and Duncan took the children so Gabe and Quinn could have a private wedding night in their own home in peace. After Kat and Alastair were asleep, Maggie found John leaning against the stairwell downstairs.

"Quite a day, huh?" she asked, rubbing his back.

"It definitely has been," he replied and draped his arm around her.

"Having second thoughts about joining up yet?" she teased.

"Never!" he replied. "I am just wondering how I am going to leave now. I have my new family here, and then there is that lovely village that I spent the night in with all of those beautiful, lonely women."

Maggie turned to John, a crazy thought coming to her. "Exactly how fond of that tribe *are* you?"

"Very much so! They live such a simple life, but they are all so happy and loved. I have never seen anything like it. Oh, to live that way." He sounded wistful.

She grinned. "What if you could?"

"What do you mean?"

"John, no one would look for you there, not that they are looking for you anyway, but if you grew a beard, changed your clothes to the type they wear, no one would ever know the difference. And, you would be here...with us. I mean the decision would be yours of course, but it is an option."

John laughed. "I can think of nothing I would like more."

"I will speak to Mingan tomorrow and see what he says."

"Alright then," he nodded. "Goodnight, Maggie." He kissed her cheek and started up the stairs. "Thank you, for everything."

Excited, Maggie kissed Duncan as she came into the bedroom.

"I am happy to see ye too, my love." He kissed her back.

"I had an idea," she said and told him her plan for John. "Do you think we could really pull it off?"

"I do not see why not. It is actually a great idea."

Maggie kissed him again. "I have those every now and then. I am having an even better one right now."

Duncan grabbed her around the waist. "What might that be?" he asked.

Her smile was devilish. "It is a lovely night, and I feel my inner goddess wanting to come out. Let's take some of those deerskins outside in the garden, and...you know."

"Oh! I like that idea," said Duncan.

They grabbed blankets on the way outside, made a pallet, and made love beneath the stars.

The next day, Maggie visited Mingan at the village, and he was ecstatic that John wanted to live with them. She explained that he was not used to that type of life, so they came up with some ideas to make him more comfortable in his new surroundings. Maggie promised to send Joshua and some of the men down to help prepare for John's new living arrangements.

Duncan met Maggie at the stables as she returned. He took her by the hand and led her to the house. "Come! There is something we need to do."

"The stables are this way," she pointed, playfully.

"We will do *that* later," he winked.

Duncan took her down into the collection room and sat her down in a chair.

Maggie looked at him, puzzled, as he pulled out a book and laid it in front of her.

"What's this?"

"It occurred to me, with all the recent additions to our family, that we had neglected to do something very important." He touched the book. "This is the family history of the MacGregors. Each birth, marriage, and death are recorded here. In all the daily chaos, we have yet to add our marriage, Quinn and Gabe's, nor any of the children. I think it is well past time that we do."

Maggie carefully opened the book, the first page going all the way back to the beginning. Any other record would have been worn away by age, but the Fae magic kept these pages as fresh as the day they were written.

"Duncan! This is unbelievable." She pointed to a different color ink. "What does that mean?"

"Those indicate where Fae blood was added, because one parent was a Fae god or goddess. In the beginning, there were many, as ye can see, but as ye get towards the end of the book, they disappear."

Maggie flipped through the ancient record, delighted to see the history of the family she had become a part of. The last recording was of the death of Duncan's father. Maggie picked up a pen and a bottle of ink and handed them to Duncan. "You should have the honor."

He sat down and started to record the additions, even adding in John. When he was done, Maggie picked up the book to blow on the ink to help it dry. She noticed the corner of something sticking out of the back. Setting it down, she pulled out a letter. "What's this?"

"I don't know. Why don't ye see?"

Maggie carefully opened it and read over the contents. "SON OF A BITCH!" she exclaimed.

She handed the letter to Duncan, who quickly skimmed over it. When he was done, he leaned back, looking up at Maggie.

"We are being used, Maggie. Finn knows exactly what he is doing, and we are playing right into his hands without even knowing it."

"What is he up to?" she asked.

"I do not know, and he will never tell." He tossed the letter on the table, frustrated.

Maggie sighed as Duncan pulled her down on his lap. She picked up the letter that Duncan had just thrown down.

"He has a right to know," she whispered.

"Do ye want me to tell him?" he asked.

"No, I will do it. It might be easier coming from me."

Maggie stood outside of the bedroom door, and hesitated, wondering if she was doing the right thing. She decided he needed to know and knocked.

John opened the door, smiling.

"John, I need to speak to you about something."

He frowned. "So serious! Does Mingan not want me at the village?"

Maggie shook her head. "No, it's not that. He is thrilled with the idea, and they have already started to prepare for your arrival."

"Then, why are you so somber?"

She entered the room. "I think you should sit down. I have some information that I just learned that involves you, and it will come as quite a shock."

He pulled up a chair.

"Duncan and I were updating the family history when I found a letter stuck back in one of the books. Kat's great-grandmother was a MacGregor who became pregnant by a man who didn't love her and, not wanting to disgrace her family, she left them and Scotland behind. That child was left at an orphanage in London while she fled to another country, changing her name, and starting a new life. That woman was Lady Aurnia's mother's sister. Years later, she wrote to her sister back in Scotland, telling her all about her life and how happy she was. She never mentioned the child she gave up, but she did mention the man whom she had married, and all her children by him. Her husband's name was Guillaume."

Maggie took his hand. "John, she ended up in Geneva, and the name she chose to go by was 'Marie Privat'." She looked down at the letter in her other hand. "I think you should read this."

John took the letter and read it, the blood draining from his face. When he was done, he looked back up at Maggie. "Is this true? Is this even possible?"

She nodded. "If I am not mistaken, you recognize some of the names in that letter?"

He stared back down at the paper in his hand. "My grandmother's name was Marie Privat, my grandfather's name was Guillaume, and my father's name was Antoine, all names mentioned here," he whispered and closed his eyes.

"Your grandmother was a MacGregor from *this* branch of the MacGregors," said Maggie softly.

John sat dumbfounded. "Well, this is quite a plot twist, isn't it?"

"I thought you would want to know." She placed her hand on his shoulder. "It seems you really *are* a part of the family."

He laid his hand on hers, took in a deep breath, and smiled. "I cannot say this disappoints me. I am proud to be a true member of this remarkable family."

Maggie bit her lip. "It also means that you carry Fae blood, so be prepared for what comes with that."

He looked at her oddly.

"Something is afoot, and we have no idea what it is, or where it is leading. We all need to be on guard at all times."

He nodded. "I understand."

Maggie found Duncan in the drawing room, drinking. "How did he take it?" he asked.

"Better than me," she replied, taking the glass from him and downing it.

"I told the rest of the family," he said. "They were all as shocked as we were."

Maggie sat down. "What is going on here, Duncan? None of this can possibly be coincidence."

Duncan laid his hand over on her thigh. "Nay, it is not. I do know that we need to tread carefully until we find out." He leaned toward her. "I know ye care for Finn, and he seems to care for ye, but we do not know his true intentions, and we must assume the worst for the sake of our children to keep them safe."

"What do we do in the meantime?" she asked.

"We live our lives, care for our babies, and love each other. We will handle the rest when it presents itself." He kissed her head and she leaned against him.

Maggie lay in bed later that night and stared up at the ceiling. "Are you awake?" she whispered.

"Aye, I am."

She turned on her side to face him. "I think we need alcohol," she said.

Duncan pushed back the covers and reached for his clothes. "Agreed. I was thinking the same thing."

They went down to the drawing room, where Duncan poured himself a whisky and Maggie a glass of rum.

Maggie took a sip. "Oh, that is so good. Now, that the babies are weaned, at least I can go back to drinking myself into a stupor when I can't sleep."

Duncan sat down next to her on the sofa. "I am not sure I will ever sleep again."

"What could Finn be up to?"

He shrugged. "Your guess is as good as mine, but I am sure he will show his hand soon enough."

"Got an extra glass for your newest family member?" asked John as he came in.

Maggie pointed to the liquor cabinet. "Help yourself. You are family now, so make yourself at home."

"I guess I wasn't the only one who couldn't sleep." John poured himself a glass.

"Get used to it in this family," replied Duncan, holding up his own glass. "I am afraid it comes with the name."

John sat down across from them.

"How are you doing with all of this new information?" asked Maggie.

"I am still trying to sort it all out in my mind. It is a great deal to process, and this whole Fae bloodline thing…well, I am just confused on many levels."

"We are happy to answer what questions we can," offered Duncan.

"What does having Fae blood mean for me? If I have children, will they float things too?"

"Nay," laughed Duncan. He cut his eyes over at Maggie. "Our babies' mother is more to blame for that."

Maggie smacked his chest. "I am fairly certain I never flew toys around my room as a baby," she said dryly.

"The MacGregor line of Fae blood has been watered down over the years. It was once very strong, but our current generation hardly notices anything from it. Maggie, on the other hand, is the daughter of a full goddess, making her blood more potent."

John looked confused. "Your mother is a goddess?"

"She was, but she gave up her abilities, her immortality, and her memories to live as a human with my father, so I was aware of none of this, and I had nothing in the way of gifts until my grandfather, the King of the Fae, somehow brought them out in me. I do not have full abilities, only some, and my human half greatly inhibits them."

"What can you do?" asked John.

"I can bring about a good harvest, cause things to grow where nothing will, and I can grant fertility."

"Fertility?"

Maggie winced. "By the way, I would be cautious at the village if I were you. I conducted a fertility ceremony there a few months ago."

John paled and downed his drink. "That would have been good information to have had sooner."

"Actually, you will find the tribe is in desperate need of men," said Duncan. "If they do not start producing male heirs soon, they will be in danger of dying out."

"I see," said John gravely. "That would be a shame."

Maggie stood and grabbed a bottle to refill their glasses.

"So, your children having Maggie's half-Fae blood and your partial-Fae blood… what will they be able to do?" asked John.

Maggie and Duncan exchanged glances.

"We have no clue," replied Maggie. "All we know is that they are special and to expect the unexpected at any time."

"And, we suspect that Maggie's grandfather is up to something," added Duncan.

"What do you mean?" asked John.

Maggie shook her head. "He has some sort of grand plan for me and the children, but he has not seen fit to enlighten us any more than that." She shot-gunned her rum.

John frowned at her empty glass. "What are you going to do?"

"We will wait and see what happens," said Duncan. "It is all we can do, and then deal with it as it comes."

"You all know that I will do whatever I can to help." John's offer was sincere.

"Thank you, John," said Maggie. "We may need you before it is all said and done."

They spent the next couple of hours answering John's questions until he was sufficiently worn out, and Maggie had finished off several glasses of alcohol.

"I think I will bid you both 'goodnight'." John stood and kissed Maggie on the cheek. "I will see you in the morning."

"We should get to bed, as well." Duncan looked to his wife after John left. He stood and offered Maggie his hand.

She giggled as she got up and wrapped her arms around him. "I have a better idea." Taking his hand, she led him to the front door.

"What are ye up to besides three glasses of rum?" he asked.

Maggie opened the door and pulled him along. "I have had *FOUR*, and I am fairly certain the stable is unoccupied at this time of night."

Duncan broke into a wide smile as he caught on to her idea. "I will get a lantern and a blanket."

They made their way to the hay stall on the side of the stable. Maggie fell back into a pile, Duncan collapsing on top of her and rubbing his body against hers as he kissed her. Over the next couple of hours, they laughed, played, and enjoyed each other. They fell asleep covered by one of the blankets and were awakened the next morning by

Onyx, who huffed and pawed at the ground to wake them up, only to appear to snicker at them.

"Dang it, Onyx, get back here!" yelled Harm as he trudged inside, waving his hat in frustration at the disobedient horse. The man instantly froze when he caught sight of Maggie and Duncan in each other's arms, clothes disheveled, and covered in hay.

"Good morning, Harm," chuckled Maggie as she attempted to get up, stopping to pull hay out of Duncan's unbound hair.

"I reckon it *is* a good morning," grinned Harm.

Maggie and Duncan went back to the main house, leaving a trail of straw all the way up the path, and once inside, one across the foyer towards the dining room as well.

Logan, John, and Lady Aurnia were standing just outside the drawing room when the happy couple came in laughing.

"Really?" scolded Logan, folding his arms in disgust. "Is there any part of this entire damn place that ye two have not had your way with each other on?"

"Nay! There isn't!" smiled Duncan, slapping Logan on the back. "Jealous, Brother?"

Lady Aurnia turned to Logan and pointed at the couple. "Pay attention! This is how I get grandchildren. Maybe ye will learn something if ye are around here long enough."

Logan scoffed. "Ye think I don't know how babies are made?"

"I think a little reminder never hurt anyone." Lady Aurnia smacked his folded arm. "For Heaven's sakes, if my youngest son, who is married to another man, can figure out how to get me two grandchildren, then there is no reason the rest of ye should not be doing your part."

Logan groaned, shook his head, and headed straight for the whisky bottle in the other room.

16 CHAPTER SIXTEEN

In two weeks time, a special longhouse, constructed for John in the Native American village, was complete. It looked like any other in the village on the outside, but on the inside, it was more like a small house, complete with a bedroom and all the other creature comforts of a Colonial home. The entire family helped him move in and a celebration was held for the newest member of the tribe.

A renewed zest for life seemed to overtake John, and everyone was glad he was close enough to the main house to visit each day. He still had the option to travel if he chose, but for the moment, he was content right where he was.

Maggie also gifted him with a new sketchbook and supplies, so he could continue to create the artwork that he loved so much.

After the family returned from seeing John settled in, they moved from the foyer into the drawing room.

Maggie noticed that Gabe looked a little pale and that he had begun to perspire a great deal. She was just about to ask him if he was feeling unwell, when he stumbled and collapsed to the floor, clutching his chest while groaning in pain.

Maggie and Quinn immediately rushed to his side.

"Gabe, what is it?" asked Maggie as she loosened his shirt. "What hurts?"

"My...chest..." was all he managed before his eyes closed, and he passed out.

"Send for the doctor!" Maggie shouted to Hettie. "Get him upstairs!" she ordered to Duncan and Logan, who carried him up to one of the bedrooms.

Maggie removed his shirt after they laid him down, while Quinn looked on in disbelief.

Lady Aurnia brought in a basin of cool water and some rags, that she wrung out and used to bathe his forehead.

"Please, be alright, Gabe," Quinn whispered through his tears, grasping his husband by the hand and smoothing his hair back.

Maggie reached for his wrist and felt for Gabe's pulse; it was beating entirely too fast. His color had gone ashen and his breathing was irregular.

"Where is that damn doctor?" she shouted.

Gabe's eyes fluttered open and Maggie touched his face.

"Stay with me, Gabe. Help is coming, you just need to hang on a little while longer."

It seemed like an eternity before the physician finally arrived. Maggie stood at the foot of the bed with Quinn, holding his hand while the doctor examined Gabe.

He looked back at them, his face grim, and shook his head. "I'm sorry to tell you this, but it's his heart. It is giving out on him."

Maggie shook her head back and forth, violently, her eyes wide and on the verge of hysteria.

"Then, fix it!" she demanded. "Don't just sit there, FIX HIM! Why aren't you doing anything?"

The doctor closed his eyes and sighed. "Mistress MacGregor, if there was anything that I could do, I would." He opened his eyes and looked back at Gabe. "I am afraid it is not within my power to save him. I am very sorry," he whispered and stood. "You should say your 'goodbyes' while you can. He does not have much time left."

Maggie blinked, her mouth agape, and her mind unable to accept the words she was just told.

"Get out!" she finally said in a low, barely audible voice.

The doctor reached out to touch her arm comfortingly, but she pulled back.

"I said GET OUT!" she screamed at him.

He nodded and left the room. Maggie turned to Duncan. "There has to be something we can do. What about the books? Is there something in them that we can use? Anything?" she choked out.

Duncan shook his head. "It would require the goddess of healing, and we do not have her here," he said, sympathetically, a despondent look on his face.

"What about the things I can do? I should be able to do something to help him. I *have* to be able to do *something*," she cried, wringing her hands frantically.

Duncan took her by the hand. "Maggie, ye are not a Fae goddess, and even if ye were, ye would not have domain over this. I am sorry, my love. I wish it were not so," and his own eyes became watery.

Duncan moved to put his arms around her, but she threw him off, moving to Gabe's bedside with Quinn on the other side.

"Gabe, you cannot leave us. You cannot leave me." Maggie wiped her tears with her sleeve. "Please! I am begging you!"

Gabe's eyes slowly fluttered opened. "I am afraid I don't have much say in the matter," he whispered. "I love you, Mags. You were the first person I could ever truly be myself around, and you have made my life so much better since you came into it. I will be forever grateful to who or whatever being sent you into my world," he said softly, weakly, squeezing her hand.

She could feel that his energy was starting to ebb from his body.

"Gabe," sobbed Quinn. "I cannot be without ye. We have children to raise...we were going to grow old together. It isn't supposed to end like this. We have not had enough time."

Gabe reached over to touch his face. "You have made me such a happy man, Quinn, and I have treasured every moment we have had together. I love you so much. I know you will raise our children well, and do not ever let them forget how much I love them."

Quinn bawled, the sound a wretched echo in the room, and laid his face on Gabe's chest, shaking his head and calling his name.

Gabe placed his hand on the back of his head as tears sprang to his own eyes. He raised up and placed a kiss on the top of Quinn's head and woefully cried.

Alastair appeared at the door, and Logan brought him over to Gabe's bedside. Maggie took him by the shoulders, the boy staring at Gabe, fearfully.

"Father?" he whimpered.

Gabe reached out his hand to him. "Come here, my boy," he said and took his hand. "You were such a welcome surprise in my life, and you have brought me more joy than you will ever know. You have been the best son I could have ever hoped for, and I am so proud of you. I need you to take care of your father and your sister for me. Look after them and never forget how much I love you. And I do! I love you so much, Alastair! I could not love you more had I sired you myself."

"I will look after them and keep them safe, Father, I promise. It is what I am meant to do."

Gabe pulled him to his chest and kissed his forehead, tears streaming down both their faces.

Alastair turned to Maggie and she took him in her arms, pulling him to her and burying her face in his hair as she wept.

She shook her head and appeared half out of her mind. Maggie managed to call over her shoulder to Duncan, who was hovering by the foot of the bed with Lady Aurnia, Logan and John, all looking miserable. "Bring Kat."

"I will get her," said John as he wiped his own face, went up the hall to fetch her, and appeared with her in his arms. He carefully placed her on the bed with Gabe.

"Thank you," said Gabe to John.

John laid his hand on Gabe's chest, directly over his heart, his own eyes rimmed in red. "Godspeed, old friend. I will see you on the other side."

Gabe turned his attention to Kat. "Hello, sweetheart."

"Father?" she asked when she saw how upset he was.

Gabe took her little hand in his, committing her tiny fingers to his memory. "My dear sweet baby girl! I am afraid I must go away, and I will not be here to see you grow up. I want you to know that becoming your father has been one of the greatest blessings of my life and that being apart from you is the last thing in this world that I ever want to do. I love you so much, my sweet princess! I want you to have a wonderful life and know that you will always be in my heart."

Kat looked over at Maggie and Alastair, not understanding what he meant.

"He is sick, and he has to leave us," Alastair said to her softly.

Kat shook her head. "Father, no go!" she said and turned back to Gabe.

"I am sorry, baby, I do not want to leave you," he sobbed. "I never want to be away from you. I would give anything to stay here."

"FATHER, NO GO!" she said louder, more agitated.

"Kat," said Maggie and tried to take her, but Kat resisted and moved closer to Gabe.

"FATHER! NO! GO!" she commanded emphatically, and as she did, Kat slammed her tiny hands flat on Gabe's chest. She looked him directly in the eyes as a strange, bright white light streamed from her palms and straight into Gabe's chest.

Gabe's eyes flew wide open, and his body clenched, a searing jolt ripping throughout his entire being. Feeling it as well, Quinn raised his head, choking up as Gabe's eyes abruptly closed.

Maggie stepped closer to Gabe, sure that he was gone, until...she noticed something odd....

...his color began to return to a normal shade, and his breathing started to regulate by itself.

She took his hand and felt his wrist only to find that his pulse rate was back to where it should be.

His eyes flew open and he took in a large, gasping breath.

"Gabe?" she asked, dumbfounded.

He looked up at her, his eyes wide open and full of disbelief. He turned to Quinn and they locked eyes.

"How do you feel?" she asked, cautious and nervous.

"Like I am not dying," he said in utter astonishment.

Maggie, Gabe, and Quinn all turned to gawk at Kat, who took her father's face in her tiny hands, smiled, and planted a little kiss on his cheek.

"Father, no go," she laughed and snuggled blissfully into the crook of his arm.

Maggie picked her up, looked at her with a puzzled look on her face, and proceeded to smother her in hugs and kisses until Kat started to giggle.

Lady Aurnia, Logan, John, and Duncan stepped closer. "Did she…?"

Maggie nodded, then broke into laughter. "She did. She healed him."

Quinn looked over at Gabe and they embraced.

"I guess you are not getting rid of me so easily after all." Gabe's laugh was half sob as he buried his face in Quinn's chest.

Quinn laughed through his tears and cried again, relief flooding his body. "Thank God. I think we are going to need all-hands-on-deck with these children."

Kat reached out for Gabe.

He took her in his arms and hugged her tightly. "Thank you, sweetheart."

"Welcome, Father. You no go!"

"That's right, princess! I am not going anywhere!"

After the shock wore off, they all left the room to give Quinn and Gabe some private time alone with the children for a bit.

Maggie pointed back to the bedroom, trying to put together the pieces of a very strange puzzle. "How did she do that?"

"That's a good question," answered Duncan and took her in his arms.

"I don't understand. You said only a goddess over that domain could do something like that," she said; he brushed her tears away.

"Aye, he is right," replied Lady Aurnia before she folded her arms and looked back toward the bedroom. "I have never seen a MacGregor with abilities that strong- not in my lifetime."

Logan stood beside her. "Well, there is obviously more to this story than we are being let in on."

"Thank God!" muttered John.

"Do ye think Finn gave that power to her?" asked Duncan.

Maggie shrugged. "Can he give powers out like that? We know our own babies have some sort of gifts, but our children carry my mother's blood."

"He has the power to make you a full goddess," replied Duncan.

Logan, Lady Aurnia, and John turned to them.

"What did ye say?" asked his mother.

Maggie sighed. "Finn made me an offer, to make me a full goddess to take my mother's place as Danu. I turned him down because the price was too steep." She turned to Duncan who pulled her closer.

Lady Aurnia snapped her fingers. "What did Alastair say to Gabe?" she asked, out of the blue.

"He said he would keep them safe," answered Duncan.

Maggie looked at Duncan and shook her head. "No! He said that it was what he was *meant* to do. I think Finn has been up to much more than we know."

Duncan scoffed, "Finn and his Fae fuckery."

Maggie leaned into him. "Well for today's fuckery, I am grateful because Gabe would not be here otherwise. I just feel like we are missing something extremely important that is right in front of our faces."

"I think you might be right." Duncan's words were spoken low and gravely, and he sighed.

A little while later, Maggie knocked on Gabe's door and stuck her head inside the room. "Up for some company?"

He was sitting up in a chair. "I am up for anything."

Maggie frowned and waved her hands to shoo him. "Oh no! Back in bed with you until we get you checked over again."

"Maggie, I feel like a new man. I am perfectly fine."

She moved to stand in front of him with her hands on her hips. "Humor me, please," she whispered.

"Alright," he said softly, after deciding that she had been through enough for one day. He got back into bed and reclined against the headboard.

Maggie laid down next to him and rested her head on his chest as she used to do all the time before Duncan came along. "I am so grateful that you are still here."

Gabe felt the wetness through his shirt from her tears. "Me too, sweetheart!" He rubbed her shoulder and kissed the side of her head. "Any idea how my daughter healed me?"

"We are trying to figure that out, but right now, we are just appreciating the fact that she could." Maggie looked up at him. "Do not ever scare me like that again. I cannot bear the thought of you not being in my life, ever. I need you like I need the air that I breathe, and I was so afraid..."

Gabe could see how upset she was getting. He tipped her chin up to better see her face. "Hey! Hey! Hey! Mags, I'm still here and I am not going anywhere for a very long time." He kissed her chastely on the lips and held her close.

17 CHAPTER SEVENTEEN

The next few weeks remained very quiet around the house. Gabe was cleared by the doctor and declared a walking miracle; unlike anything he had ever seen before. The time had come for Lady Aurnia and Logan to return to Scotland, their primary mission accomplished, but they were staying on another week to enjoy a little more time with the family.

Quinn and Gabe's horses each gave birth to fillies; one was born solid white with a black heart on her forehead and the other born solid black with a white heart on her forehead. It was decided that those two would go to Morgan and Alanna.

One night, a few days before Lady Aurnia and Logan were to leave, Maggie and Duncan prepared for bed.

"Are ye feeling poorly, Maggie?" he asked. "Ye did not eat much at supper tonight."

Maggie climbed into bed and he slid next to her.

"I am fine. I just wasn't hungry and, besides, I had other things on my mind."

"Like what?" he asked, uneasy, folding one arm behind his head. "What's wrong? What's bothering ye?"

She blew out a long breath and sighed dramatically. "I was just wondering where we were going to put the addition because we need a much bigger house," she announced.

Duncan blinked and tilted his head as if he had heard wrong. "A bigger house? That's what's bothering ye?"

Maggie nodded.

"Why on Earth do we need a larger house?"

She bobbed her head back and forth. "The babies will each need their own space soon, and we have no idea how many are coming *this* time."

"How many what?" he asked, perplexed and confused by her answer.

She took his hand and gently guided it over her stomach. "Babies, my love."

Duncan sat straight up, the full meaning of her words hitting him.

"You're not...are you?" he asked, his voice full of genuine surprise.

"I am," she smiled.

His face lit up like the sun as he laughed and kissed her. "More babies? Oh, this is wonderful news indeed, my love! Our little family is growing again."

"Don't get too excited, it may only be one baby this time," she warned.

"I guess we will find out soon enough." He stopped. "Wait! Ye have not been sick."

And as if on cue, Maggie felt a familiar feeling well up, covered her mouth, jumped out of bed, and ran to vomit.

"That's more like it," he said with a huge grin on his face, following to wring out a cloth for her to wipe her mouth.

"You had to say it, didn't you? You jinxed me," she said when she was done.

He cleaned her face. "I love ye so much, Maggie."

Gabe and Quinn brought the children up for breakfast the next morning.

Maggie pushed her plate away, a wave of nausea hitting her full force.

Gabe eyed her suspiciously as he sipped his coffee. "Not hungry this morning, Mags?" he asked, looking a little concerned.

"Not really."

"You aren't coming down with something, are ye?" asked Quinn.

"I don't think so," she replied, she and Duncan sharing a loving look.

Gabe narrowed his eyes at her, tilted his head, and looked at her closer when he caught the exchange between the two of them. He laid his napkin on the table and leaned back against his chair, stroking his chin.

A wide smile slowly spread across his face and a twinkle appeared in his eye. "Oh!" he said and waved his finger around in a circle at her. "I can see it now...it is written all over your face."

"See what?" asked Maggie, and looked him in the eye, one corner of her mouth in a sly curl.

"Oh yes! There is no doubt about it. You definitely *are*," he grinned and leaned his arms forward.

"She is what?" asked Quinn.

"She is with child—again!" he announced while never taking his eyes off her.

Everyone turned to stare at her.

Maggie smiled back at him; her gaze still locked on him.

Duncan looked down and shook his head, amused. He took her hand and kissed the back of it. "Aye, she is."

The room erupted in joyous laughter, everyone getting up and coming around to hug and congratulate them, until Maggie's stomach started to roll, and she felt it coming...she got up and dashed out of the room.

"I will make a trip to the apothecary, so we can start brewing tea again," said Quinn.

"And I will warn the staff of what's to come," laughed Gabe.

EPILOGUE

Finn appeared on the fog that rolled in just outside of the stables. He looked up to their bedroom window and smiled as he walked. She had just told Duncan that she was with child again, and they were celebrating. Things were progressing nicely.

He turned and made his way through the gate to greet the two newest additions to the family; the magical foals brought into the world to protect and serve Morgan and Alanna.

Rubbing their foreheads, Finn was saying a few words in another language to them, when he felt a hot breath on the back of his neck.

Onyx had angrily stomped up behind him, neighing and pawing at the ground, furiously, with a major bone to pick.

"Something on your mind?" he called over his shoulder.

Onyx whinnied loudly, as an otherworldly smoke rolled from his muzzle.

Finn sighed, and turned around to face him. "I know, old friend; I do not like this idea any more than ye do. Maggie is my granddaughter, and causing her pain or grief is the last thing that I ever want to do."

Onyx huffed in disgust, and Finn laid his hand on his mane to soothe him.

"If there were any other way, I would do it, but there is not. Ye know as well as I do, that we need her, but Maggie is as stubborn as her mother, and she needs an 'incentive' to fulfill her destiny." He looked back towards the house. "Aye, she will mourn him and want to join him in death, but she will eventually come around. It will be worth it in the end, ye will see."

He turned his attention back to Onyx. "Ye just make sure those children are kept safe no matter what. I am entrusting their care to ye until their own protectors are ready to take over, and I am depending on ye. The future of the world depends on them."

TO BE CONTINUED...

Book Five is Coming Soon!

ABOUT THE AUTHOR

Tempie W. Wade is the award-winning author of The Timely Revolution Book Series. She is a lifelong resident of Virginia but currently resides in Williamsburg and has a great love of history and travel. The author's writing style incorporates fantasy with historically accurate events.

The Timely Revolution Book Series in Order:

Book One-A Timely Revolution

Book Two-More

Book Three-The Complicated Life of Maggie MacGregor

Book Four-Timely Revelations

Book Five-Coming Soon

Book Six-Coming Soon

Book Seven-Coming Soon